I0557502

PROTECTING THE FLAME
BROTHERHOOD PROTECTORS WORLD

ILSA J. BICK

Twisted Page Press LLC

BROTHERHOOD PROTECTORS

ORIGINAL SERIES BY ELLE JAMES

What you're about to read is fiction except for one little detail. There's this necklace in the story that's both made up and real. That is, the necklace doesn't *really* exist and yet it sort of did. So, let me tell you the part that's real.

The Nazis came for my dad when he was seven. He doesn't talk about it much. For years, he said he didn't remember—and that's probably true. I mean, he was seven. On the other hand, I'm thinking my dad, like most traumatized people, remembers what he can bear.

I do know there wasn't much of a family for the Nazis to grab, just my dad, his parents and his dad's mom. I don't know what my grandmother looked like. My dad has his dad's hair and nose. My great-grandmother was just old. I know my dad's father sold hops for beer. I know he and his family were in several different camps because this was early 1939, right before Germany closed its borders and the Nazis hadn't hit on gas chambers just yet.

Anyway, my dad got sick. At the time, the Nazis were principally concerned not with killing Jews but keeping them healthy for slave labor. As it happened, his father was the camp health officer (remember, this is a guy who sold hops) and somehow arranged for his son to get out. Things get a little murky here, but the gist is that my dad traveled by train in a cattle car for three days and made it to either Lisbon or Casablanca. He remembers that it was very hot and there was no water. Somehow, he got on the very last ship bound for the U.S and eventually ended up with a Jewish sponsor-family in Delaware.

Not long after my dad got out, the entire camp was dismantled and all the Jews were sent to Auschwitz. For the longest time, my dad thought everyone died. About twenty years ago, though, the town where his family had lived opened a museum and invited survivors. That was when my dad found out that his grandmother—my great-grandmother—had survived and returned to live in the same town, the same house. Except she didn't know he was alive; he didn't know about her. So…

My dad's mom's name was Irma. My parents decided they couldn't do that to me, so I'm Ilsa. (They swear up and down that it has nothing to do with Ingrid Bergman's character in their favorite movie, *Casablanca*…but my brother's name is Rick.)

Another thing my dad gave me many years ago was his mother's gold brooch. The pin had this tiny ruby cabochon in the center of a small Mogen Dovid. How my grandmother managed to keep that from the Nazis, I'll never know. I also will never see that brooch again because, twenty-five years ago, someone broke into our house one Thanksgiving and stole it. I mean, think about the irony. Here's something that survived the Nazis which some jerk took without ever under-standing what that brooch signifies.

I think I included my grandmother's brooch because, well, Emma wants to belong: to a family, a tribe, a tradition. But she's also bitter and blind to how she gets in her own way and resists allowing herself to be part of a culture that's in her blood and yet in which she has little faith. She's not self-hating so much as untethered. The military's failed her; she's a widow; she doesn't believe in any god and she's done something really, really dumb. She thinks she belongs to no one and nothing.

Emma's ambivalence is something that I, as a Jew, understand. The desire to belong to something somewhere, whether that's a relationship or a country or a tribe, is just as strong as the wish to negate that difference—because when you're the minority, difference can be dangerous. Difference can get you killed. And yet, it is that difference I also celebrate. Judaism isn't just a religion but a rich and diverse culture spanning thousands of years. We're a people in a way many do not understand. We're, well…a tribe.

I'm not suggesting you feel sorry for me or Emma. I am suggesting that it might be important to be like Kim or Mattie: to recognize and respect and even cultivate a healthy curiosity and help your Jewish friends celebrate their difference. I am suggesting that if you throw a party, you might ask your Jewish friends if they eat pork or shellfish or beef stroganoff because I bet you do ask your gluten-intolerant or vegan friends what they'll eat. Perhaps this Christmas, instead of inviting your Jewish friends for eggnog, get yourself invited over for Chinese takeout and a movie. Or a latkes party. (Or a fried-anything party: it's traditional to eat all kinds of unhealthy, fried foods at Hanukkah to celebrate the miracle of the oil. Offer me spectacular fried chicken or crispy fries with mayo and I am your friend for life.)

You should not hide your joy at being Christian or pretend that Christmas is no big deal. Christmas *is* a big deal. So, yay! Enjoy! No one should ever try to shame you by getting all torqued because you've wished them a Merry Christmas either. (Full disclosure: I know fellow Jews who get completely bent about this. They're being *putzes*.)

Really, the only other thing you can really do for me? Seriously...enough with the Burl Ives already.

PROLOGUE

A little bit of light dispels a lot of darkness.
—Rabbi Schneur Zalman of Liadi, 1797

Keyner zet nit zayn eygenum hoyker.
No one sees the hump on his own back.
—Old Yiddish saying

JESS SAID he was a fool to let his cows calve this late (or early, depending on your point of view; Judd being an optimist, he liked early). *You're not getting any younger*, she nagged. *You're going to kill yourself if you keep this up. A man your age needs to act his age.*

She might be right about the killing himself part. At eighty, there wasn't a lot of spring left in this stringy old bird. But he'd be damned if he'd let himself degenerate into one of those overweight farts with their MAGA hats superglued to their scalps and spend his days down valley at Newsome's hunkered around a potbelly amongst the jars of pickled eggs and hogs' feet and jawing about this and that and what the world was coming to.

Jess was also correct about the calves. Most ranchers let their cows calve in February or March, though some went for a fall calving as late as October. Those were generally bigger outfits, those factory jobs with plenty of money for feed because there'd be no pastureland for grazing until spring and most of those factory-style ranchers had neither the patience nor good sense to let their cows eat what was good for *them* instead of what was good for the ranchers. That always ticked him off, though. Being a small rancher lumped in with the factory farms, that is. He did his level best to make sure his cows were grass-fed all year round. That meant restricting some of his prime grazing land for harvesting only, but it was a way to make sure his herd got grass, even in winter.

The problem was he'd lost fine young calves to that damn diphtheria this summer and all on account of wrecking his knee stepping off that finicky old ladder leading down from the mow. He'd slipped was all. Missed the rung and fell maybe four feet, which was enough to give him what the doctor said was a tibial plateau fracture—he had the man write it out so he could google it—and a couple torn ligaments. He'd been laid up for eight weeks, waiting to heal because, after his search, he decided no one was coming at him with a drill and a knife, no sir. This meant he'd had no choice but to allow his sister's dumber-than-a-stump boy to "help out." My God, that near about ruined him. That kid was so busy looking at his damn cell phone, he never did see when the calves wandered into thistle. Like every baby, a calf is a silly creature; everything goes into its mouth. Well, his calves' mouths got all tore up and then the diphtheria set in and, within three weeks, fifteen calves had pneumonia. Ten died.

Judd's ranch was small. Ten dead calves in a season was huge. So he'd had no choice but to try and get a jump. Was it a risk bringing out eight new calves now? Sure. Nothing in this life was certain except death and taxes.

But what was worse was to get beat. What was worse was not to try at all.

CHAPTER 2

FOR ONCE, the weatherman was right about that storm, which just proved what his grandpa said: even a broken clock told the right time twice a day. Why, all any fool needed to do was go outside, look at the leaden bellies of those clouds, and get a good snootful. One whiff of that scent of chilled aluminum, and Judd knew the storm sweeping down from Canada he'd been tracking on his weather radar for the past week was going to be a doozy. In fact, he'd told all his neighbors about it, too, though they hadn't believed him until the weatherman came out and said so, which went to show some men needed somebody else to tell them what they ought to think. (Although, yes, Jess had been right to nag him into joining the 21st century, even though that had taken almost two decades. He wasn't against progress. He was against being bullied into it, was all.)

By three o'clock, the day was already graying out, and dense curtains of clouds had descended to cloak the already snow-shrouded Whitefish to the west and Black

Wolf Mountains to the north. As he headed for his cow barn—stumping through snowpack, his dog, Carson, pogoing up and down—his bum knee yammered and complained. Well, no help for it. He clamped his Stetson to his skull. A pregnant cow didn't care about the weather, and he was sure Brett was going to drop her calf by in the next couple of days. Then it was gonna be Bart and Aaron and Jordy and Randall and *pop, pop, pop* all down the line until Christmas.

That was something Jess never understood, him naming his cows after football players. He was partial to the Packers, primarily because Green Bay owned them and not some rich hotshot. *But they're girls, Judd*, Jess said. Well, he knew that. But what difference did it make? Brett was better than Daisy any damn day. Although, well, he'd hemmed and hawed about Randall. Cobb going to the Cowboys was just wrong, like when Favre hopped over to the Jets—anyone coulda told the man that would be a disaster—before settling down for that last, almost glorious season with the Vikings. Soon as Brett let fly that last pass in the playoff game, he'd known it'd be intercepted and that would be the end. But what a wild ride it was.

As he neared the barn, blasts of icy, wind-driven grit and balloons of fresh snow buffeted and snatched at his clothes. He'd bet those ski people up at those fancy places like Big Sky were popping bottles of champagne, beside themselves with relief. After last year's scant snow, it had been a white September. Going to the Sun Road over to the west in Glacier had closed early, and they'd endured an even whiter Thanksgiving. With nine

7

days before Christmas, he bet the resorts were cranking up Bing Crosby and ho-ho-hoing all the way to the bank. Not that he blamed them one bit. The last five years had been hard. Dry when it should be wet, the streams and rivers swollen to bursting when the levels should be low, first frost coming later and later, and not enough snowmelt to sneeze at for the spring thaw.

They had seen no real warmups in the past month. This meant the forest service people had been busy setting off charges to bring down floods of sun-softened powder before some fool skiers got themselves into trouble. He'd read somewhere that California used a vintage 105mm howitzer loaned by the Army for avalanche control. My, he wouldn't mind seeing that bad boy in action, though Jess opined he'd *surely* gotten enough of that in Vietnam, hadn't he?

She wasn't wrong. Still, he wouldn't mind watching the park service people lob some of those bad boys. Watch all that snow blow up, he thought, kicking aside drifted snow so he could lever open the door. *Big white geysers and then it'd be like a river, a flood, all that snow barreling down the slopes with a—*

A faint boom grumbled to his right.

What? At the sound, Judd stopped kicking and turned from the barn door, blinking against icy bits that nipped at his cheeks and pecked at his eyes. That had come from the north, probably the Black Wolf. Unless he was hearing things? He cast a quick glance down at Carson. The big shepherd had gone still, ears pricked, snout snuffling in huge draughts of air as if he might parse the sound by scent alone.

Not his imagination, then. Odd noise. What had that been? He listened, ears straining against the whistle of the wind and he caught…yes, there was the slightest echo as the sound banged around and against the mountains.

To his right, Carson stamped and turned him a worried look.

"Beats me." He didn't know if his dog was spooked or wanted to be off because he sensed trouble. "If I had to guess, I'd say dynamite, but I'll be honest, boy. Not enough of a *boom*. More like a *bang.* Like something breaking, the way mountains will sometimes calve in a rockslide. Know what I'm saying?"

Carson whined in agreement.

"Yeah, that's what I think." Judd cocked his head and concentrated. "Let's see if it comes again."

The sound did not. He listened for another two minutes, long enough for the wind's fingers to stroke his neck and make him shiver, but heard nothing more. Even Carson's stance relaxed. Whatever had happened was clearly over.

"All right, then, let's get back to it," he said, pulling open the door, and sighed with pleasure as the barn exhaled an aroma of warm hay and manure. Inside, the cows were crunching and grumbling over their dried grass. He liked that sound. Found it a comfort, even.

At his entrance, Brett lowed from her birthing stall.

"How you feeling, girl?" A single glance at that kinked tail of hers answered the question. His own dad, Darren, always said keep an eye on that tail: *Cow goes into labor, she's gonna get restless, start turning around looking for a place to lie down, and that tail's gonna kink out to the side instead of hang straight down.* In all his years of ranching, he had yet to find a reason to doubt his father. To his practiced eye—straw wasn't wet, so her water hadn't broken, and she hadn't set to trembling or huffing like a blown horse yet—he thought Brett had a ways to go. Maybe another day and then all his girls would follow, possibly right up to Christmas. That made him chuckle. Talk about away in the manger. He wondered what his pastor would say if he missed the eleven o'clock service on Christmas Eve. Somehow, Judd thought his pastor would have a hard time seeing the poetic justice. Jess, who sang in the choir, loved the candles, the music, even the breathy toots from the church's anemic organ. If he missed the service, she might not speak to him again until after the New Year. Some men his age might not find that a loss.

He wondered now if he would mention that odd crack in the distance to her. It was...off, an almost familiar sound at a strange time. He was no expert, but he knew snow and these mountains, and if that *was* the avalanche control people setting off a charge, well, you didn't do that as a storm got going. That was plain futile.

What had that *crack* been then? Not a rifle, though the sound had been almost sharp enough, and not a shotgun either. Neither weapon was big enough to carry twenty, thirty miles. He felt in his bones that the sound was far away, which meant whatever had caused it was big.

You are not going to solve this, you old fool. That

sounded suspiciously like Jess, and, for once, he decided she was right.

So, for the time being, Judd gave himself over to caring for his eight girls and because that odd cracking sound did not come again—because he was a busy man with worries and calves coming out of season—Judd put it out of his mind and forgot about it.

For a time.

GRAVITY

"But, *Mah-awm*." The kid was gawky with a bob of cinnamon-brown hair and owlish specs. Clutching a book to her chest, she said, "I don't *have* to."

"Now, honey." The mom's belly was so bloated, give her a little white chef's cap and she could be the Pillsbury Doughboy's stunt double. "The plane's small, and we'll be in the air for quite a while. Let's try, okay?"

The kid sighed with the beleaguered air of a teacher trying very hard to help a slow student through a thorny math problem. "Mom, first off, I'm twelve, not two. I think I know when I need to go. Second, are you sure you're not projecting? You need to go every ten minutes these days."

Impressive, Young Skywalker. Emma bet when *this* girl was two, she already ran circles around the adults. She was what Emma always imagined Meg Wallace to be in *A Wrinkle in Time* (the book, not the movie; she couldn't get past Oprah's glittery eyebrows): a little disheveled, all elbows and knees. Even the braces fit. Then, too,

Emma glimpsed a shadow of herself in this girl, one who was probably smart, a loner, a misfit. A girl everyone tolerated but no one truly liked because she knew the answers or how to find them if she didn't. (Goldsmith got that *totally* right, too. Kids were completely *Lord of the Flies* when it came to a whiff of difference.) Fiddling with the small charm dangling from a thin gold chain around her neck, Emma squinted to make out the title of the kid's book. *In Search of Schrödinger's Cat: Quantum Physics and Reality.*

Okay, *most* impressive.

"Jesus." A pasty-faced guy who was all twitches and tics, stood a few steps ahead of the mom and the kid. His restless fingers drummed his thighs. "You gonna make that kid mind, Rachel, or you need me to do it?"

Interesting. The guy's anxiety almost had an odor to it, something she associated with new sweat and old cigarettes. Emma had a pretty good idea what this guy was about. Minot was, after all, a big booming oil town with all its big booming, largely imported vices. Snow wasn't the only white substance in abundance.

The girl favored the guy with a cool look. "Thank you, but no one asked your opinion. Besides, you're not my father. You're just the drug-addicted partner in rehab who married my mom because he had nowhere else to go."

"Say what?" the guy snapped.

Kim's voice seeped through an earbud. "Emma, are you there?"

"I'm here," she said, not taking her eyes from this little drama.

"What's going on?" asked Kim.

"*Masterpiece Theater*," she said.

"What?"

"You think you don't have to listen?" The guy looked as if backhanding the kid wasn't something he'd have to think about really hard or feel the least bit sorry for later. "I don't see you not eating. I don't see you not wearing the clothes I buy with the money I earn…"

"Scott, *please*," the mom said, putting a hand on the guy's chest and darting an embarrassed look around. Her dark eyes touched on Emma for a moment before jumping away. "Both of you," she said, lowering her voice. "Stop. Scott, back off, all right?"

Scott flared. "Oh, so it's *my* fault now?"

"Well, given the fact we have to move because she's pregnant and you can't stay clean," the girl said, "yeah."

"Stop," Rachel begged the girl. "Please."

Kim's voice came through her earpiece. "Is there a problem?"

"I'm not sure." If the kid weren't a kid, Emma could almost see her way to liking her, perish the thought. The only thing she knew for sure about kids was she wanted nothing to do with them. Until recently, this had seemed a really good strategy. Man, maybe it *was* time to see a shrink. She could do it on the down-low, pay out of pocket so there wouldn't be a paper trail, figure out her next moves. What she really didn't need was for anyone to find out she was getting her head examined. That happened, they'd slap her on a ward again, maybe at Andrews, maybe Lackland—*see, see, she's crazy, says so right here*—and then it was a toss-up

17

whether they put her someplace quiet or medically boarded her ass out. (She was actually surprised they hadn't done that already; it wasn't as if the past eighteen months were a dream. But, then again, everyone thought her little month-long mental health vacation was understandable. People were willing to cut her some slack because, you know, it wasn't every day a woman's husband blew his brains out all over the bathroom with his own service weapon.)

Her going after Ben's CO three months ago, shouting murder and cover-up? Supremely stupid.

Scott, it appeared, was not as impressed with the kid as Emma was. Fists bunched, he took a step forward. "You little—"

Okay, in another second, this was going to be a real story. Darting a quick look over a shoulder, Emma saw no one who looked remotely like airport security. *Hell.*

"Hang on, Kim." Whipping her phone around, Emma called, "Hey, Scott? You mind speaking up for the camera?"

Scott's head jerked around and then his jaw went slack, his eyes buggy. The look was almost comical. "The fuck?"

"Hold it." Emma's touched off a burst; her camera went *snickety-snick-snick.* "So, what's your last name, Scott?"

"What?"

"Paisley," the girl said. "Thank God, I'm still a Moore."

"Paisley? Seriously?" Emma laughed. "Panty-ass name."

"Hey!" Scott purpled. "Who the fuck you calling panty-ass?"

"Who threatens to beat up a kid?" Emma shot back. "I'm documenting all this for the record."

"That's an invasion of privacy!" Scott's ferret-like nose twitched. "You ain't got the right!"

"We're in a public space," the girl reminded him.

Ooo, that kid needed to learn when to cool it. "Last time I checked," Emma said, "it's still a free country, child abuse is illegal, you *are* in a public space, and reporters gather all the news that's fit to print."

"Really?" The girl looked at Emma with new respect. "You work for *The New York Times*?"

In my dreams. If her commanding officer had anything to say about it, her next assignment might be a permanent posting to Outer Mongolia where she'd be a regular contributor to the *Tibetan Tribune*. Did the Air Force have listening posts out there? If not, they might build one just for her.

"The *Times* might be interested," she said to the kid. "Or *The Washington Post*, that's a good one. So, Scott…" She touched off another burst and wondered when airport security was going to get its act together and storm to the rescue. "Is that Paisley like the design or with a Y?"

"Please." The girl's mother slid in front of Scott, though whether she was shielding or restraining him was unclear "Thank you, but we're okay now." She put a hand on Scott's arm. "We're good, aren't we?"

For a second, Emma thought it could go either way. But then it seemed as if the guy's common sense kicked in. "Yeah, we're good. We're *fine*." Stuffing his fists in his pockets, Scott gave them all a parting glower. "I'm going to get a coffee and something to eat, have a smoke. I'll meet you there."

As Scott stalked off, the girl looked up at her mother. "That went well."

"Do you ever *stop*?" Rachel backhanded a wisp of hair from her forehead. "You're making this so much harder than it already is. He's trying."

"I agree, he's very trying." Then, the girl sighed and leaned into her mother's side. "Sorry." She looked, suddenly, as if working so hard to be the only adult in the room was simply too much. "I'm just mad."

"I know." Looking toward Emma, Rachel gave a wan smile. "Thank you for your concern, but we're good now. Are you really a reporter?" When Emma nodded, Rachel said, timidly, "You wouldn't use—"

Emma shook her head. "Of course not. No harm, no foul." Besides, threats were only words. Threats were like the bullets in a loaded gun: lethal only if you pulled the trigger.

"Thanks," the girl said as she and her mother walked off. "I'm Mattie."

"Emma," she said. "Later, gator."

She never dreamt for a second that this might come true.

"WELL, that sounded exciting from my end." Kim's voice was tinny and thin; snow always messed with Emma's cell. "Where are you?"

"Airport," Emma said, trying to ignore the tinkle of bad Muzak dribbling from the airport's overhead speakers. If Emma had to listen to Burl Ives go on about a holly, jolly Christmas one more time, her brain was going to melt. Well, if she didn't vomit again first. Actually, she thought both were excellent possibilities. Man, instead of acid rock, they ought to blast old Burl at terrorists. After a couple of hours, those guys would be gibbering idiots.

"I got that," Kim said dryly. "But which one? Are you in Montana already?"

"Nope. Catching a connection in why-not-Minot," Emma quipped, trying for perky and chipper though she was anything but. Even after brushing her teeth a third time and swishing with mouthwash so strong her eyes watered, her mouth still tasted like something vile had taken a crap, crawled under tongue, and promptly died.

Kim laughed. "I take it Minot's still a garden spot?"

"Oh, yeah, you betcha," she said in her best Upper Midwest accent, which was really the same as North Dakota when you got right down to it because almost everyone who first settled there came from or through the Midwest. Back when she'd last been here...six years ago felt right...Minot was *Fargo* on steroids. (She thought the TV series was good, but the movie was way better, mostly because Frances McDormand not only had the accent down—really, all the natives sounded exactly like that—but even seven months pregnant, Sheriff Gunderson kicked some serious butt. Many women in North Dakota and most of the Upper Midwest were like that. Emma's grandmother, a wickedly good shot who'd schooled Emma on the ins and outs of a rifle, had learned from *her* mother, whose own family had done a Laura Ingalls Wilder but abandoned the Dakotas in favor of heading back to the Wisconsin Northwoods because, as her Bubbe Sarah often said, *Potatoes, potatoes, potatoes, oy, mein Gott, you never saw so many potatoes! The only other thing to eat was prairie dog except we couldn't—and why, you may ask? Because, girlchik, prairie dogs aren't kosher.*)

"When do you fly out?"

"Within the hour, I hope. If we don't, we'll never beat this storm." She was camped out at the Trestle Tap House on the airport's second floor...oh, no, sorry, that was the *Terrazzo* Story for the cultured among us. Whatever. Morose, bleary-eyed guys who clearly lived by the maxim that it was always five o'clock somewhere lined the bar like sardines in a can. Above the bar, three ESPN announcers splashed on a big-screen TV nattered on about college bowl picks with all the enthusiasm of manic chipmunks on speed. The air smelled of old beer, bacon, fried eggs, and warm milk.

She'd considered eggs. Protein was supposed to be good, give her staying power, but then she thought about how slimy eggs were before they were cooked and, you know, they really *did* look a little bit like snotty eyes, which was mixing metaphors but whatever. In the end, she'd ordered a cup of herbal tea—something vaguely Asian she imagined only really flexible women in formfitting yoga getups choked down—and a muffin whose raisins resembled rat turds. Sawdust would've tasted better. She managed two nibbles before her stomach heaved and tried crawling into her throat, and she gave up.

Cupping her tea, she turned her back on the tap house in favor of a view of the tarmac through the terminal's enormous floor-to-ceiling windows. The snow was more blowing than truly falling, great balloons of the stuff swirling back and forth in curtains through which she glimpsed snowplows with winking lights. The way the plows worked a grid reminded her of Pacmen gobbling energizers. Looking at all that made her shiver and want to crawl into her steaming cup instead of drink it. "I'm waiting for the pilot to text when he's ready to go."

"Really?" Kim's voice crackled through an earbud. "Text? What kind of airline is this?"

"It's not. An airline, I mean. My Delta connection got canceled. I guess it got hung up farther west, I don't know." On the tarmac, a worker in an enclosed yellow cab at the end of a long, extended boom mounted on a large white truck sprayed clouds of deicing liquid over a jetliner. Did they de-ice little itty-bitty bush planes? She hoped so. "I think they're also worried about how long they can keep the runways clear with the storm headed this way," she said, sipping at her tea, which truly sucked and no amount of sugar could possibly save. Gwyneth Paltrow always made herbal tea sound like heaven in a cup, which only went to show what a great actress the woman was. Then again, it was probably a blessing in disguise because whatever Emma couldn't get down could not come back for a visit. "Anyway, I found this private pilot who wants to get out, too. The charter was already contracted, and he had space because somebody else didn't show, so…" Actually, the guy was probably double-dipping, charging both the client who canceled and her, but being between that proverbial rock and a hard place, it wasn't as if she had tons of choices.

Well, she did have *one*. She could punt. She just wasn't sure she could live with herself after. But, man, she really did want to give up, cry *uncle*, sign her separation papers, and go find a nice cave. Roll a rock over the entrance. Order in the occasional pizza.

"A charter? How big is the plane?"

"Small. Two prop job, so it's not going to go *high*-high, which I guess is good?" She truthfully had no idea. Wasn't it better to be above a storm than in it? Yeah, but what went up always had to come back down, so it probably evened out in the end. Although having flown a couple of transports in turbulence so bad even the pilot blew his cookies—always exciting, watching a guy try to steer and barf at the same time—she knew it was the in-between that could suck. One person barfed, pretty soon everybody did. A doctor once said it was a sympathetic response. But that was crap. It was the smell. These past couple of weeks of hugging porcelain, she'd become a world authority on the persuasive powers of puke.

Jeez, quit it, will you? The image of her hanging over a bowl or blowing her cookies into an air sickness bag made her stomach lurch. She forced another sip of tea. "The plane's got room enough for eight people and luggage," she said. "The pilot does a lot of backcountry flying, I guess."

"Are you okay?" Kim sounded suspicious. "You sound weird. In fact, last night before we went out, you were *acting* weird. You actually looked kind of green there."

"No, no." Kim had insisted on treating her to dinner and drinks. She'd only wet her lips on the hot sake and, while she liked sushi, the briny smell and glistening slabs of fish and curdled lumps of raw sea urchin made her stomach flip. All she really managed was rice. "I'm okay. Just tired. We stayed out too late on a school night, I guess."

"Honey, we got back to your place at nine."

"Okay, then I'm nervous, all right?" *And sick as a dog*, she could've added but didn't.

"And snappish, too."

25

"I'm fine." She loved Kim, she really did, but she was *this* close to throwing her cell across the concourse. "Anyway, about the pilot?"

"Are we changing the subject?"

"Yes. So, he flies hunters, mainly, and fishermen all around the Mountain West and into Canada, Alaska."

"Oh. Well, sounds like he knows what he's doing then, although you wouldn't catch me dead in one of those puddle jumpers."

"I don't suppose you've considered how truly unfortunate a turn of phrase that was."

"You didn't have an alternative?"

Other than running back home and pulling the covers over my head? "For today, no. It was sort of Hobson's choice. This horse or nothing, you know? Anyway, it's the Air Force's dime, so I couldn't *not* go." Though she'd certainly considered it. There were worse things than holing up in a hotel room with a remote and a bathroom within easy reach. As she recalled, Minot had some very good pizza places that delivered. Not many, but a few. On the other hand—she heard herself give a small *urk-urk* and pressed a hand to her mouth—maybe a loaded meat-lovers of pepperoni, sausage, ham, and bacon with extra cheese was a really bad idea. (It would almost certainly cause her bubbe to turn over in her grave. Bubbe Sarah had kept a strictly kosher house, and although Emma did not, even she couldn't quite mix milk and meat or chow down on a Polish sausage—and oh, that sea urchin would've given Sarah a heart attack —without hearing her bubbe: *Nu, these American Jews eating their ham and sausages and shrimp like the goyim, you'd think they never heard their grandmothers. Tu on a khazer a shtrayml, vet er vern rov.* She agreed, of course. Putting a streimel on a pig would not make it a rabbi, but she'd pay good money to see that.)

"You *sure* you're okay?" Kim asked.

"Perfect." She forced down more tea. She was dehydrated, that was all. Low blood sugar, too. She could tell from the way her lips tingled. *I'll have to get something down before the flight or I will never last.* It would be so her luck to suddenly get an appetite at twelve thousand feet and not a peanut or bag of stale pretzels in sight.

"You aren't thinking of backing out?"

"No," she lied, running a thumb over the tiny smooth ruby at the heart of her *Mogen Dovid*. The necklace had been Sarah's. Emma never took it off, which was stupid in its way because the whole God thing was a nonstarter. People never got that, either, that a person could see herself as Jewish but secular, involved in the culture and several thousands of years of history but not the religion. No one could be, say, a secular Methodist. "If I did, I'd have to explain to you and everybody else in the group why I chickened out when there was an alternative."

"Good. I don't mind being the voice of conscience."

"Yeah, well, you're not sitting in Minot while Burl Ives gives you a frontal lobotomy." Although Burl had given way to Bing, who wasn't bad for a crooner. Her bubbe had loved Dean Martin: *And that Frank Sinatra? Those eyes? That man could eat crackers in my bed anytime.*

"Minot won't be forever."

"That's true." With her luck, they'd probably be

playing Burl Ives on every radio station in Montana. "And dogs are okay. You know, for animals."

"There you go. From what I heard, I don't think this guy...what's his name, Kurtz?"

"Kuntz," she corrected. "Joseph Kuntz. They call him Kujo, though God knows why. Makes him sound like an escapee from a Stephen King novel."

"As long as he's not Jack Nicolson coming at you with an axe, you're golden. What I was going to say is Kuntz is one of Hank Patterson's guys. They're all former military. They get it. They've all been through the shit same as us."

Except they're still around. She was also positive *none* had been through the shit she was *still* going through. "No, no, I get that. It's that I can't see a story about vets and their retired war dogs as, you know, Pulitzer Prize material." Just her luck, she'd chosen journalism when all the papers were dying. "Besides, there have been scads of books out on these guys and their dogs already, before and after. Pick up any paper, do a half-assed search, and there are stories of vets healed by horses, dogs, cats." *Probably gerbils and turtles. Goldfish.* Though she didn't say that. Kim was also a reporter, though a civilian now. Most military newspapers operated that way, with a largely civilian staff supplemented with a few active duty folks like Emma. Given how Emma's life had gone these last nearly two years, Kim believed she was doing her a favor by getting Emma the hell out of Dodge so she could get her head on straight and decide on her next move. Kim thought she knew the real story, but she didn't. Emma had decided she couldn't be responsible for one more dead person.

But she also hadn't been able to resist. When Kim mentioned southern Montana, she thought, a hop, skip, and a jump, and she'd be in Boise and forty miles from the base at Mountain Home. Ben had been working a lead in Mountain Home. That much she knew because she was the one who'd fed him the tip.

"I am positive I won't be saying anything new," she said.

"You'll never know if you don't go. When do you see that veterinarian with the search and rescue?"

"Sarah Grant?" Grant and a deputy, Hank Cooper, had made big news a year ago when they'd helped stop a band of smugglers transporting girls for the sex trade as well as a fortune in diamonds and heroin across the Canadian border. That woman…she was interested in meeting. Although it probably wasn't healthy. Ben's investigation had been shut down for lack of evidence. "Probably right away. We were scheduled for an interview in a couple days, but with the cancellation, I'll be coming in closer to her. Kuntz said he'd drive up to Lonesome where Grant and Cooper live and then we'll head down to his neck of the woods, spend a couple days at Eagle Rock. We might also go to a rehab ranch they've got down there, but we'll see."

"It sounds great. Dogs, veterans, Montana, mountains. What's not to like?"

"Right." She liked mountains, had never been to Montana, and thought the fuss about veterans was way overblown in a way that was similar to the national obsession with honoring anyone in any kind of uniform. Like every other occupation, the military had some truly stellar people on active duty, some okay people, and some complete and utter asswipes. As for dogs? She preferred cats. Dogs were okay, but they slobbered and were like kids, what with their constant need for attention. With a cat, it was understood that you were staff at best, a can opener at worst, and if a cat were larger, it would eat you. (That's where a dog really was better than a cat; you dropped dead, a dog would at least wait a couple days.)

"I'm looking forward to the terrific feel-good story you're going to turn in," Kim enthused. "Actually, it sounds like you've got enough there for that series we talked about." When she didn't respond, Kim coaxed, "Come on, Scrooge, you can't tell me the potential for some extra cash isn't nice."

"It's nice." *The Air Force Weekly* was footing the bill, although they'd also agreed that since she wasn't technically reporting on active duty folks, she could take any material she gathered and write up stories for other publications so long as they got first right of refusal. She'd already contacted an editor she knew at *The Washington Post* who'd said she'd be very interested in finding a home for Emma's series. Why, play her cards right, do a couple follow-up pieces—Patterson apparently had this whole network of vets she might be able to tap into—and the woman at the *Post* thought she could become a regular contributor.

And she did need the work, now more than ever, and especially if she did decide to separate. The military hadn't paid out for Ben. *Not of sound mind*, they said, which translated into no insurance and no benefits once she separated. (The military was interesting that way. Kill yourself, and you were automatically considered insane and the military didn't have to pay. If you *tried* to kill yourself but failed, they booted your ass out for misconduct. She knew of one Marine…back in 2010, this was…who'd slit his wrists and survived but ended up getting court-martialed because the military decided he'd harmed "good order and discipline" on account of bleeding on a sergeant, using up medical supplies when the corpsmen bandaged his wrists, and not reporting to the brig because, well, he'd been in the *hospital*.)

But, seriously, why should she stay in? Unless something radically changed, she would never make promotion and, after a couple of cycles, they'd separate her ass for her and call it *downsizing*. In fact, she had a sneaking suspicion that was the reason the *Weekly* was so accommodating about letting her shop stories. Short of a mental ward, it was a way of quietly suggesting she show herself out.

Of course, they could assign her to a story in a free-fire zone. A bullet at the right time in the right place or a well-placed mortar would do the trick. One second, she was a problem, the next, *boom*. Pink mist.

"You there, girlfriend?"

"I'm here. I was only—" *Getting morbid.* An occupational hazard when a girl went out for groceries and came back to the functional equivalent of an abattoir. "Thinking," she said.

"Yeah, I could smell the smoke coming out of your

ears from here. Listen, kiddo, I know this is hard. I know you have a decision to make. But you got this. When are you due back?"

"Christmas Eve Day." She'd toyed with jetting back on Christmas, but then she'd feel guilty making people who probably wanted to be at home with their families ask if she wanted cream and sugar with her tea and a bag of pretzels. On the other hand, the upside was that by the time her plane touched down, that excruciatingly long and boring day would be virtually over. Christmas was truly a soul-sucking experience for a Jew. Friends might invite you for a pre-party and eggnog—which had the consistency of liquid snot—but at the end of the day, you were still stuck with empty streets, Chinese takeout, and Netflix.

"Perfect. I'm having a little party at my place. A bunch of girls, no guys. You come and tell us how it went."

"Hey, so long as you hold the nog and got a bottle of Jack." Not that she was drinking these days, but a girl had to dream. At that moment, her phone chirped. "Hang on, I think this is the pilot...okay, he's ready," she said after reading the text. "I got to go."

"Safe journey. If you've got service, call when you get in. Oh, and wait. *Gut yom tov,*" Kim said, carefully. "I got that right, didn't I? Isn't it the first night of Hanukkah tonight?"

Despite everything...even Burl Ives and snotty eggnog...she was touched. She hadn't celebrated since Ben died, not that they'd ever done much either. She was marginally observant (more from guilt than anything else), and Ben was nothing, but it didn't matter because they'd had each other. Besides, Hanukkah was a minor rabbinical holiday and could be distilled into a fairly simple rubric that informed a *lot* of Jewish holidays: *you tried to kill us; you failed, ha-ha. Let's eat.* Hanukkah was totally hyped in the States, mostly so all the little Jewish kids didn't feel left out. When they were still alive, her own parents had done the candles and presents thing until Emma was bat-mitzvahed when they decided she was an adult and, *nu*, enough of this nonsense already.

She could see why. Light a candle, mumble a few blessings—except for the first night, they were the same two *every* single night—then round things out with a rousing chorus of "I Had a Little Dreidel" or "Rock of Ages" (sadly, nothing from the musical, although she'd once channeled Pat Benatar for fun; Bubbe Sarah was not amused). Other than unwrapping that night's present, that was it unless you went to the trouble of making latkes (a true pain, especially scraping your knuckles grating all those potatoes) or *sufganiyot*, which sounded exotic but was Hebrew for jelly doughnuts, big whup. Oh, and eat her way through a bag of relatively tasteless Hanukkah gelt, which was foil-wrapped chocolate shaped like gold coins. Like almost all kosher candies, gelt was truly disgusting. The stuff looked like plastic and tasted like brown earwax. Bubbe Sarah always did the *feh-feh* routine when it came to gelt. *Hanukkah is about charity,* she would say, *about tzedakah and giving to others, not about cavities.*

Whatever. In the end, really…Hanukkah just wasn't all that.

"It's the first night, yeah," she said It was also one of those rare years when the eighth day of Hanukkah and Christmas fell on the same day. "Thanks, Kim. That was nice of you to remember."

"Don't mention it. Now, go. Catch your plane," Kim said. "Go see some pretty mountains, play in the snow, pet some nice dogs. And, for God's sake, Scrooge, try to have a good time."

CHAPTER 3

SHE HAD BEEN to worse places than tiny little nothing towns in the middle of nowhere Montana. Like, you know, tiny little nothing towns in the middle of nowhere Afghanistan.

Though never officially at the front lines, she had come close. At his retirement party, a senior editor once said Afghanistan was like Vietnam. That war had been unlike any the U.S. had fought before. In World War II, there were front lines. You knew where the enemy was because all the armies were organized around the same, well-disciplined principles of front lines, fields of engagement, rear detachments. Other than resistance fighters, Churchill's SOE, and the American's own OSS, the war was conventional.

Vietnam changed all that. Everything remotely conventional was irrelevant in a country where the enemy operated as guerilla units, was everywhere and all around, and could be anyone. American soldiers fought for hills they conquered only to leave because the action had suddenly shifted someplace else, leaving the way open for the VC to return. Some hills changed hands a dozen times because the front lines were that fluid.

Her former editor also said those were the glory days for journalists, a time when a press card could get you a chopper ride to anywhere in-country. Men and women stringers could go out with the Marines at dawn, photograph them clearing a village or taking a hill, and still be back in Saigon or Da Nang for the Five O'Clock Follies, which was what the press called military briefings, and then head out for cocktails and a nice dinner. After Vietnam, the military clamped down on the press, mostly because the press reported on all the things the military didn't want civilians to see. *Now, they got embeds,* her editor had remarked, sourly. *They are gonna make sure you see only what they want you to see.*

Combat in Iraq was a lot like Vietnam, and Afghanistan even more so. The enemy was everywhere and everyone. Journalists still made it to the putative front lines but only as embeds, which meant two things: being attached to a particular news organization (no more freelancers) and to one unit, period. No more chopper-hopping.

There weren't as many women either. *Fembeds,* they were called, though she wasn't that either because she was regular military, a 3N0X5, the MOS for an Air Force photojournalist. Her job was to build up the Air Force's image, which meant that the time she did a story on women at Bagram and turned in a really nice spread, everyone zeroed in on one picture of a sign over the female head at Bagram Air Base: *DO NOT GO TO THE BATHROOM ALONE.*

My God, she'd near about been booted out for that one. A full bird shouted at her for a good fifteen minutes, most of it variations on, *What the hell are you trying to imply? Who do you think you are? Are you* trying *to give the Air Force a black eye, Corporal?* She bit back what she wanted to say: *Gee, no, sir, only pointing out that combat may not be the most dangerous thing about being a woman in Afghanistan, sir.*

They finally published her spread after gutting... uhm, *editing* out certain portions. All the interviews with women who described how weird being on a base where no woman went anywhere without a buddy got axed. Of course, that particular photograph of that particular head went into the circular file, too, in favor of nice, safe feel-goods: pics of our guys and gals in blue on 5K "fun" runs (*look at us, all grins and giggles, because we LOVE running at five a.m. because otherwise we'll MELT*). Surf 'n turf on Friday nights, Saturday and Sunday movie nights. They published her pictures of the Green Beans Coffee place and the KFC because, gosh, if a soldier had to look at one more lobster tail or fried shrimp or juicy steak, he or she might be forced to do violence.

If she hadn't still had time left on her enlistment and a desire to go to college, she'd have tried to get her ass medically boarded out. Seen a military shrink and said she was gay or something because this was back in 2009 and everyone knew that one way to a quick discharge— do not pass GO, do not collect two hundred dollars—

was to pull a Corporal Klinger on a shrink whose primary mission was to support the Air Force first and the patient second. (Confidentiality, my ass; a whiff of anything queer and you were gone.) The problem was the reason she'd joined up in the first place was for the GI Bill. She'd never be able to afford college for a journalism degree on her own.

So, yeah. She was stuck. Which sucked.

After Bagram, the Air Force pulled her stateside and put her on a short leash. She did nice, safe fluff pieces and was sent places where a photojournalist with a bee in her bonnet and burr up her ass could do little harm. Back then, when she hadn't yet been a threat, they'd only tried boring her to death and sent her places where nothing remotely controversial was going on.

One of those was Thule.

CHAPTER 4

THULE AIR BASE is in Greenland and about a thousand miles from the North Pole. The base was, when she arrived in August 2010 to do a story, and still is a spartan affair of single-story barracks, mess halls, a hospital, bowling alley, various admin buildings, as well as an air defense wing, radar tracking, and missile defense sprawled on concrete and bare brown earth right to the edge of an ice cap.

The mission at Thule is also as straightforward now as when it was first constructed on the sly back in 1951: keep an eye on those pesky Russians and their even peskier nukes. Over time, the mission's expanded to one of space surveillance via NORAD and the Air Force Space Command.

All of this boiled down to one indisputable fact. Thule was and is one of the most boring bases known to man. A place one sent new cadets and enlisted to see if they'd crack. Because, face it, if anything remotely interesting had happened, we'd have been at war with Russia eons ago.

Not expecting much—this was a fluff piece, after all—she'd flown in from BWI. She was seated on the right side of the plane, which people said was the "good" side. She had no idea what they were talking about until the plane banked over Baffin Bay and she looked down. There, in the middle of bluer-than-blue water, sculpted icebergs towered. Mount Dundas, an enormous, flat-topped tombolo thrusting up from the water, hulked over the base. She felt her throat constrict and her breath hang because it was all…beautiful.

She wandered the base in a daze that first day. Although there was still snow in some shaded nooks and crannies, the day was warmer than she expected, the mercury inching up to fifty. The personnel were a mix of Air Force, Canadian, and Danish military as well as civilian contractors. On their off-hours, guys in shorts played softball, and the few women stationed there ran endless loops around the airfield. Each dorm had its own kitchen, but the food in the chow hall was so good, most personnel ate there or splurged at Top of the World, an all-ranks club which hosted bands, dances, and special performers.

She met Ben at Top of the World. It was her second night, and she'd spent the day capturing the play of light on the icebergs and the sea. She wandered into the club, her hair smelling of icy salt, her cheeks still stinging from wind and sunburn. Slotting herself into an opening at the bar, she looked at the guy on her left. No real reason. Completely random.

What she noticed first was not his looks. She saw the book. Well, actually, the author's photograph on the cover: T.S. Eliot. Which simply did not compute. It was like finding a homicide cop who loved Jane Austen or Emily Dickinson.

"*The Waste Land*?" she asked.

"What?" He'd looked up, blue eyes a little glazed and unfocused until they sharpened on her. "Oh, no. Prufrock. You know Eliot?"

Her mother was an English teacher. Of course, she knew Eliot. Nu, was the pope Polish? (This had not been true for a couple years by then, but she still liked the line.) For the next several hours, they argued the poem over ice-cold Belvedere martinis—three olives, very dry, a glance at the vermouth bottle. He thought that the line, *I am Lazarus, come from the dead*, was an allusion to Lazarus and Jesus in John, while she pointed out that it might also be the beggar from Luke, and then that had led to a discussion of how a good Jewish girl knew anything about the New Testament. (It all boiled down to three words: know thy enemy.)

Two days later—her last on Thule, as it happened—they bundled up in parkas and hiked up Mount Dundas. It was kind of a weeny adventure. They made the seven hundred feet in an hour, more or less, though the best part was the final fifty feet straight up over sheer gray rock on a fixed rope, where he also taught her how to do an emergency belay because, well, you never knew. She teased him about being a Boy Scout. A throwaway line, sure, but also a test of sorts. She'd been raised by two people who were also *Star Trek* loons. For a school

Halloween party, her dad, who taught cinema and television at the local university extension, dressed up as Spock while her mom slathered on green body paint, donned a tattered bikini-thing, and did a pretty credible Orion slave girl while *she* near about died of embarrassment.

Anyway, if this guy had *ever* seen *The Wrath of Khan*, he knew what his line *should* be.

And he nailed it. "I may be many things," he said, managing to look offended, "but I was *never* a Boy Scout."

Then, to prove it, he kissed her—and then he did that again and again, and his lips were warm and hungry, and she sighed into his mouth. If it hadn't been forty degrees, and they'd not been on top of a barren plateau, things might have gone further right then and there. That would have to wait a few hours yet, though, but worth it because once they were in bed, they didn't have sex. They *made love*. Big difference.

Before they descended Dundas, they inked their names on a rock he'd carried up from the base and put it atop a large mound of other rocks left by previous climbers. They couldn't hold hands on the way back, not if they wanted to make it down alive. But it didn't matter. Every time she cast a glance over a shoulder, Ben was there, with those beautiful blue eyes and those lips, that face. That body she wanted to explore. The love they were in the process of making with a glance, a smile. An argument about Eliot. A throwaway line about Captain Kirk.

Thule was the beginning.

It was also, in a way, the death of him—and her.

CHAPTER 5

ON THE WAY TO THE CHARTERS' hangar, she spotted an airport shop that sold sweatshirts with bison logos, ball caps, magazines, newspapers, candy, gum, buttons, aspirin, and anything else a traveler might need so long as she was willing to cough up an obscene amount of money. The muffin was a stone in her gut, but at least it hadn't reappeared, so she might as well stock up because who knew when they'd get to Lone Ridge Airstrip, a place so tiny the charter pilot said there was no control tower and all flights were VFR only. *Visual flights rules*, he'd said. *It's one thing instrument flying in clouds. We can do that, but it's another trying to land somewhere, at night, with no tower or landmarks.* She'd already called Kuntz to let him know she wouldn't be landing at Billings. Thankfully, Kuntz—he kept telling her to call him Kujo, and all she could think of was that rabid dog —knew the airstrip, which was east of Lonesome, and said he'd get in touch with Hank Cooper so she wouldn't have long to wait for a pickup.

Maybe Kim was right. Maybe this was going to be okay after all, she thought, as she pulled two Gatorades from a cooler. She debated about a third Gatorade because hydration was important then thought that since she'd also gotten another piping-hot-but-tasteless herbal tea for her travel mug, she might live to regret that decision. She doubted the charter would have a john. Instead, she selected two sandwiches, egg salad and tuna. She wasn't the least bit hungry, but she was trying to be optimistic.

As she passed the shelves with various toiletries and over-the-counter meds, she looked for one particular item even as she told herself that a) she was being a nut and b) nothing would change. It was almost a relief when she didn't find what she was looking for but then, as she eyed a couple with two kids in tow wandering through, she considered that everything in a place like this had to be completely G-rated.

At the checkout, she threw in a bag of trail mix, Tic-Tacs, M&Ms, another travel-sized mouthwash, gum, and, finally, an Almond Joy because sometimes you just feel like a nut. The total bill came to thirty-five dollars before she also added a *New York Times* to the pile because there was something about the smell of newsprint and a real paper she liked. The downside was she'd wind up with blackened fingers. But, hey, beggars.

CHAPTER 6

SHE ALMOST MADE IT. Fifty feet from the entrance to the charters' hangar, she suddenly retched, her mouth filled with sour spit, and she knew she had about twenty seconds. Veering into a men's room—empty, thank God—she sped past a bank of urinals, slammed into a stall, dropped her pack, jackknifed at the waist, held her hair back with one hand, and hung over the bowl as she coughed out a flood of vomit. It didn't take long; other than the muffin, her stomach had been empty. When she was done, she spat, flushed, shouldered her pack, and was reaching for the latch when she heard that distinctive rasp only a zipper makes and then the unmistakable sound of someone taking a tinkle.

Shit. She glanced at her watch. The pilot had texted ten minutes ago. He wouldn't leave, would he? Quickly, she pulled out her phone and tapped out a message: *Got hung up. On my way now.* Slipping her cell into a leg pocket of her cargo pants, she waited until she heard a flush. She was about to call out a warning when the man beyond the stall said, "It's safe."

Heat flooded up her neck. How had he known? Unlatching the slider lock, she palmed the door open and stepped out.

"You okay?" He was at the sink, soaping his hands, and eyed her reflection in a mirror. "Bad sushi?"

That threw her. "I'm sorry?"

"Sushi. Does it to me every time. You'd think I'd learn not to buy sushi from anyplace that's landlocked, but…" He smiled into the mirror, and a small dimple showed on the right. "I like to live dangerously."

Despite her embarrassment, she felt her mouth kick into a lopsided grin. "No, only an upset tummy." Moving to the sink, she punched on water and soaped her hands. Her eyes strayed to his left hand. No ring. Didn't necessarily mean anything. *And what are you thinking? You, of all people, you don't get to think about things like that.* As she rinsed, she noticed a tiny pink worm of a scar peeping from the bottom edge of her left cuff. *Crap.* Quickly yanking down the left sleeve and then the right for good measure, she rinsed then dug out a plastic Ziploc with her toothpaste and toothbrush from her backpack as well as her new bottle of mouthwash. She should've bought two while she was it. Maybe emptied out the store.

He watched her reflection squirt a worm of toothpaste onto her brush. "You sure you're all right? You're pretty pale."

"I'm okay." Keeping an eye on her right cuff—she had a feeling this guy didn't miss much—she focused on brushing her teeth fast before someone else wandered in. The way the guy was still looking freaked her out a little, and when his eyes drifted to her chest, she felt a twist of disgust. *Perv.*

She was about to spit and tell him so when he said, "Nice necklace. Looks old. The stone, that is. Unusual to see a ruby in a cabochon cut."

Her necklace had flopped out when she was yorping. "Uh, yeah," she mumbled through foam. Tucking the charm back inside her collar, she spat, rinsed, swished, tugged down both sleeves at the cuffs again, and said, "Thanks. It was my grandmother's." Now, why had she bothered with that? "Anyway, thanks for, you know, being so understanding about me..." She gestured toward the stall she'd vacated.

"Don't mention it." Hefting an enormous pack to which he'd also lashed a sleeping bag and snowshoes, he slotted a folded copy of the *Minot Daily News* under an arm and moved to the exit. "Feel better and safe travels."

He had a nice smile. And his eyes—she dried her toothbrush under a blow-dryer—they were hazel, weren't they? Only they'd also changed color with the light. Shouldering her daypack, she headed for the exit. When they caught the light, his eyes were a warm shade of amber.

As she turned out of the bathroom, her phone buzzed with an incoming text. Probably the pilot, again. Tugging out her cell, she thumbed her way past the lock screen and started reading the message.

A man's voice, way too close. "Oh, good, there you—"

"What?" Her head jerked up, and she head-butted the guy. *"Oof!"* Her jaw snapped shut with an audible click. A sharp dart of pain arrowed into her tongue. The smack set a swarm of white fireflies flitting before her eyes. Reeling, she heard her cell clatter to the floor and felt her boots tangle.

"Whoa, whoa, I got you." Clamping a hand onto her left elbow, he held her steady as she regained her footing. "Are you all right? God, I'm so sorry." He nodded toward the unfolded newspaper he still had in his right hand. "I figured I'd read my paper and, you know, stand guard until you were done to keep other guys from walking in until you had—"

"I'm all right, thanks." Her head ached, and her tongue hurt, though they couldn't compete with the embarrassed flush prickling her neck. Scooping up her cell, she said, "I should've been watching where I was going. I hate it when people do that, too, you know?" She was babbling but couldn't help herself, she was so mortified. "Zombie-walking when they ought to be paying attention to—"

"You're bleeding." He made an abortive moment as if to thumb something away from her mouth then stopped. Reaching around to a hip pocket, he tugged out a packet of tissues. "Here."

"Thanks." Tweezing out a tissue, she blotted and peeked then wrinkled her nose at the spot of blood. "I'm sorry. That was very sweet of you, but I'm late, and I really have to go. I'm headed that way," she said, taking a step back and hooking a thumb over her shoulder. "I don't want the pilot to leave without me."

"Me neither." He waggled his cell. "Got another nastygram."

"You—" *Oh, this is just perfect.* She ought to give Nora Roberts a jingle. With this kind of meet-cute, she was destined for her own series. Maybe Renèe Zellweger would star. Although *she'd* already jumped to the third film in the series, hadn't she? "You're going to Montana," she said, flatly.

"As it happens." Showing that grin again, he stuck out a hand. "Will Shirer."

He had a nice grip, too, and his palm was warm, though a little calloused, as if he was outdoors a lot. From the looks of his pack, this was probably true. "Emma Gold."

"Nice to meet you, Emma." He broke contact first. "Guess we'd better hustle before the pilot takes off without us."

"Yeah," she said. "Guess we'd better."

CHAPTER 7

IN RETROSPECT?

They should've missed the damn plane.

ON TAKEOFF, the way ahead had been relatively clear, but things went south about an hour into the flight. Anvils of glowering clouds pressed down as the turbulence built, morphing from gentle swells to a fast, stomach-churning slalom. There was no escape, either. The clouds towered too high for them to clear, so the pilot had been forced to go lower, which sucked because that meant the mountains, which before had been distinct snowy ridges and crinkles in the Earth and no more consequential than a rumpled bed, suddenly grew fangs.

There was a roar and then a shimmy as another huge wave of turbulence broke against the plane. The fuselage shook, the window to Emma's left buzzed, something overhead bawled, and her seat creaked.

"Holy...!" It was Scott. Of course, it was Scott. It

would be just her dumb luck that Scott, Rachel, Mattie's grandfather, and Mattie were on the same charter. The seats were odd, too, with the two immediately behind the cockpit facing out and so, because Scott was strapped in behind the copilot, she and he had no choice but to actually make eye contact. (Earlier, when she and Will wandered up, Scott's face had screwed into a murderous clench. If looks were daggers, she ought to have bled out on the spot. His hostility was so obvious Will had turned her a puzzled look.)

"Jesus!" Scot shouted as the plane stuttered, so the word came out *Gee-hee-hee-hee-sus.* "You trying to crash us or what?"

"It's only air." Mattie was across the sliver of aisle to Emma's right. The pilot had put her and Emma in the last two seats in front of a locker and the rear cargo hold because they were both lightweights. As the plane swooped again, the girl pressed her book to her chest and closed her eyes. "It's just bad air, Scott. Bad air can't hurt you."

"Hell you say." Already sickly, Scott's pallor had gone fish-belly white with a touch of green under the gills. One hand gripping an air-sickness bag, Scott leaned against his headrest and swallowed, the knuckle of his Adam's apple rolling up and down his throat. "Blows hard enough, we're gonna end up pancakes."

"Flew worse in 'Nam. This isn't anything worth getting worked up about. Besides, I'm almost positive the pilot would like to get there in one piece." It was Mattie's grandfather, who hunkered in a seat behind the pilot and directly opposite Rachel's mother. His breath came in chuffs because, while Burke kept the windshield clear, he hadn't wanted to tax the engines by pulling heat away for the cabin. Like the rest of them, the old man was swaddled in cold-weather gear—in his case, an olive-green parka with a fur-trimmed snorkel he'd pulled up and then zipped as soon as Burke took off. In the cabin's gloom, his face was a pale, indistinct glimmer, something from a bad detective novel where the body's found floating face-up at the bottom of a well. "Take it from me, complaining won't do a damn bit of good or get us there faster. You'd do best to relax there, Scott."

"Yeah, well, I'll *relax* when I got both feet on the ground again." Leaning forward with a groan, Scott let his head hang between his knees. "I should *never* have let you people talk me into this."

Out of the corner of an eye, Emma saw Mattie open her mouth but then closed it as if thinking better of whatever she'd been about to say as Rachel, whose seat was in front of Emma's, shot her daughter a warning frown. Rolling her eyes, Mattie flopped back in her seat and returned to her book.

Having finished her *Times* and decided trying to drink her tea meant she'd likely be wearing it, Emma was bored. She'd considered Ben's much-read, dog-eared copy of *The Waste Land*. Yes, she was being morbid, but somehow Eliot's poem felt so right. She hadn't taken out the book, though. The book was a talisman, really, and how would she explain if someone…Will, for example, who was a row up and immediately in front of Mattie…asked? *Well, yes, it's all about fear and people caught in limbo, neither here nor there, and you know, the way Eliot says April is cruel because that's when life springs forth only for death to follow? Well, three guesses when Ben died...uhm, when he killed himself...er... when he was murdered to make sure he stayed quiet and his investigation went nowhere, the investigation that was my fault because I suggested it. I sniffed out a nugget of a story that everyone says isn't true.*

Yeah. That would've gone over like a lead balloon.

Instead, cinching her shoulder harness down another notch, she pushed aside one half of a set of blue fabric curtains attached to brass rods top and bottom in front of her window then gasped as the twin-engine Chieftain suddenly porpoised, rising and then dipping then rising again. Listen to Mattie, Emma thought as her stomach dropped to her toes. Her butt tried levitating for the ceiling, and she grew momentarily weightless. Her hands hooked her armrests in a death grip. *It's only air, bad air. Air can't hurt you.*

For a giddy second, there was the disorienting sensation of having nothing *but* air beneath her feet. Her shoulder strap dug as the plane fell the way a car plunges from the top of a rollercoaster. Rivets squealed; the entire fuselage squeaked; the prop's grumbles swooped in a decrescendo. If there'd been interior lights, they'd probably have winked. She heard the slosh of avgas stored in two inflatable bladders which were secured, along with their luggage in the cargo hold behind her seat. There was a third empty bladder and, when she asked about it, Burke tipped her a wink: *Well, if we get stuck and we maybe want a bunch of hot water for a bath or something.* A second later, the twin engines surged as the plane rebounded and they leveled.

Man. Slamming back down into her seat, Emma let out a grunt. Maybe it was a good thing she didn't have anything on her stomach. On the one hand, this still wasn't as bad as a chopper ride she'd taken in Afghanistan when, on his approach to base, the pilot had violently jinked the helicopter right and then left and then right again before diving because, as she later discovered, the insurgents who lay in wait with Stingers were really, really good.

"Okay." Mattie flicked a tongue over her lips. "Even I'm impressed. That was pretty bad."

"See? S'what I'm saying." Scott's head still hung between his knees. "Man, I should *never* have had those eggs."

"It might help if you stopped talking about all the food you wish you weren't going to throw up," said Mattie.

Her mother shot her another look of warning. "Maybe we should switch places, Scott?" Rachel's hand was on her buckle. "Facing forward might help—"

"Mom!" Mattie shouted at the same time that a hand shot across the aisle and gripped Rachel's wrist.

"Bad idea in turbulence," Will observed. He'd dragged on a watch cap, neck warmer, and pop-top mittens along with a dark blue parka. "You won't make anything better if you get tossed, Rachel, and in this turbulence..." He paused as another blast buffeted the plane. "In this turbulence," he continued, "you *will* lose your balance and you *will* get tossed." Relinquishing his grip, Will cast a significant look at Rachel's swollen belly straining against a rust-red parka. "You've got someone else depending on you to make the right choices. Scott's an adult. He'll be fine."

"Who the fuck asked you?" Scott flared. "What makes you such an authority, huh?"

"On which? The fact that your wife is really pregnant or that you're supposed to be an adult?"

"Real smart guy, aren't you?" The tip of Scott's nose twitched. "We crash and then we'll see how smart you—"

"Hey, you mind putting a lid on it?" It was Hunter, the co-pilot, on the righthand side of the cockpit. Snatching a quick look over his left shoulder, Hunter snapped, "Look, I get the ride's rough, but none of this jawing is making things any better. Everyone calm down."

"We're calm," Will said, mildly. "Emma, are you calm?"

"Uh." *No.* "Sure."

Mattie's grandfather gave a thumbs up. "Aces."

"Great." Will turned to look back at Mattie. "And I know you're calm."

"Well, I'm not hysterical like some people," Mattie said.

"Mattie," Rachel warned.

"As you can see, we're fine," Will reported to Hunter. "So, why don't you just concentrate on getting us there?"

Rachel raised a timid hand. "Unless, maybe, we should turn back? It's only been an hour and a half or so. We'd certainly get back faster than we're getting where we want to go."

As far as logic went, Emma had to admit it wasn't a bad idea. They were headed into the teeth of the storm, which was precisely why her original flight had been canceled in the first place.

"Whoa, whoa, none of that. No one's turning back. We'll get there." It was their pilot, Burke, who also happened to be Hunter's father. The two looked nothing alike. Squat and square, Hunter was a fire plug of a man with a thick middle, beefy hands, a Jeremiah Johnson thatch of wiry red beard, and a florid complexion that suggested he'd never met a beer he didn't want to get to know a lot better. In contrast to his son, Burke was lean and brown and tough as jerky with a voice of a longtime smoker that was as gravelly as a cement mixer. When she and Will had made their way to the plane, father and son were deep in some discussion accompanied by a lot of hand-waving on Hunter's part and a whole lot of headshakes from Burke. They'd been out of earshot, so she never did understand what Hunter was so worked up about, although Rachel mentioned he was worried about weight. *Although I don't know why. We don't have* that *much luggage, and this is a pretty big plane for a twin-prop.*

"We're still at twenty thousand. Nothing's going to reach up and bite us." Gaze focused on the milky view beyond his windshield, Burke said, "I know these mountains and this route like the back of my hand."

Yeah, you know it so well you've got to be checking that map spread over your knee every five seconds. Either he

57

didn't trust his instruments, or it might be habit. All the rides she'd ever taken, even in helicopters, were IFR, not visual though she'd known helo pilots who spread out those maps first thing, mostly when they were headed into areas they'd never flown before. When she saw Burke unfold that midway, she'd felt a small clutch of alarm. A map didn't suggest familiarity...unless Burke was searching for alternative routes? That made sense. Burke had mentioned having popped in new displays along with a set of new tanks. While she supposed instruments were comforting (though only to a degree because you were, after all, trusting a machine not to hiccup), they were useful only for flights into and out of airports with specific and designated flight routes. IFR still meant you were, essentially, flying blind, trusting machines to keep you on the proverbial straight and narrow.

What he could possibly be looking at was a mystery, too, considering they were flying in the equivalent of marshmallow fluff. She wondered if the map was a topo. Could be that he was only refamiliarizing himself with the lay of the land and how high the mountains got around here. How high was that? She was afraid to ask. Or maybe he was hoping for a break in the clouds to eyeball landmarks? Wait, didn't instruments do that? Ping a warning or something? *Crap.* She cast a quick look out her window, but there was precious little to see other than snow, the clouds, a tiny winking red light at the tip of the Chieftain's left wing. *How do I get myself into things like this?*

"Have you ever had to put down?" asked Will. "Our

ceiling's already getting pretty low. You're going to be scraping the deck on the approach."

"You a pilot?" asked Burke.

"I've flown a bit."

"Military?"

"Civilian. For fun."

"Huh," Hunter grunted. "Figures."

"Oh?" asked Will, still in that mild, unthreatening way. "How does it figure?"

"That you're a doctor. You guys are all alike. We see plenty of 'em because we're flying 'em all the time in summer. Montana, Idaho, Canada, Alaska, wherever there's game or fishing and a nice comfy lodge with a good bottle of wine at the end of the day. Half the time, they're talking your ear off about what you're doing wrong." Hunter shook his head again. "You all think you know everything."

"Hunter," Burke warned.

Will held up a gloved hand. "It's okay. Everyone's entitled to an opinion and I know a lot of surgeons who think M.D. stands for Medical Deity. They get under your skin, Hunter?"

Hunter made a horsey sound. "Not hardly. But you docs always think that because you know a *little* bit, you're like experts or something."

"I can see why that would piss you off."

"Damn straight."

"I'll try not to do that. Maybe it's that I know enough to be both dangerous and annoying, and I like, you know…" That disarming grin, again. "I like to understand things."

He's got to be a shrink, Emma thought. Only head doctors talked as if they could be everyone's friend. Interesting that Will hadn't said anything about being a physician before now. "What kind of doctor?"

"The depressing kind. Oncologist for most of my career." Will aimed a look back her way. "I finally switched specialties, though."

"To what?" asked Rachel.

"Wilderness medicine. High-altitude stuff, but I'm game for almost anything." Will shrugged. "I like the outdoors, and it was time for a change. It's where I'm headed now, actually. Wilderness Medical Society meeting up at Big Sky."

"Isn't that south?" asked Grampa.

"Yes, but I've got friends I want to see beforehand, so this is fine. I was supposed to fly into Kalispell and then drive." Will gave a good-natured shrug. "So long as I get to Big Sky eventually, this works."

Emma opened her mouth to ask why he'd switched specialties when, all of a sudden, the plane dropped what felt like ten thousand feet but was probably more like fifty. The seats shivered. The cargo locker behind her seat clanked, and from somewhere behind and beneath her feet, she heard an odd clinking and clunking. *Luggage?* Why had that sounded like glass? Or was it metal? Burke said he had a belly tank, so that would be full of gas not tools. Maybe another cargo bay, then? *Maybe that's why Hunter was so worried about weight?*

Another bounce, and Mattie gave a little cry as her book bounced out of her lap and did a swan dive onto the deck where it lay in a broken-wing splay.

"I got it." Grateful for the distraction (she did *not* want to imagine the impossibly high mountain that was probably dead ahead), Emma swept up the book in one hand. "Here," she said, stretching toward the girl. "Take—"

The plane suddenly bucked again. Emma's head snapped forward and then back like a heavy tulip on a spindly stalk.

"Oh!" Mattie's eyes went wide behind her glasses. "Gosh, are you okay?"

"Yeah, take it easy," Will said. "No sense getting whiplash."

"I'm okay." Her neck wished to suggest otherwise. *Oh, be quiet.* She realized she was still hanging onto the book. "Here."

"Thanks." Mattie made a face. "Man, what I wouldn't give for a wormhole."

"Yeah, but then we'd end up in the Delta Quadrant." At the girl's frown, Emma waved a hand. "It's a long story."

"But a good one," Will said. "Resistance is futile."

The response was immediate, the words out of her mouth before she realized because it was what she'd always tossed out when Ben came at her with the same line. "Yeah, take your best shot, Locutus."

"Because we are about to intervene." Will's grin broadened. "I always thought Frakes was a bit wooden, though I am *positive* my mother had a secret crush on him. What about yours?"

"For my mom? James T. Kirk," she said, returning his smile. "I mean, come on, the guy lost his shirt practically every episode of the first season. She once said he was considered beefcake in her day."

Mattie looked from one to the other. "What are you guys talking about?"

"Ancient history," said Will.

"An old TV show," she said to Mattie.

"Hey." Will looked offended. "Watch who you're calling old."

"I didn't say *you*," Emma began, but Mattie interrupted, "What's an old TV show got to do with a wormhole?"

"What's *Star Trek* got to do with a wormhole," Will scoffed as the plane bucked up and down. "Just *everything*."

"Jesus," Scott moaned, holding his head in a credible imitation of Edward Munch's *The Scream*. "You guys are nuts."

"No." Will said. "Only lightening the mood by sharing a mutual cultural referent. But I sure wouldn't mind a wormhole right about now. Burke, seriously, is there enough valley between us and Lone Ridge?"

"Oh, yeah." Burke made a piffling sound. "We got to grab more air, get through a couple saddles and notches. Nothing we can't handle. Maybe another hour."

"You said that an hour ago," Mattie pointed out.

"Yeah, well, the wind's picked up." Hunter scowled. "You're all freaking yourselves out."

This guy did not, Emma thought, have much in the way of people skills. "Maybe we've got a good reason.

We're flying blind in clouds and a snowstorm, and we can't turn back."

"We got instruments," Hunter countered.

"Burke," Will said in that mild way of his, "you're not worried about fuel?"

The pilot shook his head. "Like I said, we got plenty. Got ourselves new wing tanks and that belly tank… always keep that in reserve for the approach…and extra in the bladders in back to refuel us in the air if we have to, but it won't come to that. Even if we had to set down, I got enough survival gear in the cargo locker, we'd be fine."

"Wait a minute." Pulling out of his slouch, Scott twisted toward Burke. "What do you mean, if we have to set *down*?"

"Because of the clouds," Will said. "They get much lower, even trying for a notch or saddle on instruments won't necessarily be safe. Landforms aren't static."

"S'right," Burke said, easily. "But this is really not that bad, folks. Fly 'Nam, now…that was bad."

"You in 'Nam?" Mattie's grandfather stirred. "I was First Cav. Fought at Ia Drang. Didn't ever meet Mel Gibson, though."

"What?" Scott looked confused. "Mel Gibson fought in Vietnam?"

"No," Will said. "He was in a movie that was based on a book about the battle. *We Were Soldiers?*"

Yes, she remembered that film, though she was partial to Sam Elliot. A pretty good movie but a much better book. The interesting thing about deployments and bases of any kind was the many war movies they

63

did *not* show, probably for reasons of morale, although there was no shortage of the really old, ra-ra kick-butt flicks like *Midway, The Longest Day, Patton.* Even *The Bridge Over the River Kwai.* Anything where America won or was incredibly noble passed muster.

"I was based at Da Nang, mostly," Burke said, "though I moved around a lot depending on the mission. Felt like I flew out of every base and outpost along the DMZ. Spent a fair amount of time in Camp Carroll, keeping Highway 9 clear, then flew a couple missions doing recon along the Yellow Brick Road."

"What does *The Wizard of Oz* have to do with anything?" asked Mattie.

"It's what we called the Ho Chi Minh Trail," Grampa said.

"What'd you fly, Burke?" Will asked.

"These itty-bitty Bird Dogs."

Emma hadn't heard of those. "What's a Bird Dog?"

"Cessna L-19," Burke said. "Fixed-wing, all metal."

"That's a pretty small plane," Will said.

"Like being toothpaste in a tube," Burke said. "Listen to the Geneva Accords. We weren't supposed to be in Laos or Cambodia at all. If Johnson hadn't been so worried about stepping on toes, we'd have been there sooner. At least Nixon manned up to what needed to get done."

"In secret. And in an undeclared war."

"Look," Burke said, "I'm not saying he was a prince, but it was war, you know? Besides, all those South Vietnamese guys were lining their pockets, and so were a lot of our people. Black market was big business. I knew one supply guy at a PX, took in cartons of cigarettes and bottles of Scotch and fancy perfumes by the front door and let them leave out the back door at twice the price where you'd find them on the black market for half what you'd pay at the PX. It got so you couldn't walk down the streets without people trying to sell you American deodorant, shaving cream, Ritz crackers… even Spam, for God's—"

"Hey, Dad," Hunter interrupted. "The fuel gauge's kinda twitchy. I think we're sucking up a little air through the pump here. Want me to switch us to the belly tank?"

"That'd be good, Son." To Will, "All I'm saying is, you wanted a lesson in making money on the down-low, Vietnam taught you how."

"Must be a hard habit to break," Will said. "Making money on the down-low."

What? The sentence hung there for a beat too long, enough time for Emma to wonder if she'd missed something. She opened her mouth to say…well, what, she never exactly could recall…

Because, all of a sudden, both engines sputtered.

And died.

CHAPTER 8

THERE ARE many sounds one hopes never to hear. The Doppler wail of an oncoming train at the moment your car stalls on the track. That curious snap and *kerSHAW* that is a bullet breaking the sound barrier as it hurtles past your ear. The drip-drip-drip of blood on bathroom tile.

Another is the *hoosh* of wind against a plane's fuselage because the engines keeping you in the air only seconds before having stopped working.

For what seemed like a very long moment, no one said anything. Then Rachel asked, "What—"

"Hunter!" Burke barked. Without taking his eyes from the windscreen, the pilot angled the plane right in a ninety-degree turn sharp and abrupt enough Emma felt her shoulder strap catch and strain against the ball of her joint. "What the hell did you—"

"What happened to the engines?" Scott sat up straight, his hair in kinks and screws as if he'd only now rolled out of bed. "Why did they stop?"

"No fuel," Will said softly. "Must've switched to an empty tank instead of a full one. Take it easy, Scott."

"Don't tell me to take it easy! I *got* that there's no fuel!" Scott's skin had drawn down tight over his skull. "What I want to know is *why*?"

"Might be…" Burke cursed as he made another ninety-degree turn. His feet worked a set of pedals. "Could be the new wing tanks."

"Or the selector." Hunter shot a glance at his father. "Everything got yanked out and reinstalled. Could've been mounted backward."

"What does that *mean*?" Rachel asked.

"It means we got to get the engines restarted is what." Reaching forward, Burke flipped a switch and kept working pedals. "Keep this baby in the air while I do it. Everyone, stay calm," he added as if they'd all been a hairsbreadth away from screaming. "We still got plenty of air between us and the mountains."

"Where did we start?" Will glanced at his watch. "How high are the mountains we're supposed to be over?"

"Twenty-seven thousand, and about twelve. Now, shut the fuck up. Hunter," Burke said as he made another right-angle turn, "keep an eye on that altimeter."

"Altimeter? You're saying we're losing altitude?" Rachel's voice was shaking. "We're falling?"

"Yes, but we're not in a nosedive. We're gliding," Will said, though his gaze was fixed on his watch. "Small planes can glide a long time. The wind might even help us."

"Wanna bet?" muttered Mattie.

As much as Emma wanted to believe Will, the girl might be right. She could feel the wind pummel and shove them farther to the east. They were still in dense clouds, though. How fast would a plane fall? That must be what Will was trying to gauge. But how could he tell? *Wait a second.* Something burbled up from memory. Gravity made something fall faster; gravity made you accelerate. So they were falling, all right—and, every second, they fell even faster.

"Why are we flying in a square?" asked Mattie.

"Keeping us clear of the peaks." All the irritation had bled from Hunter's voice along with the blood in his face. He glanced at the altimeter and, while Emma was too far away to see the display, she imagined it was like the movies, the numbers scrolling past, counting down fast. "Twenty-one, Dad," he reported.

"Seven a minute," muttered Will.

"That's pretty fast," Mattie said.

"Yeah, well," said Burke, "it's better'n ten."

"Better than ten what?" Rachel asked.

"Feet," Mattie said.

"What, seven measly feet a minute?" Scott choked out a little laugh. "That's not so bad."

"That's thousand." Mattie didn't need to add, *You moron.* "It's gravity, Scott."

Rachel put a hand over her mouth. "Oh my God."

"A *minute?*" All the feeling, all her blood pooled in Emma's toes. *Seven thousand feet a minute?* If the mountains around here were twelve thousand feet high and they'd started out at roughly twenty-seven...

"Jesus." Scott's mouth hung open. "You're saying we got less than two *minutes*?"

No one said, *Hey, congrats, Einstein, you can multiply.* Instead, Hunter warned, "Seventeen."

Oh, God. She leaned and plucked at Will's sleeve with two fingers. "Can he do it?" she asked.

"If he has the time." Will's voice held only a tremor, which he must have heard himself because he cleared his throat. What he said next was back to steady, even, calm: the doctor keeping his shit together while all about him were losing theirs. "He has to do things in a certain order and at the right time, or it won't work. Can't try to get the starter to catch if you don't have fuel in the tank. That's what he's doing now." He offered her a thin smile. "I guess this is why one of the first things a flight instructor teaches is what to do in a stall."

She bet teachers only did that on nice, clear days with not a mountain in sight, too. Pushing both halves of the window curtains out of her way, Emma peered out. Still nothing to see, only clouds, so that was good, right?

"Fifteen!" Hunter said.

Will's fingers brushed her elbow. "You know how to brace? Can you help Mattie?"

Her chest went tight. Like bracing for an impact in this little thing would save them if they plowed nose-first into a mountain. But she nodded. "Mattie, let's get you ready. Book in the seat pocket and glasses off. Make sure your buckle's tight. Feet flat on the floor then bend over your knees." Face white, Mattie did what she was told without uttering a word. "Good," Emma said. "Now, lace your hands behind your head."

"You guys." Across the aisle, Will was talking to Scott and Grampa. "Feet flat, but don't bend over. Keep your head up and press back into your headrest."

"Why?" Scott asked.

"So your head don't pop off your spine if we hit, that's why," Grampa growled.

Scott's jaw dropped. "What the *hell*—" he began as Hunter sang out, "Twelve! *Dad!*"

With a great splutter and cough, both props caught.

Yes! Emma shot a look out of her window. They were still in a whiteout, though the clouds seemed gauzier, more like torn draperies. A shower of orange-red sparks spewed from the engine as the prop churned. *C'mon, c'mon.* Outside, the view began to tilt as her body sank into her seat, the acceleration and thrust palming her body, and she thought this was what it must be like to be an astronaut on takeoff, thousands of pounds of thrust fighting gravity, pushing, pushing, pushing, breaking free, leaving the Earth behind and shedding the past, too, while, ahead, all of space and stars and the future waited. The fuselage shimmied as the Chieftain's engines screamed, the plane shuddering and clawing for altitude. *We're going to make it. We're going to make it. We're going to make it—*

Beyond her window, the drapery of clouds finally tore and now, through sheets of snow, she saw, to her horror, colors coming on fast on all sides and below and in a blur: dark green and brown and white and gray and black—

"Dad!" Rearing back in his seat, Hunter threw up his hands. *"Watch—"*

THE GOLDEN DAY

CHAPTER 1

PLIK...PLIK...

"Hello?"

Plik...

"Emma, are you there?"

Ben, that damn faucet...

"Emma?"

Plik...

"Emma?"

Ben, that damn faucet's leaking again—

"Emma, wake up!"

Her eyes creaked open as if on balky hinges. She winced against a bright, milky light that was wrong somehow, strange, and so she squeezed her lids shut again. *I'm tired.* Her head throbbed, and her mouth was cottony and tasted like swamp water. She was also freezing, couldn't get warm. Where the hell was the blanket? *Hangover. Too much to...*

Plik.

Her face was wet. Her cheeks and forehead and chin,

her neck—*plik, plik*—were damp.

The air was thick with an oddly fruity but astringent stink that reminded her both of road trips with her parents and long nights in bad bars. Beyond the drip of that damn faucet...*my God, where was she? Which man had she let herself go to a hotel with this time?*

Plik.

She heard a strange *fwap, fwap, fwap,* the noise a sheet might make on a clothesline. This was juxtaposed against a fast, almost snaky hiss like rice on tin, sand over stone. *Or rats' feet over broken glass.* She felt the salt ball of a sob swell in her throat. *Oh, Ben...*

"Emma, are you awake?"

No. She was dreaming. She was in bed. Someone had stolen all the blankets, and she was shivering, her head hurt, and her neck *killed.* Her face ached as if she'd run into a wall. She'd done that once, too, as a kid. Talking to someone else after lunch, she hadn't watched where she was going and turned around in time to smack cinderblock. There was a shock of pain and then blood, a lot of it, spewing from her broken nose to splatter onto her shoes and the floor and go *plik-plik* onto her Mary Poppins lunchbox. The lunchbox was new, a gift for her birthday because she was a big girl now, going into the fifth grade at a big-girl school. As the rest of the kids in the lunchroom gawked, a teacher had cupped a hand to her nose and guided her to the nurse who, when she heard what Emma had done, only rolled her eyes: *Oh, for goodness' sake.*

"Don't pass out again."

Again? That meant she'd awakened once before? Her

thoughts tumbled over one another, all arms and legs and in a confused jumble like cheerleaders who couldn't hold that pyramid. Well, why the hell shouldn't she go back to sleep? She was tired. She must be lying wrong, though, because her neck hurt, and who had turned down the heat? Her fingers and toes were icy. She inhaled, tasting cold, wet air, and thought to call out…to whom? About what? Someone. Anyone. But instead she groaned against a dagger of pain above her heart. A duller burn grabbed her belly and right hip. To her right and somewhere in front came…

Plik…

that strange *fwapping* sound again. Who'd left the window open? The guy she'd let take her to a hotel, probably. That's why she was so cold. No, wait, what guy? She hasn't had a drink in weeks. She remembered it distinctly, that moment when she'd tried a whiskey and amaretto concoction…the bartender called the drink The Godfather and said a lot of women liked it, but, after two sips, she pushed it away. The drink hadn't tasted right. *She* hadn't felt right, either. Something was wrong, off, she knew it—

"Emma, come on, wake up."

She finally placed the voice to a name. *Mattie.* Suddenly, everything clicked, as if she'd been a jigsaw puzzle scattered by an inquisitive cat.

She opened her eyes.

The first thing she saw was blood smeared on the back of Rachel's headrest. Rachel herself was slumped to the right, a thick red runner of blood slicking Rachel's parka and her limp right hand from which a ruby pearl swelled and bloomed and grew heavy as a ripe grape at the tip of Rachel's middle finger before breaking away to plop into a red pool.

Plik.

"I think my mom's hurt pretty bad." A pause, and then Mattie's voice came again. "Will isn't answering either."

Will. Her gaze shifted. Will had slumped forward. He was very still. A fine dusting of snow sugared his dark hair. Drifts had gathered on his thighs and in his lap, and more snow was gusting in. White clots were humped on a short span of deck a few feet beyond Will's seat as if shoveled into the plane. Another swish of wind set the torn curtain over Will's window to fluttering again, *fwap-fwap-fwap.*

Wind. Snow? Yes, had to be. She blinked against icy bits nipping at her eyes, her cheeks. Her breath fogged. But *why?* Her stupefied gaze slid from Will to the front of the plane—

Except there was no front of the plane. Instead of Grampa and Scott and the cockpit, there was only more snow and a great white expanse broken, in the near distance, by ranks of tall pines and firs.

Oh dear God. She straightened, a too-rapid movement that reawakened the ache in her chest and belly. Where was the cockpit? A short distance away? Or was it farther, beyond them somewhere? That had happened to those boys, the ones who'd crashed in the Andes years back; the fuselage had slammed down on one part of the mountain, and the tail had broken off and slid farther downhill.

They probably hadn't slammed nose-first into the mountain. If they had, she wouldn't now be alive to even be thinking this through. She recalled seeing colors coalesce below and around them. That suggested a plateau or the top of a mountain. Maybe they'd clipped trees? Had she heard anything? She couldn't remember. Christ, it wasn't important.

"Will?" she blurted. Her voice kicked up a notch as a swell of mingled panic and hysteria threatened to over-whelm her. "Will? *Will?* Will, are you *awake*, are you—"

"Are you okay?" Mattie asked.

No. She pressed icy fingers to her lips and pulled in a shuddering, shaky breath, hitching against that white-hot dagger of pain sliding in between her ribs. *Uh, oh.* She forced herself to blow out slowly. Her breath steamed. *You've pulled something, maybe broken something. Take it easy. Someone will come looking. Someone will miss you.* She thought of her cell, tucked in the right leg of her cargo pants. Maybe she could *call* for help? No, she should leave the phone alone. It was charged. She had a spare battery bank, too. *Save it for a rainy day.* It was a line from one of her mom's favorite films, *Primal Fear*. Her mother had *adored* Richard Gere, especially when he oozed sleaze: *Guess what? It's raining.*

Mattie, again. "You're bleeding."

Shit, she was? She raised a trembling hand to her left cheek. Her fingers spidered over skin slick with cooling snow melt and something warmer, stickier congealing along the angle of her jaw. She stared at the crimson streaks smeared on her fingertips.

"You've got a cut over your eye," Mattie said. "It's not too bad, but your face is all bruised up, too."

"It is?" Gritting her teeth, she gingerly explored a ragged gash above her right eye. The cut wasn't straight but more of a starburst pattern, like a bullet hitting shatterproof glass. So much for the brace position. She must've passed out and then flopped around. That would explain the soreness in her neck and the blood on Rachel's seatback. "What about you?" Shuddering against another chill, she inched her aching head to the right. God, she was cold. They had to get warm. Start a fire, get something hot into them. "How bad are you hurt?"

"Not too bad." Mattie's face was puffy and purpled with bruises. Her eyes had swollen to slits. A black watch cap Emma hadn't seen before was pulled down over the girl's head, and she'd also flipped up her parka's fur-trimmed hood. "Really cold, but not as bad before. Mom always says if you're cold, put on a hat, and I had one in my pocket. But my face hurts, and so does my chest and stomach and especially my left hip. I think that's from the seat belt and shoulder harness, except I can't get out. The buckle's jammed."

"Hang on, I'll help you get out." She'd never been in a car accident, but she remembered photos from driver's ed: those purple swathes of bruises left by seat belts and shoulder harnesses. Maybe the same thing accounted for her aches, although that stabbing pain in her chest felt like it might be bad. Cracked ribs, maybe. "Does it hurt to breathe?"

"No. I think we're all bruised up because of the

deceleration. Emma, I'm better but still really cold. My face is getting all numb. We need to get warm."

"I know. We will." But how? Build a fire? She couldn't do that inside. What should she do first? Thrusting her chilled hands under her armpits, she shivered as more snow billowed in on a balloon of wind. What had they taught in basic about survival? Warmth, first. Right, that was it. They needed to get warm; they needed shelter, which they sort of had; and they would eventually need water that wasn't snow. But she also had to check on Rachel and Will.

Then we hunker down, wait for people to find us.

She'd done stories on rescue operations. People always talked about that "golden day," that span of about twenty-four hours, give or take, when search-and-rescue teams had the greatest chance of finding survivors. The moment they'd crashed, that clock started ticking. Had Hunter managed to send out a mayday? She didn't think so. In a way, she didn't blame him. Until the last second, he'd probably thought his father would get them out of this, and sending a distress call would've been the pilot's decision. The fact neither Hunter nor Burke had radioed sucked, but it wasn't a deal breaker. People would be looking for them and soon.

Their biggest problem, really, was the snow. The first rule of rescue was not to need it yourself. No one would risk sending a chopper or plane up in conditions like this.

How much light was left? She glanced at her watch. A little after one p.m. They'd left Minot at ten, central time. Factor in the time they'd been in the air, that put the crash about an hour ago. Okay, that wasn't great either. The plane wasn't late yet. *Which means no one knows yet.*

"Mattie," she asked, "we passed over Glacier, right? The park?"

"Yes. But I don't know if we're still in Montana. We might be north or even south. I don't remember how many turns Mr. Burke made. It's only one o'clock, but it gets dark early in winter and there are the clouds. So I don't think we have a lot of daylight left, Emma."

"Okay, hang on, I'll..." She stopped, suddenly, as more snow billowed in on a balloon of wind and carried something else with it. "Do you smell that?"

"Yes. I have since I woke up. Is it fuel? It smells kind of funny, like...almost sweet."

The girl was right. The smell conjured up images of hot asphalt and the tick of a cooling muffler but also bars and honky-tonks and spilled beer. Could that be residual fuel that had spewed out of the wing tanks? Burke had managed to restart the engine, and that required fuel, but the wing tanks couldn't possibly have been full. *Wait a second.* Turning carefully, she peered down the aisle toward the cargo hold.

"What are you doing?"

"Burke filled those bladders with extra gas."

"Oh." Mattie tried to crane her head around but couldn't because of her shoulder harness. "Are they leaking?" When Emma shook her head, Mattie went on, "Could the smell be from the wings? They're gone now, so that means when they broke off, the tanks tore.

Maybe the wings were what got caught up first. I remember lots of tall trees."

She did, too, and Mattie was probably right. Which meant they couldn't chance trying to start a fire until she hauled out those bladders and checked the rest of the plane, especially that belly tank with its odd, clunking, glassy sound. Otherwise, they might go up like a Roman candle. *Like sending up a flare.* Which was also a line Scotty had used in an old first-season episode. Scotty had thought it worth the gamble, but Spock pointed out how illogical it was because there was no one out there to see the distress signal.

"Emma?"

"Yeah." Her chest yammered a complaint as she fumbled with the buckle of her seat belt, but she ignored it. "Coming."

"No. Check my mom and Will first," Mattie said as Emma shrugged out of her shoulder harness. "I'll be okay. I think you're going to have to cut me out of this anyway. The buckle's really jammed up tight. I'm not going anywhere."

True, that. Emma slid out of her seat and carefully stood. A swell of dizziness made her head go light, and she had to grab onto her seat back to keep to her feet. Sweat prickled on her neck and face, and she smeared salt pearls from her upper lip with the back of the hand that wasn't bloody.

"Emma?"

"I'm good. I'm fine," she lied. Reaching under her seat, she tugged her pack free, unzipped a side pocket, and retrieved her wool cap, a scarf, and insulated pop-tops. After winding the scarf around her neck and fumbling on her gloves, she edged around Rachel's seat, thankful for the few feet of intact deck, and dropped to a squat before the unconscious woman.

"Well?" asked Mattie.

"Well…" There was a lot of blood. Judging from the flat, nearly dried blotch on the window, she thought Rachel's head had first connected with the jagged end of a curtain rod that had broken on impact. A deep, ragged gash on Rachel's scalp showed where the metal had ripped flesh all the way to muscle. *And maybe bone.* Emma couldn't tell because of all the blood matting Rachel's hair and slicking the left side of her face and neck. More blood fanned in a broad crimson bib on her chest. She slipped a finger onto Rachel's neck.

"Is she…" Mattie's voice quavered then firmed. "Is she still alive?"

"Yes." Though Rachel's pulse was fast. Blood loss? Maybe.

"What about my little brother? What about Joshua?"

"Is that the name you've picked out?" Her gaze fell first to Rachel's jeans, which were flecked with snow but otherwise dry. Okay, so that was good, she guessed. How to check on the baby, though?

"My dad did." A pause. "My *real* dad. He and Mom were trying a really long time after me, and then my dad died, and Scott…anyway, it's Joshua. Can you tell if he's okay?"

"I'm not a doctor, Mattie." Although she knew a baby's heartbeat could be heard through a stethoscope, which she didn't have. A baby also moved. She'd read that at about twenty-five weeks, a mother should feel those first signs, that flutter or little bubbly sensation. "How active is your brother? How much does he move around?"

"A lot. Sometimes, when he kicks now, you can see his foot."

That sounded pretty wild. She carefully placed her hands on Rachel's abdomen which was swaddled in both a wool sweater and the woman's down parka. Closing her eyes, she concentrated. *C'mon, Joshua. Give me a sign here.* She'd read somewhere that unborn babies responded to their mother's touch, but she was a stranger.

"Is Joshua all right?"

She was about to say *I don't know* when, all of a sudden, there came a teeny-tiny *thump* against her right palm, and her heart leapt.

"You felt him. I can tell from your face."

"Yeah, I think so." Both Rachel's sweater and parka were thick, and so it was tough to be certain. In a few seconds, there came a second, harder thump, and she saw the parka move from right to left. "He's rolling."

Mattie smiled. "Mom always says it reminds her of making a cat up in a bed. You know, under the sheets?"

Despite everything, Emma grinned because the description was so perfect. *Well, hey there, Joshua.* As the baby shifted and Rachel's belly bunched, she wondered what it must be like never to be alone. Wake up in the middle of the night, stroke your belly, and there was someone there, floating up to—

Will moaned.

CHAPTER 2

"WILL?" Emma's heart kicked. Scuttling across the aisle, she put a hand on his. His skin was icy. "Will?"

"Is he awake?" Mattie asked.

"Getting there." She hoped. She got right into his face. "Will, can you hear me?"

"Uhhh." He stirred and then, as he pulled his head up, he sucked in a sharp, hard breath that came out in another panting groan. Sudden tears leaked from the corners of his eyes. "Oh, *shit.*"

"What is it?" Mattie demanded.

"I don't know. Will, Will, what is it? Where are you hurt?" He was scaring her. *Jesus, no, you can't die. You can't be hurt. You can't!* Hot panic bolted up her throat. She gripped his hands. "What is it?" Her frantic eyes darted to his face, his head, his chest. Was he bleeding, was something broken? "Where do you hur—" The word evaporated on her tongue.

"Emma?" Mattie called.

His parka was askew, the garment draped oddly as if

arm of the hangar on which it hung had broken. But, of course, the equivalent of a hangar on a *person* was his shoulders.

Will's shoulders were all wrong. Where the hump of his right shoulder should be, there was, instead, a steep drop-off. An odd bump poked midway between where his shoulder had been and the center of his chest.

"*Dis*located." Will forced the word between clenched teeth. Despite the chill, his forehead was beaded with sweat. "Can't *move* it."

"Can you fix it?" she asked and then wanted to kick herself. That was like asking if he could take out his appendix by looking in a mirror.

His head rolled back and forth on his headrest. "Not by myself." He fixed his eyes, glazed with pain, on hers. "I'll talk you through it. But how are you? I don't like that cut over your eye. How's your head? Are you hurt anywhere else?" Before she could answer, he asked, "What about Mattie?"

"I'm okay," Mattie called. "My seat belt's stuck, that's all."

"I have something in my pack we can use to cut you out. Won't take but a jiffy. What about your chest, Mattie? Your stomach?" Will looked at Emma. "Did you check her?"

"No," she said, a little stung as if he'd caught her in a mistake or falling down on the job. "I was worried about Rachel."

"I told her to, Will," Mattie called. "I'm okay, really. I'm cold, but I'm good."

"Are you feeling sick?" Will persisted. "You going to throw up?"

"No, I told you, I'm *fine*. It's my mom who's hurt bad. You have to help my mom."

"We'll help her." Panting, Will let his head fall back against his seat. "Emma will do it, and then we'll get you out and fix me up, get a fire going or at least block off this wind."

"What?" Emma asked. "Will, I don't know what to do for Rachel."

"Then it's good I'm here. I'll talk you through it. Emma, you have to. No choice. Now, tell me about her." He listened, cheeks still moist with tears of pain, as she told him about the cut on Rachel's scalp, the baby's movements. "What about her pulse?"

"It was fast." She couldn't remember a number. Had she even bothered to count? "Is it because she's lost a lot of blood?" That slick on her face and puddling on the floor sure looked like a lot.

"Maybe. Head wounds always bleed like stink. We'll stop the bleeding first."

"We?" A bad line from *The Lone Ranger* floated through her brain. "I'm not a doctor."

"But you're military. You know battlefield first aid, right? Hemostatic dressings?" When she nodded, he said, "Great. I've got a bunch of QuikClot in my pack. You should put some on that cut you've got, too."

"Okay. Then what?"

"Then we get my arm into a sling, slap a couple splints around her neck to brace her spine, work her out of her seat, and lay her flat."

There was that *we* again. "Will, your shoulder's dislocated."

"My left arm still works. Don't worry, I'll let you do most of the work. I'll even let you superglue her wound."

Superglue? "That is *not* funny."

"Trust me when I say that, at the moment, I am completely incapable of humor."

"Get me out, and I can help, too. And don't tell me that you have to check me out first," Mattie added. "You're letting Emma move around and do all this stuff. You're not yelling at her to lie down even though she's cut and her chest hurts and it took *forever* for her to wake up."

Despite everything, Emma felt her mouth curl into a grin. "She's got you," she said to Will.

"Of course, I do," Mattie said, irritably. "Now, cut me out of this thing before we all freeze to death."

CHAPTER 3

"HUNH." Will's grunt smoked in the chill as he sat back on his heels. "Well, that's interesting."

"What's interesting?" Emma kept her gloved palms firmly clamped on a wad of QuikClot layered over Rachel's scalp wound. Although Will had already checked for a fracture, feeling carefully through blue latex with his good left hand as she swabbed away blood so he'd have a decent view, she was still leery of pressing too hard. A lot of her training had come back, though. Most of the medical stuff was pretty basic: applying a neck brace and then hefting Rachel out of her seat and onto the sleeping bag Mattie unfurled. Will did the best he could, and he was strong, but with every move that jarred his shoulder, which meant about every move he made, she could tell from the way he sucked in through his teeth that the pain had to be bad. (After dry-swallowing two acetaminophen, he had her slip on a sling from his emergency medical kit so that right arm wouldn't flop around. He said they'd fix him as soon as he checked *her* out. Oh. Joy. She was looking forward to both with about as much enthusiasm as a root canal.) She was actually too cold to be much interested in anything except something hot to drink…*Wait. I still have that disgusting tea.* "What is it?"

Draping his stethoscope around his neck with his working hand, Will regarded Rachel's abdomen with a speculative eye. "I don't know."

"Is it the baby?"

"What?" Mattie was at the front of the ruined fuselage where she'd been dragging luggage from the cargo hold to block off the opening but now turned and said, with a new note of alarm, "Joshua isn't hurt, is he?"

"As far as I can tell, your brother's fine. Good movement, heartbeat's steady, but there's something." Will's frown deepened. *Haahing* into his left hand to warm it, he placed his palm along the lower margin of Rachel's belly and gently followed the curve. "I think only your mom can tell us for sure."

She didn't like the sound of that. Emma watched Rachel's abdomen swell and shift as the baby responded to Will's touch. "Tell us what?"

"If the baby's dropped at all. It's been a long time since my ob-gyn rotation. I know how to deliver a baby, but as for whether that's imminent…"

"Imminent." The word dropped from Mattie's mouth like a stone. "You mean, Joshua's going to be born? *Now?*"

"I don't know. Maybe? Or maybe not, and this is the

way she carries him. The problem is this is the first time I've examined your mom. I don't know where Joshua likes to hang out, on the second floor or the first. We'll have to wait for your mom to tell us."

"What if she doesn't wake up to tell you?" Mattie's eyes welled. "What will happen then? Why are we awake and not her?"

"Because as far as I can tell, she's got a really bad concussion."

"Scott watches football. Players with concussions get up all the time."

"And sometimes they don't. Sometimes they're knocked out. That's what's happened to your mom, but I don't think anything worse is going on."

Mattie looked stricken "What could be *worse?*"

"A couple things," Will said. "None of which I think your mom has."

Mattie's eyes narrowed. "But you don't know for sure."

"No, I can't possibly. To be sure, I'd need access to a whole bunch of diagnostic tools I don't have. But let's not panic yet. It's only been a couple of hours. Your mom could wake up by nightfall or in the middle of the night or tomorrow morning."

Or maybe not at all. Emma studied Rachel's placid features. If this were a Hallmark special, a week would go by, and they'd be on the brink of starvation. Wolves would descend at the moment Rachel went into labor, leaving Emma to deliver the baby because something would've happened to Will or maybe he was fending off the wolves or rescuing Mattie or fending off wolves *and* rescuing Mattie when—cue soaring music—a helicopter miraculously appeared, scattering the wolves and whisking them all away in time for Christmas but *not* before Emma had swaddled a perfect baby boy in a blanket or something and handed him over to Rachel. She was, in fact, almost positive there'd been an episode like this several years back on NCIS, only Gibbs had delivered the kid while Ziva David kicked butt as only a Jewish Mossad ninja warrior could. God, what a great character. Ziva being Israeli was icing on the cake. For a while there, when she'd been with Ben, and he was doing his undercover work, Emma had toyed with the idea of learning how to fight like that on general principle. She'd even daydreamed of she and Ben taking on the bad guys together.

You're an idiot. She had to get a grip. Not everything had its correlate in a movie or show. *This is reality, Greg* —and then she had to wrestle the smile into submission before it settled on her mouth. Gosh, *E.T.* had been one heck of a good flick.

"Is my mom in a coma?" asked Mattie.

"I'm afraid so, honey. Here, let me show you, okay?" Pulling out a penlight, Will clicked it on then flicked the light into Rachel's open eye and then away before repeating the maneuver. "There, see how her pupil doesn't get smaller when I shine the light. That's what happens to people in a coma. And if I do this?" Pushing up a sleeve of Rachel's jacket to reveal bare skin, Will gathered a healthy pinch between thumb and forefinger and squeezed. Rachel's face remained placid, and her arm didn't move away. "Unconscious people respond to pain. Comatose people don't."

"So this is really bad."

"It's better not to be comatose, yes. I would love it if she would wake up, and if I knew why she was out or how long she'll stay this way, I'd tell you. But that sometimes happens in traumatic brain injury. The body's not dumb. It knows when to take a rest."

Well, woo-hoo. Let's hear it for the body. So long as Rachel kept making like the Eveready Bunny, the baby would keep ticking, too. But what if Rachel's body up and quit? What would they do about the baby then? Will knew medicine, but did he know how to save an unborn child even as the mother's body gave up the ghost?

And then there was this, the fact of the crash, that they were stranded in the middle of nowhere. She glanced toward the front of the fuselage. There was precious little to see, other than snow. The light had gone a bluish sharkskin gray as the day slid toward dusk. A little while back, Mattie had stamped outside to look for the cockpit, but the snow was too thick, and Will shouted at her to come back before she wandered off and got lost. Even so, Mattie had lingered, yelling for her grandfather, for *anyone*, but all she got back was the hiss of snow on metal and plastic, the hollow groan of wind, her own voice. Hours had passed with no thump of choppers, no hails from intrepid rescuers risking life and limb.

So where *was* everyone? Their plane was overdue. All of them were expected and now hadn't arrived.

Hank Cooper should be waiting, and so should this Kujo character. When it got dark and no one showed up…when someone tried calling Burke's plane and got dead air…they'd know to start looking, right?

Right?

"Snow's still getting in," said Mattie, hunching her shoulders against a fresh gust as Emma ducked back inside. The girl had positioned herself between the barricade and her mother, whom they'd cocooned in Will's sleeping bag. Clutching Emma's travel mug in both hands, Mattie gave the low barricade she'd formed with their luggage a forlorn look. "There's not enough to keep out the wind and stuff."

"We'll find something." Maybe unbolt the seats and use them? That would at least give them more room. She huffed out a breath, grimacing against the grab along her left ribcage.

"Are you okay?"

"I'm fine." A lie. Her head ached, probably a combination of her scalp wound, being banged around, and hanging out in air that was brain-freeze cold. She was also winded from having dragged the heavy avgas bladders from the fuselage. She'd worried every step of the way that she'd snag fabric and spill fuel everywhere. If she'd done that, they'd be sunk. While she'd been outside, she'd caught that very odd scent again, the one reminiscent of smoky late-night bars, which, though not as strong as before, seemed concentrated near the tail. There weren't any standing puddles of spilled fuel or anything on top of the snow at all. Still, maybe a leak in the belly tank? She'd have to check, especially if they decided they needed to start a signal fire.

Brushing snow from her shoulders, she felt melt trickling down her cheeks. The fuselage wasn't toasty in the slightest, though it was warmer than before, and that was already an improvement. Now, with the bladders gone, they could at least fire up Will's portable cooking stove, a Jetboil Flash which was essentially an insulated cooking cup screwed onto a small fuel canister which could be lit with a match. What she really wanted was a soft bed, a good pillow, warm covers, and a steaming mug of hot cocoa. Oh, and to be off this bloody mountain.

But she had to take care of Will now. No getting around it. Relocating his shoulder really was the last thing she wanted, but they needed Will. She didn't know a damned thing about arms and even less about anatomy, but she assumed the shoulder was put together the way it was for a really good reason. There were nerves there and blood vessels. Who knew what kind of damage had been done already? Will was important. The rest was…

"What are you smiling about?" Will said.

"Nothing," she lied. Her bubbe once told a story about Rabbi Hillel who'd been challenged by a heathen to teach him everything in the Torah while the rabbi stood on one foot. Hillel reportedly thought a second then said, *Do unto others as you would have them do unto you. The rest is commentary.*

Will was important. The rest was commentary.

"I got to do your shoulder, Will. It's worse for you the longer we wait, right?" When he nodded, she said, "Then, okay, tell me what to do."

Mattie piped up. "Can I help?"

"No," they both said at once and then Will continued, "This isn't a job for you, Mattie. I appreciate it, but you're not strong enough." Will looked back at her. "I'm not sure you are either."

"No better time to test that theory than right now. Come on. I presume you got to be lying down for this?"

"Normally," he said. "But that won't work here."

"Why not?"

"It's mechanics," said Mattie. "It's a ball-and-socket joint, right?"

"So?"

"*So*, his arm is long. Think about it. In order to slip the ball of his shoulder into his joint, there has to be enough room for his arm to dangle and then some. Otherwise, you can't stretch the muscles enough to get the joint to slide back in."

"She's right," Will said. "I need to be higher off the ground. If we were in a hospital or ER, I'd be on a gurney or in bed. You're also not strong enough on your own."

"What does strength have to do with it?" she grated. She felt vaguely ganged up on, too. These two were starting to get on her nerves. "We're not going to arm wrestle, for God's sake."

"With an injury like this, the muscles go into spasm and don't relax. They can't because they're being stretched, and a stretched muscle responds by applying a counterforce. My muscles are trying to help by making themselves as rigid as possible so they can hold my arm in place. It's protective. They're trying to keep the damage to a minimum."

Damage? "How *much* damage? Will you be able to use your arm at all after we get it back into its socket?" Because, please God, she had to.

"Within limits, but I'll have to be careful. First things first, though. You have to relocate the shoulder and then I can reassess. Check pulses, sensation, strength, that kind of thing. Normally, we dope people up pretty good so the muscles relax."

"Do you have anything like that?"

Will shook his head. "Even if we did, I'm not sure it would change anything."

"Why not?"

"I told you," Mattie said. "There's not enough room for his arm to hang down."

Will nodded. "In other words, no gurney. But I know another way. It's more involved, but it should work."

Should was not the same as *would.* "What do I have to do?" she asked.

"Be strong," he said.

CHAPTER 5

WILL MOVED TO HER SEAT. While Mattie unbuttoned his flannel shirt, Emma grabbed a coil of nylon rope from Will's pack. Looping the rope across Will's chest, she threaded it beneath his right armpit and behind his back while Mattie got busy removing the fabric cover from Emma's seat back. Then, Emma knotted the rope into a kind of tourniquet, only instead of a stick, she used one of Will's collapsible hiking poles from his pack. When Will was good and tight, she tied the legs of a spare pair of his waterproof pants into a snug knot then carefully fed his bad arm through until the loop rested on his right biceps. Then, cocking his arm at the elbow, she placed her booted foot on the knot she'd made in the pants and put her weight into it, bearing down, applying more and more pressure.

His body resisted. His muscles hardened. His face blackened with blood, and the veins of his neck and arms and chest stood in thick cords. She knew she was hurting him. He was panting, hard and fast, trying to ride the crest of the waves of pain that shook his body. *Sorry, sorry, sorry*. She bore down.

Then, all of a sudden, there came a dull *thunk* that was the sound of a butcher's cleaver against a carving board, and Will screamed.

"Oh!" Mattie's hands flew to cover her mouth. "What happened?"

"I think it worked." Sweat matted her hair to her face. Her neck was slick, but Will was bathed in perspiration, his thermal shirt soaked through. He'd flung his good arm over his eyes, but she could see the shine of tears. She touched his damp cheek. "Will? Did we—?"

"Yes." The word was a croak. "Give…give me a second," he said, voice tight. "Mattie, get the…the sling I was wearing, okay?"

"You bet." Snatching up the sling, she slid past Emma and knelt in the space between Will's legs and the back of her mother's seat. "Here it is, Will."

"Thanks, honey." Will cupped the girl's head with his good hand. "Emma, if you'll bend my arm across my chest, then Mattie can slip on the sling."

"Sure." Her insides had turned to jelly. A good thing her stomach was empty, too. She kept hearing that *clunk* the bone made as it socked back into place, and the memory made her a little queasy. "What can we do about the pain?"

"It's already not as bad. But I think I should probably take some more acetaminophen."

"I'll get it." She put a hand on his good arm. "We have to get you out of those wet clothes. You have extras, right?"

Face still ashen, he'd fallen back against her seat and closed his eyes. "In my pack. Side pocket. I've got another shirt in my luggage. But I'm not sure I can move my right arm enough to get it out. Don't want it to dislocate again."

"Do you have surgical scissors?"

"In my kit. Why?" Then his mouth twitched into a tired half-grin. "Cut me out?"

She'd seen medevacs in action. "That's the plan." Retrieving the scissors along with a fresh top, she said, "You let me do the work. Don't help."

Beginning at his waist, she cut straight up the middle to his neck and then flayed open the arms. From there, it was a simple matter of peeling the fabric away from his torso. As she did, her pulse gave an absurd little thump. Will was toned and tanned and much more muscled than he appeared. In the chill, his nipples puckered, and when her fingers brushed his sides, his skin jumped.

"Sorry!" Flustered, she took an involuntary step back. My God, someone would think she'd never seen a man's chest before. "Did I hurt you?"

"No. Ticklish." He closed his eyes as she wiped away sweat from his chest and neck with a camp towel before making him sit forward so she could dry his back. "Stop worrying," he said, his eyes still shut. "All pain passes, Emma."

He said that so gently, with such kindness, and yet the words were arrows to her heart. It was as if he somehow saw *into* her, read all her grief and regret.

Before she could respond, though, Mattie handed her Will's clean thermal. "Here. Trade you for the towel."

"Thanks. Okay," she said to Will and rolled his fresh top to the neck. "Ready?"

"As I'll ever be." He remained motionless as she worked the top over his head and down to his shoulders. "I can do the left arm," he said, though his jaws clenched and he sucked air through his teeth as he cautiously threaded the arm through its sleeve. "Now for the hard part."

"You let me do the work," she said. "Go limp. Dead weight."

"I've got to help a little," he protested. "There's no way you'll be able to both keep the arm bent *and* pull on the top. Maybe I should make do with half a shirt."

"That is not an option." She already didn't like that he wouldn't be able to get his arm through a parka sleeve for a day. But his quip about half a shirt gave her an idea. "Mattie, I saw a roll of duct tape in Will's pack. Go get it, okay?"

As Mattie scuttled off, Will gave her a narrow look. "What are you going to do?"

"Give you half a shirt," she said as Mattie trotted back. "Okay, here's what we're going to do."

In the end, she cut Will's thermal top on his right side straight up from the waist to the seam at his sleeve and then down the inner seam to the wrist. Then, draping the shirt over his bad arm, she had Mattie cut lengths of duct tape which she smoothed into place from his waist to his armpit and then down to his wrist.

"Okay, I'm impressed," Will said as she worked. "It's like a vest with side ties."

"Or chain mail," Mattie said.

"Whatever works." Securing the open flap of shirt at his wrist with a last piece of tape, Emma took a step back. "How's that?"

Mattie favored Will with a critical eye. "He looks like the time my dad dressed up like the Mummy for Halloween. Except he started really coming all undone when we were only halfway. Mom used tape to hold his costume together on account of he only had on his underwear underneath." The girl stopped to consider a moment. "And only the top half. He said he didn't mind the breeze."

Will and Emma looked at one another then broke up. "Ow, ow, ow!" Will said, grimacing but still sputtering. "Stop making me laugh!"

Better than you looking like Death warmed over. Laughing made her ribs hurt, too, but it was worth it because Will would be okay. She had to believe in that. As long as Will was okay, they were, too.

CHAPTER 6

A SHORT TIME LATER...

"HERE." She handed her travel mug to Mattie, who crouched between her mother, still in Will's sleeping bag, and their pitiful barricade. "Drink this."

"I'm okay," Mattie protested.

"Oh, right, says the human windbreak. Drink it. We'll figure out a way to keep the wind from getting in." As the girl took the mug, she said, "How's your mom?"

"The same." Mattie brushed a finger along Rachel's left cheek. The woman didn't flinch. "I wish I knew if it was good or bad."

"Is Will worried?"

Shaking her head, Mattie hugged her knees. "But he's a grown-up. I don't think he'd tell me if he was."

"Hey." Will looked up from the rear, where he knelt before the open cargo locker behind Emma's seat. "I heard that."

"Well, would you?" Mattie demanded.

"Have I been straight so far?"

Mattie gave him a look. "Answering a question with another question isn't answering the question."

"Give it up, Will. You're doomed. And you," she said to Mattie, "drink some more of that before it gets any colder."

"It's actually still pretty hot." Taking a dutiful sip, Mattie pulled a face. "But it tastes like grass," she said, handing the mug to Emma.

"That's because it is. On the other hand, it's better than nothing." Depressing the mug's auto-seal button, she tipped a swallow into her mouth. The tea was no better than it had been back in Minot, but at least it wasn't icy cold either and she sighed as a warm finger traced its way down the middle of her chest. *And it is still hot.*

"What are you smiling at?" asked Mattie.

"The last line from an old kid's book my mom used to read to me." She made a mental note to write to the travel mug's manufacturer if they ever got out of this. Maybe Gwyneth Paltrow, too, if she was feeling charitable. She looked toward the rear of the plane. "What'd you find?"

"Buried treasure," Will said. "Burke wasn't kidding about having survival gear."

"Please tell me there's a satellite phone in there." While she'd been outside earlier, she'd tried her cell more out of habit than actual hope and had gotten what she expected: the equivalent of an electronic raspberry and a message in tiny capitals, *NO SERVICE.*

"Afraid not." Will had strapped on a headlamp from his pack and was laying objects onto the deck: flashlights, batteries, a hand axe, a black-bladed fixed blade in a leg sheath. Hefting a rifle in his good left hand, he said, "But it's still not half bad. Almost makes you believe in Santa Claus."

At this point, she'd be willing to attend a Burl Ives solo concert in exchange for a seat on a rescue chopper. "Wow. Here," she said, holding out the travel mug. "Trade you." As he drank, she hefted the rifle, a bolt-action Savage. Slow-rolling the bolt made her smile. Burke had maintained the weapon well. Even in the freezing cold, the action was buttery-smooth, and she caught the slightest whiff of gun oil from the barrel. "I call dibs on the Savage," she said, setting the weapon aside. "And I want that blade."

"They're yours. I've already got a knife in my luggage, and there's no way I'll be mucking around with a rifle anytime soon."

"That's a pretty big knife." Mattie, who'd followed, watched as Emma strapped the sheath to her right thigh. "And that gun looks dangerous."

"Only if you're on the receiving end," Emma said.

"My mother says guns are bad."

"I think that depends on who you are and what you use them for."

"Guns are only for killing."

She was not getting into this. "Yes, they are. But if it's a choice between going hungry and eating deer stew, I'll take stew." The knife was a KA-BAR BK2 and, she could already tell, sharp enough to slice paper. She usually carried a knife, a nice Ken Onion Leek Ben had bought that she could clip to a pocket when she was off-duty. The knife was a comfort thing more than anything else; it wasn't as if she was skilled in fixed-blade fighting, and there wasn't much call for, say, shaving tinder, splinting out kindling, skinning game, or carving out a handy-dandy hand drill to make a fire in her apartment. But Ben had always carried a knife. She had a sneaking suspicion it was a nod to NCIS—Gibbs's Rule Number Nine—a show he'd loved and never missed, although he always made fun of it, too. Being a special investigations officer, he knew what agents could and couldn't do. (A Mossad agent like Ziva David, he said, was a non-starter, but hey, it was fiction.) One thing Ben always said: you never knew when you'd need a knife. For this trip, she hadn't thought to pack her Leek. Why should she? She was supposed to be only interviewing veterans and their nice dogs, not trying to figure out how to stay alive long enough for someone to rescue her ass. Besides, the airlines would only have given her hell, and she'd been traveling light, with only her pack.

"Do you know how to hunt?" Mattie asked.

"I'm from Wisconsin. Even my grandmother hunted." Straightening, she dropped her right hand, felt her fingers brush the sheath's release strap. No good wearing a knife you couldn't get to in a hurry. She wondered if there was any game at this elevation. In winter, the answer was probably no. Deer, rabbits, raccoons, opossums...except for mountain goats, anything they could reasonably hunt would be at a lower elevation where food would be easier to come by.

Well, they wouldn't be here long enough to have to worry about that anyway. "What else do we have, Will?"

There turned out to be quite a bit. Besides the rifle, two boxes of ammunition, and the BK2, there was a coil of wire, three flashlights, extra batteries, a hand axe, a folding saw, a collapsible fishing rod, a folding shovel, a coil of rope, a small military-grade stove, nesting cookpots, fire sticks, three lighters, three packets of waterproof matches, a packet of jerky, and eight civilian MRE-equivalents (full meals, Emma noted, and not simply entrees, which was good; with the cold, they'd need calories to keep warm). There were also extra packets of tea, instant coffee, sugar, and creamer, as well as an inflatable raft, two sleeping bags (one a double-ton, which made Emma wonder if Burke took trips with lady friends), an extra men's parka and gloves, snow pants, a pair of men's snow boots, and another of snowshoes.

"Interesting." Will inspected a long orange tube topped with a white cap. "Well, I guess if your radio's busted and you want to get someone's attention, this would be a way. Or maybe mark out a landing zone at night? He's got several."

"I can see that." Turning over a second, Emma read the label. "But why a marine flare? Why not a regular roadside doohickey?"

"Is that a technical term?" asked Mattie.

"Yeah, right up there with thingamajig. I suppose there's a distance component. That is, a marine flare is brighter and produces a much larger flame." Then Will's face cleared. "Now I remember. It was during a lecture on bear attacks. An instructor said these are pretty handy against grizzlies. It's the noise and the fire that scares them away, and they're better than roadside flares because you don't have to worry about fiddling with a striker. With this baby, you pop the cap and pull the string and you're got fire. Might come in handy if there are bears up here." At the expression on Mattie's face, Will laughed. "Don't worry. This late in the season, grizzlies already have been denned up for a month." He paused then added, "Unless it's been a bad fall."

Mattie gave him a withering look. "Come on."

"Scout's honor. Bears don't necessarily sleep all winter if they haven't eaten enough in the fall, or something can cause them to wake up."

"Yeah." Emma nodded solemnly. "Like a plane going boom."

"*Especially* a plane going boom," Will seconded.

"Oh, ha-ha. I'm glad you're having so much fun torturing a kid." Mattie plucked the flare from Emma's hands. "Seriously, should we carry one around or something? Just in case?"

"If it makes you feel better, I don't see why not," said Will. "There are enough for each of us. Might be prudent."

"Wait," said Emma. "You were serious about grizzlies waking up?"

"As a heart attack. But the chances are small. It's more likely we'd need one to signal a rescue team. In a pinch, you could also start a fire."

"Cool." Setting her flare to one side, Mattie read the

label on a long blue box that also sported a graphic of a boy in a white sailor suit. "What's pilot bread?"

She knew this one from Thule. "It's another name for hardtack. They're really hard, thick crackers without salt. People in Alaska and way up in Canada and Greenland eat it instead of bread because bread's too expensive to make and pilot bread doesn't spoil. Most people have it for breakfast along with, you know, jerky or fish." It also tasted vaguely the way she imagined the paste they'd used in kindergarten might, and the stale ones could break your teeth, but details, details. Pilot bread was fine in a pinch, and if ever she was in one, this was it. Thinking about crunching into a cracker made her mouth water. Wait, she had her sandwiches, her trail mix—she nearly groaned aloud—and her Almond Joy.

"Jerky? For breakfast?" Mattie wrinkled her nose. "What about eggs?"

She forced herself to stop thinking about chocolate-covered coconut and almonds. She wasn't going to touch that bar until they were rescued. "Chickens don't do so hot in the cold. Plus, you have to fly eggs in, and that gets expensive. It depends on what you're used to. I know people who like canned Dinty Moore stew for breakfast."

"Could you guys please stop talking about food?" Will said. "If you'll recall, none of us has had anything to eat since this morning."

"Speaking of which," Emma said, "we should dig through our packs, pool our resources." And get some calories in and have something hot to drink and shore up their barricade and maybe start gathering wood for a fire...The list was endless.

"Hey, look." Setting aside the box of pilot bread, Mattie reached in again, and this time pulled out three rolls of duct tape. "That's a lot of tape. Can we use it?"

"Apparently." Emma inspected the packaging. "Says it's specially formulated for use in snow and ice." A few pointers burbled up from memory. "I think you can make rope from it and use it for bandages and stuff."

"Are you kidding? Duct tape's a godsend. Say," Will said, trying but failing to lift out what looked like rolls of plastic, "grab that for me, will you? I only have the one hand."

The plastic was clear, thick, and very heavy, and wrestling one of the four rolls from the locker set her ribs to complaining again. "What is this?" She let it fall with a hefty *thunk* to the deck.

"Visqueen. It's polyethylene," Will said. "This is a total jackpot. Normally, you use this stuff in construction work. You know, drop cloths, vapor barriers..."

"Dexter."

"Who?" asked Mattie.

"A very good show until the last season when it went completely off the rails," she said.

"True," Will agreed. "But beyond walling off blood spatter..."

"Blood?" Mattie asked.

"We'll explain later."

Mattie stuck out her lower lip. "Grown-ups always say that."

"Sometimes they even mean it. As I was saying, you

can also use this for an emergency tent or a tarp." Will nodded toward the front. "Be a nice way to block off the rest of that opening, too."

"Wait, we won't suffocate, will we?" asked Mattie.

"Well, the fuselage isn't going to be airtight, but we'll leave a way for us to crawl in and out, like a snow tunnel. Speaking of which," Will asked Emma, "how buried are we?"

"Not bad, but the snow's really coming down, so it's going to get worse," she said. "That might not be a bad thing, though, Will."

"For us to get *buried*?" Mattie's eyes were wide behind her glasses. "No one will *see* us."

Will's tone was soothing. "But snow's a good insulator, Mattie. Come on, a smart girl like you, you have to know this."

"Yeah." She gave a cautious nod. "We learned about igloos and stuff."

"Exactly. It's why snow houses keep you warm. And I hate to say it, honey, but no one will be looking for us tonight. It's almost dark, and it's still snowing, so…"

Mattie's teeth snuck out to gnaw at her lower lip. "But what about my grandfather?"

Probably dead. Funny, how that thought was so… dispassionate. Very matter-of-fact. *It's snowing. Oh yeah, he's toast.* Except for a few moments when she'd finally comprehended their situation, she'd not wasted a lot of time thinking about the others. She'd been so busy taking care of Rachel and worrying about Will and trying to set up a shelter that would actually give them a shot at surviving the night. There was also a very small

ILSA J. BICK

part of her that actually felt a tiny bit...well, *relieved.* She didn't need to be responsible for yet one more person. She had a hard enough time taking care of herself and, frankly, with their scarce resources, they had a better shot at making it with fewer mouths to feed.

And, yeah, it was also true that she wasn't all broken up about Scott. Good riddance to bad rubbish. Mean but accurate.

"There's nothing we can do about your grandfather tonight," Will said. "I'm sorry, honey, but that's the truth. If he's smart, if the cockpit is anything like the fuselage, he's holed up, trying to stay warm, same as us."

"But he won't have any of the stuff we do." Mattie's eyes filled again. "It's not fair."

"I know. Now, come on." Will waggled Emma's travel mug in his good hand. "Let's fire up my Jetboil and make something better and hotter to drink than this swill."

It was on the tip of her tongue to snipe that she resembled that remark, but she caught it before it could leapfrog from her mouth and let the words curdle. *Getting punchy.* There wasn't anything the least bit fun, funny, or even mildly amusing about this. Yeah, cool, she and Will could toss glib one-liners; hooray, they knew the same bad pop-cultural icons; but she felt as if all that were something born of a mild hysteria. It was easier and better and even more constructive to make stupid jokes than to give into panic and how she really felt as if there might be nothing better to do than run off screaming into the wilderness.

"I'll work on the shelter," she said, more sharply than

114

she intended, her tone suggesting one of them needed to do something useful before they all died. But she had to get out of here. She had to move, to do something. If there was enough plastic left over, and there should be, she was going to put that hand axe to good use building a lean-to for a woodpile. *If we're here that long.* "Why don't you guys start going through the rest of our crap, pool our stuff, see what we've got?"

From his expression, she knew Will caught that caustic edge. "Sure." Clamping his good hand to the edge of the locker, he pushed to his feet. "But Mattie can handle that. Let me give you a hand."

"Well, considering that one is all you've got at the moment, not a chance." They needed Will, especially if Mattie's brother decided he was really sick and tired of a womb without a view, ha-ha, and that now would be a good time to blow this crackerjack joint.

"All right." Will favored her with a long look. "I still need to examine you, though, and that gash on your scalp needs cleaning out."

"Yeah? Lessee, she'd already gotten Will's arm into a sling, cut Mattie out of her harness, had Will talk her through supergluing and then bandaging Rachel's scalp, mostly built a barricade to keep out the damn snow… "Well, it's always something," she said in her best Gilda Radner imitation, and that made her even angrier. SNL was a stupid show. "We'll get to it." Hefting a roll of Visqueen—ignoring the yammer of her damn ribs—she grabbed a roll of duct tape. "As soon as I finish."

"Okay," Will said easily. "But at the risk of pissing you off even more…"

"I'm not pissed."

"Yes, you are," Mattie said.

Jesus. She blew out in exasperation. *"What?"*

"Have you checked the antenna?" asked Will.

"What antenna?" said Mattie asked.

"Emergency locator transponder." She should've remembered to check this. "All planes are supposed to have them. They're designed to go off on impact." She decided not to go into all the reasons why, sometimes, an ELT would not go off. "The ELT broadcasts a signal search and rescue teams can zero in on." She looked back at Will. "You think that's why we haven't heard anything? Why no one's come looking?"

Will inclined his head in an abortive shrug. "It's possible."

"What are you saying?" Mattie looked from her to Will and back again. "What does that mean?"

"He's saying that might be a reason we haven't heard a search plane." She kept her eyes on Will. "It's snowing, Will. No one's going up in this to look for us."

"Still, best to check," Will said. "Better safe than sorry."

And if something's wrong with the antenna, then what? She didn't even want to think about it. She'd think about it tomorrow, and fiddle-dee-dee.

"I'll do that," she said, and left.

THE DAY BLED AWAY, taking the wind with it, though the snow didn't let up. Smoothing a last length of duct tape to the fuselage, she took a few steps back and ran a critical eye over her handiwork. Not too shabby, actually. The arrangement of luggage along the base reminded her of sandbagged fortifications at forward operating bases and bunkers. A small but soft light diffused along the opaque plastic sheeting through which she could make out Will's hunched form and, to his left, Mattie's back as they worked at sorting through the contents of their various packs. The sheeting wasn't air-tight, and although she couldn't make out the words, she heard the rise and fall of their voices, the lighter, slightly anxious note as Mattie asked a question and then Will's low, slow baritone. She also caught a whiff of warm chocolate. Will must have made hot cocoa. The smell made saliva pool under her tongue, though of course her bladder took that moment to remind her that she had other business to attend to.

Might as well scout that out now. If they were here for longer than this evening, they'd have to designate an area well away from the fuselage. *Wait, what are you thinking?* Turning aside, she slogged through snow in as straight a line as she could manage, heading for a denser, darker area that might be forest. She didn't know why she had that feeling, but it was the same as when a person carefully wandered a dark cellar or bedroom and sensed a wall coming up, a tower of boxes. Every few steps, she paused to eyeball the plane through dense, heavy snow that fell straight-down, like water gushing over a falls. Several inches already blanketed the fuselage. Will was right about insulation, but all that snow also would make it tough for anyone to see them from the air. Worse, Burke's plane was white with black-and-red markings on the sides. She couldn't remember what color the vertical fin and rudder were, but any color was better than none. Clearing snow away had to be a priority for tomorrow and maybe stamp out an SOS in the snow, too. The pack was certainly deep enough. If the sun deigned to make an appearance, perhaps they could use bits of the plane to catch the light?

There was a lot to think about. She bet Will would know the best course of action. He was the wilderness guy, after all. She pushed away the thought that followed on the heels of that, but she couldn't help but consider that Burt Reynolds's character in *Deliverance* was a big outdoorsy guy, and he'd been the one who needed rescuing.

She had to stop thinking so hard.

The going was tough; every step was a posthole into fresh snow that came to mid-calf. She didn't think what she felt beneath her boots was ground or rock, either, but more snowpack. She was reminded of stories her grandmother told about blizzards and following guide ropes from the house to the barn that were right out of *Little House on the Prairie.* Getting lost out here would be bad. Tomorrow, they would have to scout out the place, figure out where the cockpit was. The chances anyone was alive were, as her dad always joked, slim to none, and slim had left the building. (It was a dumb joke then and a dumb joke now, but her mom always laughed. That was, her dad once said, why he'd married her.) But there might be maps, like the one Burke had been consulting, or the radio might work.

There has to be something we can do other than wait.

As she waded through calf-high snow, she fanned the beam of one of Burke's flashlights right and left. She saw nothing fresh or dug out, no trough made by something as large as a cockpit skidding through hardpack, but she was moving at a right angle to the wreck, too. All things considered, if the cockpit was anywhere, it probably lay in front of and on a line with their wreck. That's what had happened to that rugby team in the Andes. Of course, where Burke and the cockpit were also depended on how the plane had come down. If a wing had clipped a tree, that might have spun them around.

She was still thinking too hard.

She wondered if animals might come to explore and see what all the fuss was about. She guessed that depended on how high they were. This was grizzly and wolf country. Mountain lions, too. Of the three, she put her money on cougars, not because she actually knew anything about the animals—she'd never seen one in her life—but because she'd seen it in a movie...which was it? The one with Jeremy Renner that took place on that reservation. That poor native girl who ran as fast as she could through air that flash-froze her lungs. On the other hand, the mountain lion in the movie came down from a mountain to feed; it didn't hunt in the mountains.

They might not be able to hunt up here either. Which meant they would have to move to a lower elevation. Maybe they should do that sooner rather than later.

God. Freak yourself out. They hadn't even passed the twenty-four mark yet. The end of their golden day would come soon enough, at about midnight, one a.m., but it wasn't here yet.

When she figured she was far enough away to tinkle in peace, she stopped and turned back toward the wreck. The light was still there but very faint. She hadn't come to any trees, either, which should've embarrassed her but didn't because, well, beggars and all that. Wedging her flashlight into an armpit, she quickly unzipped and squatted. Her bladder wasn't as full as she'd imagined. From the ammonia smell, she must be dehydrated. Her lips were dry, and her tongue felt huge. Water would taste good right now. Better yet, a mug of hot tea or cocoa.

As she was pulling up her pants, she happened to

glance down—and saw something on her panties in the white beam of her headlamp.

Shit.

When she was twelve, she'd slipped on the balance beam and come down in a hard straddle. That had torn her up a bit on the outside. She'd also not been able to walk for a week, what with that melon between her legs. Yet another time when the school nurse had taken a look and rolled her eyes.

The spot on her panties back then had been red.

This one was pink.

She must've stared for a good minute before her brain started working again.

It's trauma. She ran the zipper up then secured her pants with decisive snap. *Nothing more amazing than that.* What the hell? She'd been through enough in one day to last a lifetime.

Face it. You're one accident-prone chick.

The thought made her laugh. Because wasn't it the truth that accidents kept happening—

Something, somewhere, screamed.

CHAPTER 8

W<small>HAT</small>?

Her heart crammed into the back of her throat. The hackles bristled along the nape of her neck and up and down her arms. Had that been a scream? A real shout from a person? She listened hard, trying to hear above the continual dull patter of snow hitting snow. The sound had been very high, almost womanish, but coming from where? Which direction? It had been so unexpected, she couldn't really tell.

She opened her mouth to call out—

And stopped herself.

Did she *want* an answer? Anyone looking for them wouldn't scream. They would call. They would shout. More likely, they'd use a bullhorn or blast something down from a loudspeaker mounted on a chopper. But other than snow, the air was still.

If she called and someone *did* respond, what then? She'd have to go look. She'd have to tell Will and he'd insist on slogging out into this storm and then *anything* might happen and if something happened to *Will*…

Wasn't it better to say nothing?

My God, no, what was wrong with her? It might be Mattie's grandfather or Scott. It could Hunter or Burke. The cockpit might be very close by, although, no, that cry, that solitary scream, had sounded far away.

She turned in a slow circle. *If it comes again, I'll go check it out. Otherwise, it was nothing. It was my imagination.* It could've been an animal, for all she knew. Rabbits screamed; their screams were actually quite bad, almost human, like the scream of a little kid. She knew because once she'd been at her bubbe's house when a red fox had made her den under a shed in back. She liked to watch the baby kits chase one another and play, although Bubbe Sarah's cat, Thomas, had to stay inside because he was too curious and would end up in a fox's stomach. One afternoon, she'd been startled to hear a series of blood-curdling screams. She'd nearly jumped out of her skin, but Sarah had said only, *Oh, sounds like rabbit's on the menu.* Sure enough, a short time later, she watched as the kits took the rabbit their mother had brought and spent more time playing with it, tossing it up and down, than actually eating.

If it comes again, I'll tell Will. She listened now, nerves fizzing. *If not…well…*

No harm, no foul.

CHAPTER 9

"Hey." Wrench in his left hand, Will turned as she peeled back the plastic and wriggled inside on a raft of cold air. "Thought you got lost."

"What are you doing?" He was sweating again. His eyes, shiny with pain, seemed to have sunk back into his skull, and the smudges beneath them were the color of old coffee. Those pills had either worn off or not done much to begin with. "Why aren't you resting?" she snapped.

"I'm okay."

"Like hell you are." She heard the quaver. "You need to be careful."

"Take it easy." He gave her a close look. "Did something happen?"

"No. Why should anything happen?" She cast around for something to say that wasn't a retort. "I checked the antenna. As far as I can tell, it's fine."

"What about the unit that powers it? It would be located inside the tail."

"I don't know. The panel's locked. Were there keys in Burke's stash?" When he shook his head, she said, "Then I guess we take it on faith, unless you want to take a rock to it or something."

He opened his mouth to say something else, but she was saved by Mattie. "Will made hot chocolate. We saved you a cup." Carefully pouring from Will's Jetboil, the girl held out a blue-enameled mug. "You should drink it. Will wanted to wait to eat something until you got back."

"Okay. Thanks." She almost groaned when the chocolate washed over her tongue, the taste was so good. She had to calm down.

"Everything okay?" Will asked.

"Isn't that just another way of asking if something happened?" Draining her cocoa, she gestured at the wrench with her mug. "What's with the wrench?"

"Seeing if I can get a couple of these bolts loose. If we can move the seats, we'll have more room to—" He stopped talking as she plucked the wrench from his hand. "What do you think you're doing?"

"What does it look like? You need to stop. You're hurt. You should rest. I can do this, and I will," she added as he opened his mouth.

"I wasn't going to fight you about it. You're right. What I was going to suggest is that we eat something. What do you say we did into those sandwiches you bought? I've got an apple, too, and we can all have tea. We'll all feel better."

"Is that a promise?" Because she sincerely doubted it.

ILSA J. BICK

"No." He gave her a lopsided grin that showed off his dimple. "But there's no harm in finding out, is there?"

She fired up Will's Jetboil and they ate by flashlight. It was almost cozy, like camping minus the fire. Emma took small bites and chewed carefully as she waited for her stomach to rebel. It didn't. Perhaps even it understood she needed fuel. As they shared a mug of tea, Will said, "I still need to check you out."

"I'm fine," she said then yelped when he poked a finger into her left side. "Stop that!"

"Right. Fine." Will tipped Mattie a wink. "Does she sound fine to you?"

"No," Mattie deadpanned.

Emma scowled. "Whose side are you on?"

"Mine. I suppose it's too much to ask if there's dessert. Because when we were going through the packs, I saw this, like, really *nice* Almond Joy bar."

"Touch that, and you're a dead woman." Digging through the nylon carry sack into which Will and Mattie had pooled their food, Emma unearthed her Almond Joy and reached to tuck it back into her own pack for safekeeping. "We can have it when we're rescued."

"And I suppose you can be trusted."

She really was starting to like this kid. "I resemble that remark."

"Thank you, Curly," Will said. His color was better... well, through the bruises and swelling. They all looked pretty gruesome.

"You guys." Mattie executed an impressive eyeroll. "What does that even mean?"

"Three Stooges," they said at the same time.

"God." Mattie covered her ears with her hands. "Now they're in stereo."

Emma's mouth cocked in a grin. "Stick with me," she said, pushing Ben's copy of *The Waste Land* to one side then slotting her candy bar into her bag. "I'm a font of irrelevant effluvia…" She frowned.

"What?" asked Will.

"I don't know." She withdrew a plain brown paper packet about the size of her hand but oddly shaped: something square that felt like a box on top and an odder, heavier object on the bottom. It felt a bit like a very large lipstick case. "I don't remember packing this.

"I saw that when I went through your pack. It's a present. See?" Taking the packet from Emma, Mattie turned it over and pointed at a message done in fine black Sharpie .

For dark times, Emma read. *Kim.*

"Who's Kim?" asked Mattie.

"A friend." Kim must've slipped this in last night. She remembered now that Kim had asked to use the bathroom right before they went out.

"Here." Will slipped a knife from a front pocket where he'd clipped it. "Never know when you might need paper to help start a fire."

"Thanks." She could've used Burke's KA-BAR, but it was too much knife for the job. Will's pocket carry was a Ken Onion Blur. Ben had a knife like this. "Nice knife."

"Wow," Mattie said as Emma thumbed open the

speed-safe and the Blur's blade locked in place. "It's black."

"Yup," Will said. "It's one of my favorites. Rule Nine."

"What?" Then Mattie did another eyeroll. "Don't tell me this is more irrelevant cultural effluvia."

"Television show." She wouldn't have pegged Will as an NCIS-type. "Never go anywhere without a knife."

"Oh." Mattie thought about that. "*Sooo*...do I get a knife?"

They looked at one another, and then Will said, "I don't see why not, especially since I'll be resting this hand for a couple days anyway. You ever use one?"

"Well, gosh, no, my mom cuts up my food all the time," said Mattie.

"I told you. She's got you." Folding the knife, Emma held it out to Mattie. "All the same, we'll go the basics in the morning, okay? The last thing I need is to explain to your mother why you no longer have an opposable thumb."

"Fine." Mattie heaved a put-upon sigh. "What's in the package...oh!" Mattie exclaimed as Emma peeled back paper. "Is it your birthday?"

"They're not that type of candle." She was amazed her voice was so steady. She also saw that what she'd thought might be a really large lipstick case wasn't. She turned the length of lacquered wood in the wash of blue-light from their flashlight and studied the green vines, red flowers, and white coves painted onto a lapis-blue background. A tiny brass hinge was set in one end.

"What is that?" Will asked as she pulled the hinged wood open to its full length. "Wait, is that a menorah?"

"What's that?" Mattie asked.

"A special kind of candelabra." She cleared her throat. "It's what Jewish people use on Hanukkah to celebrate the miracle of the oil and the Temple."

"A miracle?"

She decided on the Spark Notes version. "There were these guys, the Maccabees, that led a revolt against the Seleucids. This was, like, a really, really long time ago. When they retook the Temple in Jerusalem, they found there was only enough of the right kind of oil to keep the eternal flame, the *ner tamid,* burning for a day, which is bad because you're not supposed to let that go out. Anyway, the miracle was that the oil lasted eight days and eight nights, long enough for them to get more. It's really a minor holiday, honest. Something the rabbis decided on."

"Which started tonight at sundown, actually," Will put in.

"Yeah, but you know, it's like every other holiday around this time of year. It's because it gets so dark. That's why you have Christmas trees and lights and Hanukkah candles. Even people who celebrate Kwanzaa have a special candelabra."

"Seven total instead of nine," Will said. "The middle candle, which is always black, is lit first and then used it to kindle the others. You add a candle for each night, and each new candle stands for a different principle or idea, like unity, creativity, faith."

"Oh." Mattie peered at Emma. "Well, if it's the first night, are you going to light the candles?"

"You don't light them all at once. I mean, you're

talking forty-six candles," Will said. "The idea is you light a new one for every night to symbolize all the nights the oil lasted."

"Forty-six?" Mattie frowned. "That's eight more than you need."

Will pointed at a hole in the smaller of the two hinged portions. "That's because this holder on the far left is for the helper candle."

"Like the black candle for Kwanzaa."

"Well, Hanukkah came first, but yeah. It's called the *shamash*," she said, picking up the thread. Shirer was German; Will had to be Jewish. Even if he wasn't, he knew a hell of a lot. Why did that make her feel...well, not *good*, but better? *No, less alone.* "It doesn't count as one of the nights. Its job is to light the other candles."

"Cool." Mattie made a get-rolling motion with a finger. "So, light them."

"I don't know. We should probably save them."

"What for? We've got Burke's firesticks," Will said. "We'll find wood, and we've got plenty of matches and lighters."

"And you're forgetting we're going to get rescued. Besides," Mattie added, "isn't it kind of a miracle we're all alive to be talking about this? I wish my mom would wake up, but she's alive, and Joshua's alive, and those are all miracles." Mattie's voice went a little watery. "Aren't they?"

Will threaded his good arm around Maddie's shoulders and pulled her close. "That is an excellent point."

"Yeah. Okay." She was not going to get out of this.

She didn't know how she felt about that either. The last time she'd lit candles, Ben was alive.

The multicolored candles were made of beeswax, the kind that didn't drip and make a mess. Fitting a dark-blue candle into the hole for the *shamash*, she stuck a white candle in the hole to the far right.

Mattie was watching closely. "How come you put it all the way out there?"

"Because that's how you read Hebrew, from right to left. It's not like English, which goes from left to right."

"Did you know that Shamash was also a Babylonian solar deity?" Will said. "He held the power of light against the forces of darkness and evil."

"That's us, then." Mattie looked solemn. "Maybe not against evil…Mr. Burke wasn't bad or anything…but it's really dark, and my mom won't wake up, and I'm kind of freaked out." She burrowed closer to Will. "I don't want to be here, but if I have to be, it's better than being here alone."

Oh, boy, could she tell this kid a thing or two about that. Flicking a Bic, she held the flame to the *shamash's* wick, which caught with a small *pfft* and spray of orange sparks before blooming in a hot-yellow flower. "There you go," she said, using the *shamash* to light the first candle.

"That's it?" Mattie's eyebrows arched in surprise. "You don't say anything? You only light candles?"

"That's it." Avoiding Will's eyes, she reseated the *shamash*. The blessings were on the back of the box for the forgetful and even transliterated for the Hebrew-challenged, but she knew them by heart. "You can say *yehi 'or*, I guess," she said with false heartiness. "That's Hebrew for, 'Let there be light.'"

"Is that all? Well." Suddenly pushing to her feet, Mattie brushed past and headed for the cargo hold where her mother lay. "That's not so much."

CHAPTER 10

You are a horrible human being.

Working a wrench with grim efficiency, she cranked loose nuts and bolts, trying not to feel the grab in her side, working hard not to listen as Mattie cried. She didn't wail like a little kid but sobbed in soft, angry hiccups as Will tried to comfort her. Would it have hurt her to embellish a little, say the stupid damn blessings, maybe even teach the kid a verse of "The Dreidel Song" or "Rock of Ages"? *It's a matter of principle.* Saying the blessings would be hypocritical, an empty gesture to an even emptier and more bankrupt concept because that's all a god was at the end of the day, wasn't it? An idea? She'd have better luck putting her faith in Spiderman.

Wrestling her seat and Rachel's from their rails, she butted them against their barrier of luggage and Visqueen. Once morning came, presuming it stopped snowing, they could reassess and figure out where to put the seats for the duration. God, she hoped that wouldn't be more than another day. Any longer and, hell, they could set the seats out in the sun, catch a couple rays, work on their tans.

When did you get this way? The voice was half hers and maybe a little of Ben mixed in. Whatever the case, it was a good question. Perhaps she had always been a glass-half-empty kind of person.

Yeah, yeah, yeah. She went to work on Will's seat. *I dare anyone to come home to what I did and still look on the bright side of life.* This was probably the reason she despised romance novels—all those size two women with the flyaway hair and their drop-dead-gorgeous guys on the covers...and none of the men seemed to have heads, did they? *No, only rippling, well-oiled six-packs.* She snorted as she dislodged a bolt and thumbed out a monster screw. *Fantasy land.*

Once she was done with the seats, she spread Burke's double-ton bag, shucked her boots, killed the flashlight, and then, still wearing her watch cap and the rest of her cold-weather gear, slipped inside, and lay on her right side. She listened to Will's low murmur. The sound was comforting, almost a lullaby against a counterpoint of snow scurrying and hissing over plastic and metal. Eventually, he fell silent. She felt him waiting, could imagine him with Mattie, perhaps sitting quietly with his good hand pressed to her back. After a time, there was a soft rustle and then Will slipped into the sleeping bag where he settled with a small groan.

Without turning, she said in a low murmur, "Does it still hurt?"

"Yeah." A long sigh. "Not as bad. I might have a small fracture. Hard to tell without an x-ray. Have to be careful not to use the hand or arm much."

"Can you? Use it, I mean."

"Within reason. I'm not going to be doing any rappelling any time soon, though, or splitting wood. Better hope we find a lot of downed branches. Thank God, Burke packed that folding saw."

"Which you are not going to use. With our luck, you'll saw off a thumb or something."

"Thanks for the vote of confidence."

"I'm serious." She turned onto her back, a move she regretted an instant later as the pressure on her left ribcage sent a spike of pain zinging into her spine. "We can't afford for you to get hurt more than you already are."

"You always sell yourself short?" Before she could reply, he went on. "I heard that groan, by the way. I never took a good look at you."

"Tomorrow." She rolled a bit onto her right side to take the pressure off her back. The pain fell to a low grumble.

"Is there a reason you keep putting me off?"

"No. It's that there's nothing to see. You really think we're going to be out here long enough where chopping down trees becomes an issue?"

It was dark as pitch in the fuselage. She couldn't see his face or even a glimmer of his profile. "I think we need to be prepared for that," he said.

A clot of panic formed where her heart rested. "Come on. Will, even at minimal rations, we'll run out of food in a week. Maybe less."

"Let's not catastrophize yet. We'll know more in the morning, once we've got better light. Even if the snow doesn't let up, we'll need to do some exploring, find fuel for a fire."

"I thought about that." She told him her idea for using Visqueen and building a lean-to. "I think we're close to trees. We can probably gather a lot of wood. We won't be able to start a fire if the snow keeps up, but we can be prepared." Starting a fire *in* or *on* the snow would be difficult but not impossible once the storm let up.

"We'll need it. If we are near trees, that also explains why the wings are gone. They wouldn't normally shear away like that unless they get caught up on something."

"How long do you think we'll have to be here?" It was a stupid question. "That was dumb. Ignore me. You can't possibly know."

"True. But I've certainly asked myself the same thing. We'll have to hope for a break in the weather sooner rather than later. Weren't you going to do a story on a bunch of military guys?"

"Ex, but yeah. Why?"

"The military has a better capability when it comes to search and rescue, even in storms. They've got choppers that can navigate in the equivalent of pea soup. And there are drones. They use them way up for here for patrolling the border because it's more efficient and easier than navigating mountains and forests on foot."

"Heat signatures, you mean." That put a new spin on things. "They could look for us even in snow."

"That's the theory."

"How long do you think we should wait?"

"Before…?"

"Before we leave." She didn't want to do that at all, but it paid to think ahead. There were three of them—four, if you counted Rachel—and they would need to start thinking about calories. Staying warm burned a lot of them, and they had limited rations. As it was, they'd be skimping if this went on for more than a day, as seemed likely. When Rachel woke…*if* she woke…that would be another mouth.

Will listened and then said, "We'll burn a hell of a lot more calories walking in the cold than staying put. I read a story not long ago. *Outside* magazine, I think. It was about this thru-hiker on the Continental Divide. Veteran, knew what he was doing, but also went ultra-light so he could make better time. He told people where he was going and when he ought to arrive; he even had a sat phone, I think. Then it snowed. One of those freak October storms. A helluva dump, I guess. Anyway, when he didn't show, people started looking along his route. Search planes, the whole nine yards. Turned out they were looking in the wrong place. Even so, this guy managed to survive until late February."

"Holy cow." Five months? "How did he do that?"

"Luck. He kept a journal. It's all in there, what he did, how he tried to get out. Because he knew the area, he made it to a campground and eventually sheltered in one of the cement-bottomed latrines. In a woodshed nearby, he found a couple pounds of horse oats. He still had a camp stove, so he lived on oatmeal and water for months. He tried making skis, too, but that didn't work. All he could do was sit there and write in his journal and daydream about food. As time went on and no rescue showed up, he started thinking maybe suicide was an option. He tried, too, by cranking up the wood-stove so he'd asphyxiate. Only the latrine was drafty, and he survived. Another time, he cut his wrist with his portable saw. When he woke up still alive, he sewed himself up with fishing line."

My God. "What happened? Did they find him?" They must have. Will said the hiker kept a journal.

"They found him…in April. An early spring hiker came on the latrine and there was this note warning people not to open the door because there was a dead body inside. They finally brought the body down in May."

"If you're trying to boost my morale, you're totally failing. Why are you telling me this?"

"Because that guy was an experienced hiker in an area he knew well, and he still died. *We* are lost. We haven't a clue where we are except, probably, some-where in Montana. But we could have crossed the border into Canada. I know you keep thinking I'm this indispensable guy, but I know wilderness medicine and basic survival skills. I know how to navigate but need a map or some idea of which way to head. So, I'm not a Superman here. I'm only a guy who knows things. *You* know quite a few things, too. Don't tell me they don't teach you basic survival in the military. You're the hunter, too, not me. I know how to fish and set a snare, but that doesn't mean I've ever caught anything. Plus, we have Mattie to consider. She's a tough kid, but if she's spent one day on a trail, I'll eat my hat." He let out a small grunt. "I might do it anyway if we get desperate enough. We also have to worry about Rachel. I sure don't want to be delivering a baby on the trail."

"It's better to deliver it here?" But it was a rhetorical question, and she knew it. "Have you ever done a long-distance hike?"

"If you mean days, yes. But months?" He wagged his head in an emphatic negative. "You?"

"No." But how hard could it be? Hadn't there been some woman who'd up and decided to hike some really long trail? Yeah, that was right. Reese Witherspoon had starred in the movie. She'd read the book and, if she were honest, the book had ticked her off. Like, that woman would *never* had made it if a bunch of people on the trail hadn't rescued her butt several times over. (Seriously, who tossed away a hiking boot because they were pissed?)

Will was right, she did know a few things: how to build a fire, make a solar still to turn her pee into water, construct a basic debris shelter, catch fish with a safety pin and line made out of her hair. If she had to, she could choke back a worm (a task assigned by a truly sadistic sergeant; the worm had been disgusting, but she learned you didn't chew worms. You swallowed them whole and tried not to think about it). She could ice-fish and set a snare; she knew how to clean whatever she caught. Sarah had taught her well, too.

So, if I had to, I might make it...if I knew where I was going, if I tried hard enough. And to hell with his stories of experienced hikers caught in snow. She was *already* in the shit. They all were. "We can't wait too long, Will. We'll never be stronger or in better shape than we are right now. Waiting means we only break down more."

"As anxious as you are to be moving and *doing,* and believe me, I understand that, I'm saying that if we do decide to leave, we need to pick the right time. We shouldn't leave too soon, but we don't want to wait so long that we're boiling bark to stay alive either."

Or eating each other. She pushed the morbid thought aside. "Well, we're not there yet. We may not get there at all."

"From your mouth to God's ear." He paused, and she sensed he was thinking about the menorah, how she'd not said the blessings or even admitted there were any to say. Or that could be her guilt talking but, seriously, no matter what Mattie said, miracles were in kinda short supply. Finally, he said, "Okay, we've had enough doom and gloom for one night, don't you think?" She was about to agree when he went on. "Before we settle down, I want to do a quick exam, make sure you're okay. Good time for it, now that Mattie's asleep. Just because you keep saying you're fine doesn't mean you are. Trauma's funny that way. You can have a splenic or liver tear and not know it until you've bled enough into your abdomen where you're in more pain than you can possibly imagine."

She thought back to that tiny pink smear on her panties. "But blood is an irritant. If I was bleeding into my belly, I'd be pretty sick already." She remembered this from basic. "Besides, I don't have stomach pain. My ribs hurt, that's all. They might be cracked, but there's nothing you can do about that either, right?"

"No, not really. You get a pneumo because one of your ribs makes shish-kabob out of your lung, *that* I can treat. Is there a reason you don't want me to examine you?"

She lied for the second time in as many minutes. "No. Can I ask you a question?"

"Is it a diversionary tactic?"

"Yes."

He let out a low laugh. "At least you're honest about it. Shoot. I've got nothing but time."

"How come you switched from oncology to wilderness medicine?"

"I told you," he said, easily. "I got tired of death."

"But why? You must've known going into it from the beginning that you'd see a lot of death."

"I did." He was silent so long she was about to ask more when he said, "I started out in the military, too, as a matter of fact."

"You're kidding. Which branch?"

"Air Force. I know, small world. I was a flight surgeon for a while because what I wanted to be an astronaut. Actually, I really wanted to hang out with Captain Kirk or Jean Luc-Picard, but I was about two centuries too early, so…you take what you can get."

"No way." She laughed, though it was cut short by a

needle of pain. "I wanted to be Luke Skywalker, and *that* wasn't happening, plus I needed college first, so…" She concentrated on taking a breath that didn't hurt. "I went in because I didn't know what else to do."

"That was my dad's story. He was originally Air Force, mostly so he could go to school. Once he took his first college biology class, I think it was all over. I guess the military wanted scientists back then for the space program, so they footed the bill for grad school, too. Eventually, he switched over to the Public Health Service. Worked out at Fort Detrick on stuff he never could tell me about because it was all top secret bioweapons stuff. He's retired now, but if you google him, you'll find my dad on a couple conspiracy websites. Anyone in your family military?"

She shook her head. "Media studies professor and English teacher. Total pacifists. I think they were appalled, actually. They wanted me to go straight to college, but I wasn't ready yet, I guess. I didn't see the point of going into debt without a direction. I think they were relieved I chose the Air Force, though."

"Why did you?"

"Because I looked a lot better in navy blue than khaki."

He let out a short bark of laughter he quickly smothered. "Where were you stationed?"

"I was detailed to D.C. as a photojournalist, but they send you all over." It struck her that she hadn't checked out her camera or lenses at all. Well, she *had* been a little busy surviving a crash. Besides, other than a few glimpses of the terrain below snatched between clouds, there really hadn't been much to take a picture *of*. Even if the clouds hadn't been so thick, the best terrain for aerial photography was south in the Dakota Badlands. She'd taken, maybe, five or six pictures, max, before they crashed. "What about you?"

"Besides wanting to be in the astronaut corps? Money. College was bad. Medical school was obscene. There was no way I'd afford it without help, so I joined up. The Air Force put me through and then I became a flight surgeon for a while. Went all over with my guys. Everything they did, I did, too. It was a good experience. I might even have stayed in."

"Why didn't you?"

"I got married. We wanted kids. Remote assignments aren't exactly conducive to a stable life, and a flight surgeon…well, you go where your flight goes. Don't get me wrong. I really loved it. By and large, pilots are a healthy bunch. If I did my job, I kept them that way."

"So, why leave if you liked it so much?"

"Becca. My wife. Some people are good at managing the separation, the long tours, the unexpected calls when your flight's ordered somewhere you can't tell your spouse about. Becca wasn't good that way, and she…like I said, we wanted kids. So, I got out and did a fellowship in oncology. Don't ask me why. It was a weird choice for someone like me. All that death. Yes, there are cures, and you do the best you can, but there were a lot of days when I realized my job was also to help people die."

"How many kids do you have?"

"None." Before she could respond, he clicked on a

penlight. "Okay, enough chitchat. Come on, let me take a look, and no more deflecting. It's a good time now, anyway, with Mattie asleep. Nyuh-uh." He shook his head when she started to roll up her shirt. "All the way off."

Crap. "Why? I'm cold."

"You'll be warm a lot faster if you stop arguing and do what I ask. Come on, shirt off."

"Can I leave my bra on?"

"No, but it doesn't have to come off right this second."

Damn. Shrugging out of her shirt and then her tighter-fitting thermal was harder and more painful than she'd thought it would be, but she worked at keeping that off her face.

"Okay, that's good," he said, screwing his stethoscope into his ears with his left hand. "Stay sitting for right now." She kept her eyes averted as he listened to her heart and lungs and then stiffened when he took her left arm and began to walk his fingers down its length. "Any discomfort?"

"No." But she felt when he came to the scars midway up her forearm and over her wrist. Her scars weren't sensitive. The ER guy said she'd trashed a couple cutaneous nerves and would probably always have a few dead spots. But she could feel his surprise and then the questions in his fingers, as if he were parsing something drawn in an unknown language. The scars on her right forearm were fewer and not as deep because she was right-handed, and by the time she'd gotten to her left wrist, her hand was slick with blood, and it was hard to hang on to the razor. The ER guy said that was lucky because she'd clearly meant business, cutting up and down over the arteries instead of sawing straight across the way most people did. *Amateurs*, he'd said.

She waited for a question or a remark, but Will only scooted around to her back. "Let's have a listen." After a few moments with his stethoscope, he said, "You're going to feel my hand now." He began walking the fingers of his left hand along her ribs, first the right and then left. "Tell me when...*okaaay*," he said as she grunted and cringed away from his touch. "I guess that hurts."

"Well, yeah, when you *bother* it."

"Uh-huh. How did it feel when you were on your back?"

"Not great."

"Is it better when you lie on your right side?"

"Yes, although I noticed I can't take a really deep breath either and...*ouch*." She flinched away again. "Go easy, would you?"

"Sorry." He was still behind her. Finally, he sucked in air between his teeth, exhaled, and said, "Listen, you've got some pretty impressive bruising here. It's not only your left chest in front but the shoulder, too, and along your back. No wonder your bra is killing you."

"I was going to lose the bra when I was building the barricade, but then—" She pulled up abruptly, the words *but then I thought I heard a scream* jamming up behind the gate of her teeth. "There hasn't been the right time."

"You might be more comfortable out of it." And then he added, more gently, "I also need to get a better look. I would do it for you, but I've only got the one hand."

"No, that's fine. I'll get it." Her muscles screamed as she reached around to work her bra's hooks. Sliding down the straps, she shot a look down at her chest and felt her mouth drop. From the top of her breast down to the angle of her rib cage was one large purple-black bruise. "Wow. I didn't realize it was so bad."

"Yup." Still behind her, he feathered his fingers over her ribs. "Might be nothing more than soft tissue, but... sorry, sorry," he said as she flinched. "You've got a great big hematoma here, too." He touched an area farther down, right below her left ribcage, and then abruptly gave it a thump with his fist. "Does that hurt?"

"Yes." She shifted forward, blinking back sudden tears. *Jesus.* "Why did you do that?"

"Trying to figure out if you've got an injury to your kidney. Any blood in your urine?"

She remembered that pink smear. "Why?"

"Well, it's your left flank and where your kidney rests, and you near about jumped out of your skin, that's why. The kidney is actually retroperitoneal...nestled outside your abdominal cavity and along your spine. A blow or even a well-aimed kick can sometimes bruise or even fracture it. I honestly think you'd be in a lot more pain if the latter were the case, though, but that, in addition to your ribs, probably explains why you can't get comfortable on your back. Listen, I know this sucks, but I *do* need you flat. Can you do that?"

"Yes. Give me a sec." After she slowly worked her way onto her back, she kept an arm draped over her breasts as he gently probed and prodded. "Well?"

"Like I said, we might not know anything about rib

fractures unless you drop a lung. You've done a lot of heavy lifting already, though, so you'll probably be okay if you take it easy from here on out."

"Says the guy with one functional arm," She rolled her eyes. "Like that's an option."

"Truth, that." Fitting in the earpieces of his stethoscope again, he said, "I'm going to take a quick listen to your belly. You haven't been sick, so you're probably fine but…"

"Yeah, yeah, better safe than sorry." She studied him as he closed his eyes and bowed his head to listen. "Well?"

"Some squirts, some growls." Then he smiled and opened his eyes. "Noisy in there."

She was starving. "That's a good sign, right?"

"Better than silence." He breathed in his left hand and then placed his palm on her stomach. "Going to palpate here, see if there are any areas of tenderness."

"Okay." She kept a careful eye on his expression as he pressed and prodded from the bottom of her ribs to her pelvis and hips. She caught something as he felt around her navel: a slight but sudden cock of his head which was what a person did when surprised. "Is there a problem?"

He answered her question with another gentle prod, his hand cupping the slight swell of her belly. "Any pain?"

"No."

His face was in shadow. If suspicion or sudden knowledge or even curiosity played on his features, she couldn't have said, although she felt the questions forming in his mind from information her body might have yielded without her even knowing. He was silent for another beat and then took his hand away.

"Well, then," he said, drawing the sleeping bag over her belly, "I guess no news is good news."

CHAPTER 11

WHICH WAS NOT TRUE.

THEIR GOLDEN TIME WINDOW PASSED, the snow kept on, and Rachel didn't wake. The next day, Will insisted they all wash and brush their teeth; they had toiletries and plenty of warm water. It was, he said, the little things that would help boost their morale, and they'd feel better. Emma had her doubts, but after dashing out with the excuse of having to pee but really because she needed a few minutes' peace to puke, brushing her teeth seemed awfully attractive.

While Will shaved, an operation Mattie watched with interest, Emma took care of Rachel. While she was drying Rachel's face with one of Will's camp towels, Mattie came up with a small toiletry bag in hand. "She likes to put on a little lipstick," she said.

"Sure." Emma backed up. "Why don't you do it?" She

watched as the girl carefully applied the color, a soft muted russet, to her mother's lips. "That's a nice color."

"It's my mom's favorite."

"I bet it would look nice on you, too."

"Me?" Mattie scrunched up her nose. "It would be weird."

"It might also be fun." Reaching for her pack, Emma rooted around and came up with a small travel toiletry case. "Or we could use mine. It's mauve, which is kind of soft purple."

"I know what mauve is." Popping the top, Mattie twisted the stick and inspected the tip for a long time. "It's pretty."

"Thanks. I think it's best for girls like us with dark hair. Go on, give it a whirl," she said, opening a small compact of powdered blush and turned it so Mattie could see herself in the mirror. "I promise, I only have a couple cooties."

"Cooties are for kids," Mattie muttered. She worked the lipstick with all the concentration of a brain surgeon. "There. What do you think?"

Emma cocked her head. "I think mauve is your color. How about a little blush with that?"

"Like our cheeks aren't going to be red enough?" But Mattie let Emma feather a muted taupe blush along her cheekbones. Peering into a mirror, she said, "Not bad."

"Are we missing something?" Emma came up with another compact. "Eye shadow?"

"Maybe. Do you really wear all this stuff, like, every day?"

She shook her head. "Only if I'm going to interview

someone. The rest of the time, a little lipstick, a little blush, I'm good."

"Then I think we're good right now," Mattie said.

"I think you both look terrific." Will grinned from the front. "And now if you are done preening, probably time we get to work."

They worked all day. Emma and Mattie built a lean-to with Visqueen and stout branches then gathered wood for the fire they couldn't start because of the thick snow while Will stayed by the fuselage and kept shouting so they had a point of reference and couldn't wander off. They kept the tail and ELT antenna clear— and the second day passed, with no helicopters, no rescue teams, no miracles.

By the third day, the snow was getting deep enough to cover up the shelter's opening, so they carved a tunnel to the surface the way the Inuit do. The rest of the time, they huddled together, melted snow in the Jetboil and with their body heat, and tried to stay warm. They still washed, and Emma and Mattie put on makeup (Mattie even allowed for shadow), but that day, they ate almost nothing at all. Will had a deck of cards, and they played a lot of gin rummy. Mattie started a journal in a composition book she'd brought along. They read every scrap of the *Minot Daily News* and *The New York Times*, even the obits and ads, and pored over the crossword puzzle (thankfully the tougher Saturday offering) and the word scrambles and sudoku and even the bridge hints with the intensity of archaeologists studying hieroglyphs. They took turns reading Mattie's book on quantum realities. Will and Mattie started *The*

Waste Land, rationing stanzas, trying to make the poem last, though Emma couldn't bring herself to read it. For starters, she knew the thing better than her own name. For another, a poem about limbo suddenly felt too damn real. In a way, they also were in the same pickle as the cat in Schrödinger's box: gone and yet not-gone, dead and alive at the same time. To the world beyond their box, they would stay that way, too, until someone —a helicopter, a drone, a rescue team—crawled through that tunnel, looked inside their box, and collapsed probabilities.

They lit a new Hanukkah candle every night. They all said "*yehi 'or*," but that was it. She wasn't feeling it. Like, surviving the crash only to slowly die of starvation or maybe freeze to death if they tried to walk out? Some miracle. On the other hand, when people did find them, she and Mattie would look good.

By the evening of the third day, when still no helicopters had descended and no rescuers braved the mountain and the deadening snow was unrelenting, Emma decided Will, who was right about so much, was wrong about one thing at least.

No news was bad.

AFTER THE STORM

CHAPTER 1

"EMMA."

She came awake but slowly, her awareness swimming up from a deep, dreamless well of unconsciousness, as if attached to a ball and chain and as likely to sink again as break the surface.

"Emma." A hand on her left shoulder. "Don't fall asleep again."

"Uh." She'd meant to say she wouldn't. It still took her another few seconds to actually open her eyes. Instead of only gloomy as it was during the daylight hours, the fuselage was completely dark because they'd let the snow mound up against the windows. She was curled on her right side, as close to Will as she could manage since, with his bad right arm and her noisome left ribcage, they couldn't spoon. Carefully rolling onto her back, she glanced at her watch. A little after five in the morning. *Holy cow.* She'd been out since seven the night before. They were all starting to sleep more. Will kept saying it was normal and a way of conserving energy, which was another way of saying when you weren't eating and using up all your calories to stay warm, the body shut down whenever it could. *And it's been only three days.* How much worse would it get? She had a feeling that answer was a lot. "What is it?" she whispered.

Mattie could have been a ghost sighing from the night: only a voice and nothing more. "Do you hear it?"

"Hear what?" A jolt of hope made her sit up, a move she instantly regretted as her head emptied and the darkness seemed to wrinkle.

Mattie's hand clapped around a biceps. "Are you okay?"

"Yeah." Slicking her tingling lips, she shook away the cobwebs. "What did you hear?" Had Mattie heard a helicopter? A plane? *No, wait, it's night. They can't possibly be looking for us now.* Besides, snow was still coming down when they'd gone to bed. "Did you hear a plane?"

"Wuh?" Next to her, Will stirred then cleared the sleep from his throat. "Something wrong?"

"Mattie says she heard something."

"No, I didn't say that. Listen. No," Mattie admonished as Will clicked on his flashlight. "You don't need that. Just listen without anything to distract you."

They did. Emma listened so hard, a high whine started up in her ears. "I don't hear anything," Will said.

"Yeah. There's nothing." Mattie heaved an exasperated sigh. "Don't you guys get it? I think it stopped snowing."

"What?" asked Emma, though now that Mattie had said it, she knew the girl was right. She'd gotten so used to the moan of wind and relentless susurration of ice against metal and the creak of trees as they swayed and then the scrape of ice over hardpack as the snow got deeper that she'd ceased to actually hear any of it. "Will, I think she's right."

"We might be buried so deeply now, we can't hear," Will remarked, though his tone was halfhearted. "If it has, this could be really good news."

"Right. It means they can finally look for us. I'm going out." Snapping on a flashlight, Mattie clumped for the exit tunnel. "I want to see."

"Wait for us," Will called, but the girl was already squirming out.

"I'm going." Clambering out of their bag, Emma grabbed her boots. "Are you coming?"

"Right behind you. I'm going to check on Rachel first. You go ahead."

She could tell before she even wormed out of the exit tunnel that the snow had stopped. There was no wind, but the air felt much colder. When she took a breath, the small hairs in her nostrils seemed to crackle.

Mattie was waiting as she made her feet. The girl was staring straight up, a mittened hand to her nose. "I see stars. Why is it colder?"

This one she knew and was surprised Mattie didn't. "Because there are no more clouds. Clouds are good insulators, too." The snow glimmered from a combination of starlight and a bright eyelash of moon. There was enough light for her to see that they'd crashed onto a wide plateau hemmed by black walls of thick forest.

At a distance, the fuselage was mostly a suggestion with only the tail sticking out of the snow.

"There are a lot of stars." Mattie let go a relieved sigh. "It's kind of nice to finally see them."

"Yes, it is." She knew her constellations, especially the winter ones, but the night sky was glittery with so many hard, diamond-bright stars she was completely disoriented. She couldn't even figure out where the North Star was. Wait, where was the Milky Way?

"What are you doing?" Mattie asked as, eyes fixed on the sky, Emma did a slow pirouette.

"Trying to find the Milky Way." The view was a little dizzying, as if she were a ballerina in a snow globe. Having had only a half an energy bar from Will's stash the day before probably didn't help her wooziness either. "December's out of prime season for seeing it, but if you're in the northern hemisphere, it's always in the southern part of the sky. If I can find it, I'll know which direction to look for—" She pointed to a spot to the right of and behind the fuselage. "There it is."

Mattie followed Emma's finger. "I see it. So, that's north?"

"That's right." There was a dull thump of boots in snow as Will made his way over, and she said, without glancing his way, "Found Polaris."

"Well, I could have saved you the trouble," he said. "I've got a compass."

"Ouch," Mattie teased. "Way to deflate."

"Yeah," she said, adopting a tone of mock outrage. "Let me own this moment, Mr. Wilderness."

"Far be it from me." They all stared at the sky a few

more moments and then Will said, "And you're getting your bearings because? Don't tell me it's because you wanted to be Luke Skywalker."

Maddie piped up. "You did?"

"Briefly. A long time ago in a galaxy far, far away." She was annoyed, but mostly because she knew what Will was fishing for. She saved him the trouble by coming out with it. "We need to think about getting out of here. We need a plan at the very least."

"What?" Mattie's alarm was instant. "But what about my mom?"

Will's face was a nacreous oval in the starlight. "The weather's only cleared up a few hours ago. You have to give the searchers time to actually look for us."

"I get that," she said. "But we need to think ahead, too. In their calculus, we're already past our window of survival. First off, it's cold. Second, with the snow, they'll figure the odds we made it this long as close to zero. "

"It doesn't mean they won't look for the plane. With the ELT, they might find us pretty fast. I think we need to give them a chance to do their job first before we panic."

That rankled. "I'm not panicking. I'm thinking ahead. Look, I hope you're right. I hope we get to the point where you can say you told me so. But we also have to be realistic here. Their odds of finding us depend on how off-course we were from Burke's flight plan when we crashed."

"I'm not disputing that, but the first thing they taught us in the Boy Scouts was if you're lost, sit down.

We need to sit tight. If we move, even if we leave markers showing them our direction, the likelihood's much less that they'll find us. Plus, with the snow gone, it's colder now. The sun will help, but we'll use up a lot more calories if we're humping over mountains and also trying to stay warm."

"The exercise will help keep us warm. We'll make fires. We'll melt snow and drink hot water or tea or whatever." She knew about dogsledding from her time in Thule. "Mushers do it all the time."

"They also have food and know where they're going. We might not find any game, we have no idea where we are, and hypothermia is hypothermia. We could be in big trouble pretty fast."

Everything he said was correct. But she'd shot a story on military search-and-rescue operations. Even knowing exactly where a plane went down wasn't a guarantee of finding people fast. About the only times people were found within the first twenty-four was either if they were wearing a personal locator beacon— or dead. Dead people tended not to go far. Well, unless they were in pieces. Many animals liked to cache their prey for a rainy day.

Besides, sitting around and waiting was making her crazy. For a woman who'd spent a month cooling her heels on a military psych ward, that was saying something.

"I didn't say we shouldn't give the search teams a chance," she pointed out. "What I *am* suggesting is we need to think about the future and how long we wait until—"

"Hey, do I get to say something?" Mattie's shout was loud enough to echo, and they both turned, surprised. "Because it's not only about you guys! It's about me and *my* mom! What, are you guys going to *leave* her here?"

"No, no," Will said. "Of course not."

"Then *what*? Because if we do what Emma wants, if we leave, like, *soon*, my mom might not be awake."

"Then we take her. We have Burke's raft. We can make a stretcher out of it if we have to or take turns dragging her. It's not ideal, but whatever works."

"Over *mountains*?" Even Mattie was incredulous. "Through *woods*?"

"People have done it. We'll pick a direction and keep to it. I've got a compass. Burke has a compass. We have to come on somebody somewhere eventually. We do the best we can. Guys," Will said, "both of you, calm down. It's been *three* days."

Which can easily turn into three weeks. "All the more reason to be thinking ahead, Will," she said. "About what's realistic, about what we can really do so we can all look back on this in a year."

"Well, then…maybe then you and Mattie go," Will suggested. "I stay with Rachel. We divide up the food, you ladies take the rifle, pick a direction, and start walking."

"What?" Mattie cried at the same moment Emma said, "You're out of your mind if you think I'm leaving—"

Someone shouted.

They all went rigid. Almost as one, they turned toward the distant woods in line with the fuselage.

Mattie whispered, "Did you..."

"Hush." The word smoked in the starlight. Will put a finger to his lips. "Be quiet, honey."

The silence stretched and crackled. What had that been? Years back, she'd seen *The Blair Witch Project* at a Halloween party. At certain points in the film, a character would shout something fleeting and formless. No matter how many times they rewound the stupid thing, they couldn't make out the words, not even the tone.

This was like that. Something so formless, it might have been anything or nothing. Emma cast her mind back to three nights before when she'd been alone and heard that...that something that could've been anything: a rabbit, a bobcat. Even a *person?* And she had said nothing, mentioned nothing because she hadn't wanted the responsibility. God, she was a monster.

"Hello?" Will's bellow made them jump. Cupping a hand to his mouth, Will shouted, "Is somebody there?"

Nothing came back, not even the wind. "It could've been an animal," Emma finally said.

"Or it might have been a person," Will replied.

"Could it be someone who's come to save us?" Mattie asked.

"Not at night and not like that. *Hello?*" Turning, Will shouted into the darkness and the direction the fuselage pointed. "Is there anybody there?"

They all listened. Emma's skin was fizzing with apprehension. After what felt like forever, she said, "I don't think—"

The sound, short and sharp, came again. It had no more personality or form than before, and there was no way of knowing if it had been made by a human. But it was there.

"Will, even if it's a person, we can't do anything until daylight and then only if the snow holds off. It's not safe," she said and then added, almost hating herself, "Bobcats sound like a person screaming. Coyotes scream. So do wolves."

"I know. Mountain lions do, too."

"Well, which one is it?" Mattie demanded.

"Without seeing it or a print? I don't know, but if I had to guess, I'd say wolf or mountain lion. Maybe a bobcat. They'll all go into the mountains if that's where the game is."

"What does *that* mean? Emma said deer probably don't come this high in winter."

"We don't know what that is or was." She had a feeling she knew where this was going and didn't like it one bit. "We should go back inside. I'm getting cold. It could've been anything. Rabbits scream, too." So did anything getting its throat ripped out.

"But if it is a mountain lion or something," Mattie persisted as they trudged back, "what does it mean?"

"Two possibilities," Will said. "One is its den might be close by. The other is what Emma said. Maybe that lion, if there is one, found dinner."

She should say nothing. She should make like Spock. An omission wasn't the same as a lie. Besides, she'd thought of something Will had not mentioned.

Yes, that might be a mountain lion, and it might have found dinner.

But who said a person wasn't the main course?

CHAPTER 2

"I CANNOT BELIEVE YOU," Will said, his long strides on his personal pair of snowshoes lending him an almost easy grace despite his pack. Stopping, he scanned the woods dead ahead. He held a hiking pole in his left hand because, as he'd pointed out, even with his snowshoes and those they'd taken from Burke's locker for her, the snow was deep, and there was no way to know what really lay beneath their feet. Still, now that the snow had stopped, the path the cockpit had taken was clearly marked by a rough trench of humped snow and shattered limbs that ran away through the woods. "You are a real piece of work, you know that?"

"What are you talking about? I'm out here, aren't I?" God, she was *this* close to stabbing him with a hiking pole. This should teach her that honesty was not always the best policy. The only bright spots this morning so far were that they'd gotten a signal fire going and she'd only puked once, quite possibly because there was precious little in there to begin with. Her stomach was as shriveled as a raisin. "I told you, didn't I? Say I had said something earlier about *maybe* hearing someone… something…whatever. What did you think you were going to do, Will? Run off to the rescue? First off, you had a dislocated shoulder; second, it was snowing and visibility was crap and *stayed* crap until today. Third, it was dark. So, what, you're going to rush out and put the save on somebody?"

His jaw set. "We could have gone out the next day."

"It…was…*snowing*," she reiterated. "We couldn't have helped anyone, if there even *is* anyone. I was thinking of what made sense at the time."

Will shook his head in disbelief. "You don't get it, do you? Say, it was you out there…"

"No." She gave the air a karate chop. "Don't pull that bullshit because it isn't me or you or Rachel or Mattie. You don't think I thought about that? Well, I did. But think, Will. We've been out here for the last fifteen, twenty minutes, right? We shouted, we called. Has anyone answered? No."

"Maybe that's because they can't." Will paused. *"Now."*

She gave him an incredulous stare. "Don't be such a sanctimonious asshole. For your information, I really did think it was the wind or an animal or, you know…" She fumbled for the right term. "Wishful thinking."

"You sure about that?"

That stung. "What the hell does that mean?"

"Exactly what it sounded like. But then, again, I'm a sanctimonious asshole, so…whatever."

"Fine. *Fine.*" She was cranky, winded, huffing like a

blown horse from floundering around in snowshoes made for a man with larger feet. The pointed metal rear end of her shoes kept catching and snagging, flipping up clots of snow as she wallowed. She was about two seconds from ripping the stupid things off. "We don't know if there *is* a them."

"I agree. It might have been nothing. Tell me something, though. Three days ago, did you bother giving a shout?" Before she could reply, he added, "Because I wasn't asleep when you went out, and I'm pretty sure I would've heard you."

She blinked, her eyes swimmy with angry tears. "It was snowing," she said, forcing the words through clenched teeth. "It was windy. You were inside the fuselage, and I was a good hundred yards away. You wouldn't have heard me yell either."

His reply was nearly as frosty as the air. "Well, I guess we won't be able to test that, will we?"

"Why are you being like this?"

"You honestly want to know?" His bruises were an ugly shade of green and yellow, and there were coffee-colored smudges under his hazel eyes which held none of the warmth or easy charm they had even last night. "I think the responsibility of caring for even one more person right now completely freaks you out and, believe me, I understand, I really do. You think I'm not scared?"

"You? You're always so calm."

"Not inside. I'm scared to death. But I also think Kipling was right."

If you can keep your head when all about you are losing

theirs... Her mother would be proud. "I'm not losing my head. There's a difference between panic and dealing with, you know, with facts and things you can't change no matter how much you wish things were different." If he only knew what *she* was dealing with... The funny thing, of course, the bust-a-gut *hilarious* thing was this: working up the courage to do a little slicing and dicing had been a piece of cake compared to what she faced now. She thought again about the pills in her pack. Why was she hanging onto them? She should chuck them before, God forbid, Mattie found them. She could see it now: Mattie, holding up those blister packs. *Gee, Emma, what are these?* And what would she say? *Oh, those little things? I'm saving those for a rainy day.*

Richard Gere's line played on the soundtrack of her mind. *Well, guess what? It's raining.* Will was a doctor. One look at those pills, and he'd know. Wait, what did it *matter* if he knew?

"I think all this talk about responsibility is a bunch of baloney, too," he said. "I think it's a cover for something else that's eating at you. You're a much better person than you're letting on."

Was there an invitation to confide something in there? "Don't be too sure. You don't know me."

"I know you well enough. Mattie told me what you did in the airport."

"Oh, that?" God, that seemed to have happened to another person. "That was nothing. Scott was a turd, bad news. He's no loss."

"That's brutal. Rachel *was* married to him."

"I can't help that his being an asswipe also happens to be true. He was like all bullies. They're all bluster and no bite if you're their equal." If you weren't, they squashed you under a combat boot, threatened your family, and killed your husband to show they meant it.

"Except," Will said, "he is the father of Rachel's child. There must have been something in him she once loved and probably still does."

She had nothing to say to that. Her mistake hadn't been one made because of love. Hers had been one of loss. Vulnerability. She'd trusted the wrong person. Some great judge of character she was.

"What if it was you?" Will asked.

"What if it was you what?"

"Out there." He inclined his head toward the woods. "What if the situation had been reversed? If you were the one stuck out there alone and afraid, hurt, maybe dying?"

"Is that a trick question?"

"Something's really bothering you."

"You *think*?"

"Stop that." He scrubbed the air with his good hand. "You don't have to play tough with me. As a general rule, I don't like bad people. I think you're a much better person than you're letting yourself be right now."

"Oh?" She heard the tremble and wanted to slap herself silly. She'd be damned if he made her cry. "So, you're a shrink now?"

The air was so cold, the words seemed to turn to ice the instant they left her mouth.

"No. I already told you. I know a lot about death." Something shifted beneath his face, and his gaze fell to her wrists and their scars, hidden by sleeves and gloves. "And I know grief when I've touched it."

CHAPTER 3

"You know what this reminds me of?" Will said, suddenly.

"What?" she asked, grateful he'd broken the silence. Neither had spoken in the last ten minutes as they'd followed the trail left by the cockpit. She hadn't known what was safe to say, though she wasn't stupid. He'd invited her trust in him—and she *couldn't*. God, there were days when she wondered who that fool in the mirror was.

"Those kids in the Andes. Look at this and then look at the fuselage." They turned back to face the way they'd come. Through the trees, she could make out the bright orange flicker of their signal fire; the wind was with them and laced with a scent of resin and burning wood. "Their cockpit ended up some distance away, too, as I recall. I think that's what happened here. Burke kept turning us in a square, remember, to keep us clear of the peaks? But then the engine caught and he started pulling up. I remember him yanking back on the yoke.

So he came in from the north." He pointed at a faraway saddle between mountains. "He threaded us through that. We might have made it, too, if he'd only been able to pull us up faster and higher."

Which Burke obviously hadn't. Judging from a series of broken, splintered trunks thrusting up from the snowpack behind the fuselage, the plane had smashed into tall spruces, which had caught them by the wings, shearing those away and sending them spinning before the plane had slammed down in a hard belly flop and then slalomed down an incline. The impact fractured the plane and their portion, which wasn't as stream-lined, had plowed to a halt, while the cockpit had bulleted into the forest.

"But how does that remind you of the Andes crash?"

"The slope. It's a natural chute, maybe even a some-time waterway, you know, when there's spring melt? I can feel the incline. With the momentum the plane had built up, once it got going on this, it would be like bombing down a ski run. Same thing happened in the…"

He stopped as a small, static-filled fart blatted from a pocket of his parka. Pulling out a small yellow walkie-talkie, Will depressed a button. "You okay, Mattie? Is there a problem? Over."

"No. I'm checking in to make sure you guys are all right." There was a long pause. "Oh. Over."

Will grinned. "Well, we still see you. In fact, I'm waving, even if you can't see it. Is your mom still asleep? Over."

"Yes. How long are you going to be? What if she wakes up while you're gone? Over."

"If she wakes up, you get on the horn, and I'll hustle back. You know, you'd probably feel better if you got outside into the sunshine. Over."

A pause and then Mattie came back. "If she wakes up and I'm outside... Over."

"Set up a schedule. Thirty minutes out, fifteen in, something like that. Keep an eye on the fire and don't forget to keep drinking. Over."

"Okay. Will you be back in time for lunch?"

She was not going to hang around and listen to them talk about food. Catching Will's eye, she mouthed, *Going to check something out* then, at Will's nod, turned back to study the cockpit's trail, thinking Will had something there about water. Approaching the trough from the side, she used the hiking pole as a probe, trying to feel the terrain through her too-large snowshoes, silently cursing when a shoe flopped and threatened to trip her up. She studied the spray of snow from the cockpit's passage, the way the cockpit had carved a runway for itself. *I could swear this is a bank or...* She felt the tip of her pole skid and skip. *Rock?* Kneeling, she swept at snow, swishing the flat of her gloved hand back and forth.

She heard Will come up behind her. "Find something?"

"I think so." She pointed at a sheet of dense white ice that had been hidden by snow. "That's pretty solid. I think that probably answers why they kept going. Nothing to stop them, really, and it's wide enough." The cockpit simply wasn't that large. Like all aircraft, the Chieftain's cockpit had been big enough for two men and a central console with enough maneuvering room along the sides left over so neither was constantly was banging an elbow. "With no wings to stop them or get them hung up, they'd have shot down this like a luge."

"To wind up where?" Will asked.

"I guess we follow and find out." But she already had a suspicion, which also probably meant she really *hadn't* heard anything. Because if she was looking at a frozen waterway carved by years of snowmelt or simply a run-off channel, there were only two possibilities. One was that the water emptied into a lake, which might not be a bad thing for *them* because lakes, unless at very high altitudes, usually meant fish, didn't they? Whether that lake was also iced over enough to hold the cockpit's weight…well, that was a separate question.

The other possibility was, well, gravity.

After another several minutes, she felt the woods pulling away and the way ahead opening up. Through gaps in the trees, distant peaks thrust toward the sky and, closer in, she glimpsed the snowy tops of tall spruce.

"Uh-oh," Will said.

"Yeah." The fact that they were looking at treetops meant a drop-off. *Hell.* Stopping a good distance back from the edge, she gazed down into a very wide, U-shaped valley.

"So the stream ends in a waterfall," said Will.

"Or a cliff." Which was another way of saying a waterfall without water. There'd been that show years back people had loved about an airplane that had crashed on this wacky island and blah, blah. She and Ben had streamed the entire series. She'd liked the first couple of seasons but finally got pissed when nothing was ever *really* explained and then the whole thing turned out to be a dream which she'd always suspected because, in the very first episode, when the Matthew Fox character woke up on the beach, she remembered turning to Ben and saying, *You watch. It'll all be a dream.*

The sight of the cliff ahead reminded her of the episode where John Locke found that drug smugglers' plane—a Beechcraft, as she remembered it—mired in trees over the jungle floor. The smugglers had stuffed heroin into statues of the Virgin Mary and then…well, she couldn't remember the rest, other than the plane eventually fell out of the trees.

"Looks like they went over," Will said.

"Looks that way." It also seemed to her that if anyone had survived—a miracle, in and of itself—she couldn't possibly have heard them. The woods were dense, and they had to be almost a quarter mile from the fuselage. Sure, sound carried in the wilderness, and especially at night, but *that* far?

Will must've been thinking the same because he reached his good hand to touch her arm. "I'm sorry. About what I was saying before. I was being unfair. This is pretty far from the fuselage and, in a storm, I'm not at all sure the sound would've carried." He didn't say that the reverse was also true: if there had been someone who survived, they might not have heard her calling.

"Thanks." If they could spot the cockpit, though, and

somehow reach it… "Will, if it's down there, I think we have to try and check it out, don't you? Burke had a map. Maybe it's still there or he had others." Maybe there was more—batteries, a radio, something. God, a satellite phone would be a real miracle.

"Well," he said, sidestepping carefully to the edge but steering well clear of the ice slick, "I guess that depends on how far down they…" He stopped talking.

"What?" She forced herself to move slowly to avoid taking a spill, already dreading what she would see.

The cockpit was directly below, shrouded in snow and hung up on a very wide, snow-covered plateau in a tangled cradle of the stout branches of tough, gnarled pine. Because it had smacked onto its belly instead hitting nose-first, there was no way to tell how many bodies were still inside or if anyone had been thrown. She didn't see anyone lying on the snow nearby, but with the storm, that meant nothing. The drop was at least a hundred feet and probably a lot more, so it was hard to imagine that anyone had survived first the actual impact of the plane careening into trees and then plummeting over a frozen waterfall. The valley itself was odd, though. It was as if there were two valleys, the one the plane had landed in and then, beyond, yet another U-shaped expanse.

"Hanging valley," Will said when she pointed that out. "I've heard of them. There's one at Glacier. But I'm not sure of the mechanism. All I know is it has something to do with one part eroding faster than the other. This might help us, though."

"How do you figure?"

"Getting down there. This part with the waterfall is a sheer drop-off, but…" He wandered to the right a short ways, studying the snow. "I think if we walk along the edge for a time, we might find a more gradual way down."

"And if we don't?"

"Then, I guess we're screwed." He stopped then pointed down at snow that seemed oddly trammeled and bunched. "But if critters can do it, I figure we can, too."

"What kind of critters?" she said, but she was already thinking of those odd screams and, when she got a good look, a sudden chill that had nothing to do with the cold shuddered down her spine. "How many do you think there were?"

"I'm thinking at least three." He used the tip of his pole to prod at something that looked like a discarded blackened cigar butt. "That spoor's still soft, too, so it hasn't been long." He gestured with his pole. "The prints head back into the woods not far from where we came out."

Crap. She turned an alarmed glance back into the trees, though, of course, no self-respecting wolf was going allow itself to be seen. Kneeling alongside Will, she stared at the spoor and spotted tufts of what looked like hair. Probably from whatever…*whomever*…the wolf had last eaten. Rabbits? Maybe? If that was true, what she'd heard might not have been human at all. She wished that made her feel better. "You think we scared them off?"

Will shook his head. "I doubt it. Look at these

prints." He used a gloved finger to trace the outline of a much-larger print with four rounded toes and a wide central pad. "No claw marks."

"What's that mean?"

"Mountain lion, more than likely. A pretty big one, too. I'm no expert, but see here?" He indicated several yellow splotches melted into the snow. "The wolves got spooked and beat feet. So did the mountain lion, but I'll bet it left because it heard or smelled us coming." Rising, he turned to look toward the dense forest to the west. "Might have a den close by or be watching, waiting for us to leave. Could be that's what you heard that first night and what we heard this morning. It would also explain why no one answered when we shouted back."

"Seriously?" Mattie was all by herself in the fuselage with her unconscious mother. My God, what if it came after them?

As if reading her thoughts, Will said, "The barrier will discourage any predators, and so will the fire. Besides, I don't think they'll bother us for a while, not when there's a buffet down there."

"God." She shivered from fright and the cold. "And I thought *I* was morbid." The sooner they got out of here and back to the fuselage, the better. "Can we get the hell out of here now?"

"Not until we check out the wreck. We've come all this way. It would be stupid not to try. I don't think anything's going to bother us in broad daylight and, like you said, there could be things down there we can use."

"Will, it's at least a hundred, maybe two hundred feet down. How are we going to do that?" Thanks to Ben,

177

she knew how to rappel in a pinch, but Will didn't stand a chance with his shoulder. She could probably get back up, so long as one end of the rope was fixed, but she'd really rather not have to prove that, thanks.

"Well, the animals gathered here for a reason. If they wanted a snack, they needed a way down." He studied the slope. "How much billy goat blood do you have?"

"Oh, ha-ha." But she spotted what he'd seen: the narrow meander of an animal trail through snow. She followed it with her eyes and saw how it wound away before curving back east, toward them—and the wreck. Despite those odd cries, she wondered if any animals had been down there already. Possibly not; the snow over the wreck looked relatively undisturbed.

"Hello?" She jumped as Will cupped a hand to his mouth and shouted again, "Hello, is there anyone down there?"

"God, some warning next time, please? You about gave me a heart attack." She listened to the crash of his words echoing and bouncing off rock before dying. The wind was a hollow moan and from somewhere came a *whump* as snow tumbled from a bough. It hit Emma she hadn't heard any birds at all. Maybe they didn't come up this high?

"Hello?" Will called again. "Can you hear me? Is there anyone there?"

She wanted him to stop. She wanted to put her hand on his good arm and pull him away from the edge. She wanted to get back to the fire and that damn fuselage and have some hot tea and hunker down until someone found them. "Will, can we—"

"H-hullo?" The word seemed to float on a whisper of thin air. An agonizing pause and then: *"Hello?"*

"Oh, Jesus." Cupping his hand to his mouth, Will leaned so dangerously close to the edge, she grabbed a fistful of his parka. "Hello?" Will shouted. "Hello, who's there?"

"Help," the voice said. *"Help."*

God, it figures. Because she recognized that voice.

Scott.

CHAPTER 4

FIVE HOURS LATER, Will said, "There's no easy way to say this."

No shit. "I know." She was exhausted, hungry, light-headed from working nonstop, but there'd been little choice. Time was not their friend. The sun had long since passed overhead and now hovered above peaks to the west, coloring the sky pink and blush orange as it began its slide toward sunset. She checked her watch. The day before the light had lasted about eight hours, before dusk around 5:00 p.m. *Two more hours of daylight, and that's it.* The sky, too, had remained quiet, with not even a faraway jetliner sketching a white trail across a blisteringly blue sky.

Where was everyone? Why were there no planes, no helicopters? The answers were unknowable, even rhetorical.

She glanced at the bright orange flames of the fire she'd gotten going. She wondered when the animals might come back. Maybe, with the fire, they wouldn't.

Their predicament at the moment was a Catch-22 if you were into Heller. Trekkies called it a Kobayashi Maru, that proverbial no-win scenario; Ben always said that the Kobayashi Maru of marriage was if your wife asked whether that dress made her look fat. There was no real right answer for that, was there? If your wife was asking, it was because she thought it did, and if a guy said it didn't, well, he was a liar, which meant the dress made her look fat and therefore, she *was* fat...like that.

Most folks in the military said *C-F*, but only when there were civilians around and everyone was being politically correct.

Seriously, their situation right this very moment, given what she and Will had found at this second crash site? Total Kobayashi Maru, no-win cluster-fuck.

"I'm sorry," Will said in an undertone. "I really am, but we're going to have to divide and conquer here. I can't be in two places at once. I need to get back to check on Rachel, but by the time I make it there with Scott..."

"Yeah, yeah," she said. "I get it." There hadn't been any way to speed things up either. They'd spent the better part of an hour traversing the two hundred-plus feet to the wreck, scrambling over snow-covered rocks and stepping carefully along that narrow, icy animal trail. Since then, they'd worked nonstop, checking out Scott, tending to Hunter and Mattie's grandfather, building up a fire, stacking rocks in a low wall which Will had covered with a large rectangle of aluminum foil he carried in his pack and buttressed with slabs of metal from the plane to reflect the heat back toward the cockpit while she worked at gathering enough wood to last the night. Will also had checked in with Mattie at intervals, to be on the safe side and make sure he didn't have to hustle to get back to Rachel. "I get you have to go, but I'd be lying if I said I was overjoyed."

"I'll be back as soon as I can to spell you…wait, why not?" he asked when she shook her head.

"Are you kidding? I get you're Mr. Wilderness, but you are not indestructible, and unless I'm missing something, I'm pretty sure you can't see in the dark. Because that's what you'll be doing, trying to get back here at night." She'd watched him like a hawk as they worked their way down to the wreck. He'd done all right, though he'd had to take that right arm out of its sling or risk being pulled off-balance on the narrow trail, part of which had been more of a rock scramble than anything they could really walk. That meant he had to use the arm. From his expression, she knew that had hurt. "There are too many variables, and most of them are bad. First off, you will never make it down, even with a headlamp and especially with a bum arm. Second, it means that *I* would have to climb back up in the dark. Again, even with a headlamp, I slip and that's bad." She held up a third finger. "And there's still the little problem of a bunch of really hungry animals out there one of us would have to deal with without a weapon because we have only the one rifle."

"They haven't come back."

"Oh, please." She gave him a withering look. "You saw the tracks out there."

There had been many, in fact. Once they were down, they realized that the cockpit hadn't really landed on a ledge at all but a very wide, very long table of snow-covered rock that reminded her a lot of Mount Dundas. The western slope was more gradual and gentle than the eastern edge and, from all the trammeled snow and spoor on that side, the wreck had had a lot of company. Advance scouts, probably checking things out.

They had also found a few, very faint boot prints, mostly filled in with snow, that petered out after fifty yards. Scott had said he hadn't wandered out that way and that Burke had been gone when he regained consciousness. So, had Burke walked off to find help? Will had doubted it. There was frozen blood smeared on the pilot's side of the console, and the window on that side had shattered. Whether Burke had bulleted through and then awakened to wander off, dazed and disoriented, or he'd crawled out was almost of no consequence. What mattered was the man was missing. Chances were good Burke was either out there, buried under fresh snow, or dinner.

"Those animals aren't going to leave all this good meat lying here." She imagined she could feel the press of their eyes even now. As soon as darkness closed in, those animals would be back. From her bubbe, she knew that the movie notion of wolves gathering around for a kill, as had happened in *The Gray*, was fiction. (Although it had still been a *fine* movie, and she totally wanted Liam Neeson on her side in a zombie apocalypse.) A pack would chase down a moose or deer, though, and while she'd never heard of a pack doing the same to a person, a) that person certainly wouldn't have lived to talk about it and b) Jack London couldn't have gotten it all wrong either. It was like his story about a guy trying to build a fire. The pack picked off the guy's dogs until there was only one left and then waited around until the man had nothing to protect him: no weapons and no way to start a fire. A wounded animal was a wounded animal and potential prey, even if that animal was human. "It's not safe to be out alone in the woods after dark, and I'm not really eager for either of us to end up as a Happy Meal."

"Scott managed to make it this far, and without a fire."

And more's the pity. Fine, call her spiteful. True, Scott was a jerk, but he didn't deserve to wind up as kibble either. Huddled near the ruined cockpit under one of Will's space blankets, Scott was on his fourth or maybe fifth mug of hot broth, which he cradled in cupped hands. Other than the same pattern of mottled bruises they all sported, Scot also had a nasty cut over his left ear that had dried to a rust-colored crust and a huge knot where the side of his head had smashed into his window. He'd wrapped himself in the curtains that had separated the cockpit from the cabin and also stripped the cover from both his seat and Rachel's grandfather to stay warm. She wondered if he'd thought of stripping Rachel's grandfather out of his snorkel jacket, for spite. On the other hand, while the old man's legs were para-lyzed, there was nothing wrong with his arms, and she bet he'd give Scott a couple black eyes before surren-dering that parka. Scott probably could have overpowered the old man, but maybe even he wasn't that bloodthirsty. Besides, she had the suspicion that Scott had done the math. Snuggling up to a warm, *living* body gave him a better shot at survival than getting cozy with a really cold corpse.

"Are you sure?" Will asked. "You can handle this? I'm not talking only the animals now."

She knew what he wasn't saying. "They've made it this long." Which also didn't translate into either Rachel's grandfather or Hunter making it through another night, and it was a toss-up who'd exit first unless help got here, like, yesterday.

And where *was* everybody? There hadn't been a search plane of any kind all day. Not even a distant *brrr* of an engine. God, and to think she'd been freaked by the idea of Rachel going into labor. That would be a cakewalk compared to this.

"In the immortal words of Scotty and language you can understand, Cap'n, I canna change the laws of physics," she said. "I got this. Leave the rifle and the walkie-talkie and don't ask me again if I'm sure because there's really no choice, is there? Sure, I can go back, but hell if I'll know if Rachel's better or worse. Grampa and Hunter really only have one way to go, right?" A brutal way to put it but the sentiment also had the virtue of being true. "What are you going to tell Mattie?"

He'd been in touch with the girl only twice to tell her that they found survivors and ask after Rachel. "I don't know. Let's see if he makes it through the night first. I could be wrong, you know. People are stronger than you think, and they sometimes recover. It might not be a complete break..." He passed a hand over his eyes. "I'm operating in the dark here."

He looked so haggard, she put her arms around him in a fierce hug. "Stop. We keep putting everything on you and it's not fair."

"No, it's all right." He'd stiffened at first and she almost let go, but then he slid his good arm around her waist and buried his face in her neck. "Thanks. Feels good. You forget how nice..."

He let the rest go, though he held onto her and he was warm and solid and, for the first time, she felt not only her need but *his*. Which was strange, wasn't it? He was married. His wife's name was Becca and they'd wanted children. *Except he's not wearing a ring.* Many men didn't, though she imagined a man like Will would wear that ring with pride. So, divorce? She left him? No, that wasn't it. *Something else happened.* Because Will had said it: he knew grief when he touched it. She ached to ask the question but instead let her body relax and mold to his. "We're all scared," she said. "It's all right to be scared, Will."

She felt his mouth move in a smile against her skin. "Isn't that my line?"

"Yes." She held on for another few seconds then let go even though she didn't want to. "I know you'll do your best. All anyone can ask." She could tell he had something else on his mind. "What?"

"How much experience have you had with death?" His eyes searched hers. "I'm talking worst-case scenario."

More than you can imagine. "I helped take care of my

grandmother. Kidney failure. She'd been on dialysis for a long time and then she got tired of going in four times a week and not eating what she liked." Bubbe Sarah thought she'd go fast, too, but she was a sturdy woman and lingered for almost a month. By the last week, so many toxins had built up in her grandmother's body she'd become delirious and combative, paranoid to the point of lashing out with fists when Emma tried giving her a sponge bath. After that, they'd put her bubbe on morphine. This was almost as bad because while she lived three more days, there was only her body lying there. A mannequin would have more personality.

"I can handle it," she said. "As long as I keep the fire going, the animals ought to stay away. Leave me some food and bouillon and tea, and I'll be golden."

It was all bravado. But she couldn't decide which was worse: being alone with a comatose woman and her slimy second husband who hated her guts or out here, in the wild, with two dying men and any animals who might happen by hoping for a midnight snack.

There was no other logical course of action, though. They all needed Will.

And the rest is commentary.

"Go," she said, "before you lose the light."

"DRINK A LITTLE MORE," she coaxed. Before Will left, they'd maneuvered Rachel's grandfather as close to the fire as they could without the poor man actually catching fire and then used a seat from the wreck to prop him up. This, Will said, would help him breathe a little easier. She held a cup of broth to his lips. "A few more sips, and I promise I'll leave you alone."

"As if." The old man heaved a noisy, beleaguered sigh that turned into a wheeze. "Isn't that what all you young people say?" He sucked in a breath and then pushed out the next sentence. "As if?"

"I'm not *that* young, but yeah."

"Give me...that," he grumped. "It's my legs..." He struggled to pull in air. "That won't work..." Breath. "Not my arms."

"Maybe you shouldn't try to talk so much," she said

"Don't tell me...what to do." He sucked. "I can still feed myself. But...I'm cold. Can't get warm. Damnedest thing. That doctor said...it was on account..."

"That you broke your back, yeah," she said. *Spinal shock* was what Will had said. Depending on the level of the break, it was normal after a spinal injury for the body to have trouble regulating blood pressure, pulse, temperature, and for every breath to be a struggle. Given the huge bruise over his spine midway up his ribs, Will though Grampa's break was high thoracic. This was all so much Greek to her, but the gist was that the nerves controlling the muscles between Grampa's ribs were out for the count, which meant it was hard for him to cough, clear secretions, and otherwise avoid pneumonia. She knew without Will having to say a word that, even kept warm and hydrated, the old man probably wouldn't survive another twenty-four hours. That he'd made it this long, three days post-crash, was a miracle. Maybe snuggling up to Scott had been a two-way street.

"All right then." She made sure he had a good grip before relinquishing hers. "Drink up." She watched the old man carefully guide the mug to his mouth. His hands shook with cold, and she almost warned him to be careful because the broth was hot but bit that back. She was a stranger; he was helpless. No need to humiliate the man.

After several loud, moist slurps, he held the cup out for her to take back. "That's enough for now...and don't even think...about it, young lady," he warned as he caught her expression. "I know I gotta...drink. But you're forgetting." He managed a wink. "Everything that goes in..."

"Has to come out. Right." She managed a smile, even

though it really wasn't funny. She couldn't imagine what it might be like for this old man to be both paralyzed from the waist down and stuck with a stranger to clean up after him. "You know, I don't even know your name, sir."

"Earl." He held out a quaking hand. "Hollister. You call me Earl."

"Pleased to meet you, Earl." His hand was work-hardened and rough with callous. She had a sense Earl had lived through a thing or two himself. Releasing his hand, she said, "Better put your gloves back on." Dumping the broth into a small thermos (and to hell with cooties), she rose. "I'll be back. I have to check on Hunter."

"Make him drink that," Earl called after. "Him...you need."

What we need is a damn rescue. As soon as she left the fire, the drop in temperature made her wince. Crouching, she scuttled through a short tunnel in the snow she and Will had heaped around the cockpit along with slabs of the plane in an attempt at constructing a snow-shelter. They hadn't had a lot of time, and the effort was half-assed but better than nothing, and the air inside was warm enough that when she skimmed a gloved finger over a side window, the fabric came away damp with condensation.

"It's me, Hunter," she said as she pushed inside. "I brought you something hot to drink."

"Okay." His voice was tight with pain. "Don't suppose you got something better than aspirin?" There came a crinkle of paper as he shifted. "Right about now, I'd take a good whack in the head."

"This is all I got." Slipping into his father's empty seat, she uncapped the thermos. "You need to drink this. Then, maybe you'd like to wash your face and brush your teeth? Will left an extra toothbrush."

"Yeah, yeah, Mr. Be Prepared. You know what's driving me crazy? This damn beard." He dug with a gloved hand. "Itches."

"Would washing it help? We could do that."

"Cut the damn thing off for all I care. But, yeah, maybe." With his hood cinched down tight around his face and that beard, it looked as if he were peering with deep-set, glittery eyes out of some deep cave. Will had brought *The Minot Daily News* to use for a fire, though the majority he'd wadded then stuffed into Hunter's coat for added insulation. Already chunky, Hunter was bulky enough now to give the Michelin tire guy a run for his money. Whenever he moved, he crinkled. He held out his hands. "Give that mug here."

She watched as he drained the broth in nothing flat. Tipping out the rest of the thermos for him, she asked, "Are you hungry?"

"Yes, but I'm not eating a fucking thing until we cut me the fuck out of here." He gave the fiddleheads of steam rising from the mug a morose stare. "If that even happens." His face suddenly crumpled, and he turned away, but not before she caught the shine of tears. "Having to fucking sit here in my own shit. Worse than a fucking baby. At least a kid gets his ass wiped."

"I'm sorry we couldn't get you out today." They'd

debated before Will emptied out his water bottle. She'd been against it because the odds were against Hunter, but Will argued that keeping up Hunter's morale was as important to the man's survival as warmth and water and food. *Bad enough he has to stew in his own crap. No point in making him constantly pee his pants.* "Will's going to bring tools from your dad's cargo locker in the morning. Like you said, everything in the console is pretty much a drop-in, right?"

"Yeah." He gave his side of the console a baleful look. "I told my dad not to buy this fucking thing. Took all his savings and then a loan and then he goes and does an upgrade, and now we're more in hock. I told him to be satisfied with what we had, but no, he had to keep going bigger and better. I always knew this business would come back to bite us if we stayed in too long."

It was a curious thing to say, and she didn't know how to respond. That the plane had bitten down on Hunter wasn't too far from the truth either. While the pilot's half of the console was still relatively intact, Hunter's had crumpled to trap his legs at mid-shin. For the first thirty-six hours, he could wiggle his toes, but now had no feeling in his feet at all. Will thought that meant frostbite and another set of problems. But, as he'd said, one crisis at a time. First they had to free Hunter's legs, then they could worry about whatever they found.

"Sorry." Hunter blew out a shaky laugh. "I'm lucky you guys found the cockpit at all. That fucking Scott, man, he was no help. Like he didn't even *try*. Took one look and left. And my dad...Jesus...hell did he go? I told him it was crazy, middle of a fucking storm, told him he shouldn't go."

They hadn't talked much before now. She'd been too busy, and this was new information. "Do you know when he left? Where he thought he was going?"

"Naw, he was out of it. Stove in his head here." Hunter touched his own forehead. "Bleeding like crazy."

Well, that explained the blood on the console. "He was probably confused." Which meant Burke had likely died fast and was out there, somewhere, entombed under new snow. Maybe that was a mercy.

"Kept going on about meeting the guys," Hunter said. "I told him they wouldn't be here."

"Guys?" She eyed Hunter. "You mean, like friends? At the airstrip? Were you guys meeting up with someone?"

"Yeah," Hunter said, and she saw the shift in the set of his face when he decided to say something other than what he'd intended. "Friends at the airstrip."

He was lying. She'd done enough reporting to spot that. But why would Hunter lie about something like that? Instead of asking, she said, "Hunter, your dad was looking at a map right before we crashed. Why did he do that if we were instrument flying?"

She saw his eyes shutter. "I don't know. There was a lot of turbulence, and we didn't stick to the route."

That set up a little *ding-ding-ding*. "How far off his flight plan were we?"

He gave an irritable shrug. "Beats me. I can take over in an emergency, you know, but he's the pilot."

So they might be well off whatever flight plan Burke

had filed. When the engines stalled and Burke piloted the plane into a series of right-angle turns to avoid the mountains coming up fast as they shed altitude, they might also have been shoved even farther from their projected route.

Maybe that explains why we haven't heard any planes or helicopters. A talon of dread dug at her chest. They might be looking in the wrong place.

That reminded her, too. They'd been so busy, neither she nor Will had thought to look very carefully before now other than to check a slot for papers in the pilot's side door. That had been empty and the map Burke had been consulting must've blown away in the crash. "Hunter, are there other maps? Something that might tell us where we are?"

Again, she listened to the silence he let continue for a beat too long. "If there are, they'd be in there." He gestured toward the center of the cockpit. "Underneath and behind the engine throttles. There's a safe. He keeps a lot of paperwork and stuff in there. It's locked, though," he added as she panned her light in that direction. "I don't have a key."

"Okay." The safe was maybe a foot long and as deep. It reminded her of a car's glove compartment. A couple of whacks with a hammer might pop it open, or there might be a spare key in Burke's cargo locker. On the other hand, the safe was a weird place to keep a map. She imagined a pilot might want that handy and not have to fumble around with a key. "Hunter, did your dad have a satellite phone?"

She saw the roll of his throat as he swallowed. "Yeah. He did."

A sparkle of hope. "Do you remember the last time you saw it? Did he have it on him?" Actually, she was positive Burke had not. What she remembered was walking up with Will to where Burke and the others waited and the pilot, his cell in hand, saying, *I was gonna give you people two minutes.* He'd slipped his cell into a breast pocket, but there had been no satellite phone. She'd probably remember that because a sat phone was so big.

They were breaking open that safe if it was the last thing they did.

"Be back in a jiffy." She turned to go. "I'll bring some hot water so you can wash and brew up some tea."

"Well, great," he said. "What a pisser."

WILL'S walkie-talkie burped as she was melting a potful of snow, and then Mattie's voice sounded, "Emma, are you there? Over?"

"Hey, Mattie. How's your mom?" she said, dropping to a sit next to her grandfather. "Over?"

"Still out, but Will said her color's better so that's good and she...you know, she went to the bathroom." Pause. "So we made her another diaper. Over."

"Too much information," Earl grumbled.

She grinned. "You want to talk to your grandfather? Over?"

"Oh, can I? Over?"

"Sure, hang on." She showed the old man how to work the handset then scooped up Burke's rifle and moved away from the fire to give them some privacy.

Something weird is going on. The glow from the fire at her back was a muddy orange on the snow but only reached a few feet before darkness shrouded the world beyond. The stars were out again, though, and this time, when she tilted her head to peer up, she spied the moon, now more like a thumbnail, midway up the sky to her left. With the crackle of the fire and the low drone of the old man's voice, it was almost peaceful. Of course, if this were a novel or horror movie, right about now she'd snap on her headlamp and the green coins of a million eyes would leap from the blackness.

Don't do it. Her hand strayed to her headlamp. In movies, a person had about a split second before the animals leapt. *But this is reality, Greg.* She flicked on her headlamp. A silver lance pierced the night.

No eyes. No slavering wild animals.

Idiot. Switching off her headlamp, she let out a soft snort. *Freak yourself out, why don't you?*

But she was troubled. Her reporter's instincts niggled. There was a disconnect she wasn't seeing. Hunter said his dad, confused and disoriented, had gone off to meet "some guys." She was pretty certain these were not friends. She stared into the darkness so hard her eyes ached with the strain. They were *guys*. And that whole thing about upgrading the plane, going into debt but expecting the investment to pay off? What had Hunter said? That their business would come back to bite them if they stayed in too long. What did that mean? Why would ferrying rich people around to expensive and distant locations be a problem?

"Hey." She turned to see the old man holding up the walkie-talkie. "She wants to talk to you."

"Sure," she said, though she also felt the tiniest squirt

of disappointment. Will had to be listening. He didn't have anything to say? Of course, Scott would also be listening. So, maybe just as well. She wasn't going to discuss anything Hunter had said within Scott's hearing. Hunter had told her to watch out for Scott, which was not news. But had Hunter meant something else or more? "Hey, Mattie, what do you need? Over."

There was a mild background fizz and then Mattie said, "It's the fourth night. Over."

"Ah. Sure thing." *Yippee.* "You and Will got the candles ready?"

"We do," Will said. "You say when."

The sound of his voice made her heart leap. She wished they could talk things over. Instead she said, "When. Tell me when you're ready."

"Hang on...Okay, go for it."

"Yehi 'or." She could feel the actual blessings jostle for space on her tongue. What would it really cost her to say them? Nothing. They were only empty words that would dissipate into an even greater void. "Over."

"Let there be light," said Mattie.

"That's right." Emma cleared her throat. "Okay, talk to you guys in the morning. Over and out."

As she clicked off, Earl said, "You going to share... what that was about?" He listened as she rattled off a thumbnail version detailing the holiday. "I heard...of that one. But there's got...to be more to it. More words. Especially..." He drew in a long, rattling breath. "If we're talking a miracle."

"Yeah, well." She gave a tight smile. She had heard

that kind of rattle before and didn't like it now any more than when it had issued from her grandmother and she had discovered that the sound was not a metaphor. "If we are."

CHAPTER 7

SHE SNAPPED upright from her slouch, pulling her head up from where it had come to rest on her knees. *Feel asleep.* She smeared drool from a cheek. She wasn't aware she'd dropped off. She aimed an anxious look at the fire, which had not dwindled much at all. She wasn't toasty by any means, but she wasn't freezing either.

So what had awakened her? Not the cold. Something else. Earl was still, his features arranged in what looked like sleep. She laid a palm on his chest then felt her shoulders relax a smidge at the rise and—

Something, somewhere, made a very faint but very audible sound.

She froze. The hairs rose on her arms. What was that? She listened hard over the snap of the fire, the pop of a log. The sound had been so fleeting, it might even have been her imagination. She willed herself to hold still. That had sounded like…

Something growled.

Oh hell. Her heart kicked. She inched her head over a

shoulder to peer into the darkness to the east. The noise came again, a soft growl followed by a scuffling, a hissing noise that could be ice against ice or stone. The sounds were coming from the direction where she'd found those faint impressions of boot prints and fresher, deeper animal prints. But there hadn't been anything to find, no body, no bits of clothing, nothing.

But I didn't think about digging beneath the new snow to check now, did I?

It had been snowing when Burke wandered off. He could have fallen fifty feet from the wreck or five hundred, and she and Will had been too preoccupied with doing what they could for the survivors.

Rifle in hand, she slowly made her feet. What could she possibly do here? Bringing a body into camp would be inviting the wolves in for a buffet. *And there's a mountain lion out there, too, don't forget.* Killing the animals wouldn't be right. They were only doing what animals did. Would a single shot over their heads scare them away? Or, wait…she felt for the flare in a parka pocket…she could touch that off and accomplish the same thing or simply use a log from the fire. No matter what she did, the solution would be only temporary. The wolves would be back and pick up where they'd left off—or that mountain lion might take their place.

She crept around the cockpit, wincing every time snow squeaked and squealed. She knew the animals must hear her coming, too, because at every misstep, the sounds ceased, the air quivered, and she could imagine them all pricking their ears and pausing in their feeding to look, as one, in her direction. When she'd drawn even with the cockpit's ruined nose, she could make out the animals' shadows as they fed. Her ears caught the dry tearing of cloth and the deeper, meatier, wetter sound of ripping flesh. Heart booming, she flipped on her headlamp and socked the rifle's butt into her shoulder.

Four wolves, three a mottled gray and one larger wolf who was the color of jet, leapt from the darkness. In the light of her headlamp, their eyes were green cinders. Muzzle dark with blood, the jet-black wolf's lips peeled back revealing orange teeth and the dangle of something pink and stringy. The snow, chunked and churned, was red. The rest was a fractured kaleidoscope of torn clothing, tangled guts, a cage of rib bones partially stripped of flesh. Burke's body lay at an angle, his head cranked impossibly far back on the stalk of his neck because they'd torn out his throat and eaten the flesh down to bone.

She should use the rifle. That had the best chance of really spooking them. But it was stupid to shoot. This wasn't their fault. But wasn't it also true that once an animal had the taste of a human in its mouth, it wouldn't stop but would hunt down what was, in the end, very easy prey? She wished she knew what to do. Should she call Will? No, that was stupid, too. She was supposed to *have* this.

She took aim for a spot over the animals' heads and fired. The rifle cracked; a bright yellow flare of muzzle flash leapt from the barrel. Yipping, the wolves jumped and backed off but didn't leave.

"Go away!" She let go of another shot and then

another. This time, two of the wolves wheeled about; a third jumped in a high, frightened hop. At the fourth shot, even the black wolf finally broke and ran off into the darkness beyond the range of her headlamp.

Her pulse thundered. Sweat trickled down her neck, and she shivered. She was panting, though she couldn't hear much over the ringing in her ears. Her grandmother had always warned her to wear ear protection.

She felt a vibration at her hip. Pulling the walkie-talkie from her pocket, she depressed the send button. "Yeah?"

"Emma? Are you all right?" The words, barely intelligible over the roar in her head, spilled from the speaker in a hash of static. "I heard shots. What's going on?"

So, it was true. Sounds really did carry at night in the wilderness. "W-wolves," she managed. Her mouth didn't seem to want to work. The smell of spent gunpowder was sharp and turned her stomach. Swallowing, she pressed a hand to her mouth then said, with a weird little laugh, "I found Burke. Well, the wolves did. He was buried under the snow and they…they…he's all torn up and…"

"Oh Jesus." Maybe he heard that slight hysteria, maybe not. "I'm sorry. I'm so sorry, Emma. I wish I could make it better for you. Are you all right?"

"N-no. I mean…" She forced a swallow. Now that the adrenaline was tailing off, fear gnawed her neck. She didn't dare fall asleep again. She wasn't *supposed* to have drifted off at all. Some great helper bee she was. One little thing, and she couldn't get it right. "I didn't shoot them, Will. Was I supposed to? It didn't seem right. It's not their fault we're here and Burke's dead and…"

"Hush, honey, hush. You didn't do a thing wrong. They were doing what wolves do."

"Will they come back?'

"Doubt it, but I don't know. I'm not an expert on wolves. You did the right thing. I've heard that in some places, they shoot the wolves so they don't get used to being around people."

"I didn't shoot them," she said again.

"You did fine."

"I fell asleep."

"You're human. We're all exhausted and scared and half-starved. It's okay. You're safe. Earl and Hunter are safe."

A sob balled in her throat. "I think Earl is really dying."

"You're doing what you can do." A static-filled pause. "I can come be with you. Rachel will be okay, and Mattie will have the radio. I can be there in an hour, maybe less."

"No. It's not safe. I'll be all right." She added in another burst of illogic, "I'm sorry I woke you. Go back to sleep. Both of us can't stay up all night. Only one of us is allowed to be a wreck." And tag, she was it. She hoped she hadn't awakened Mattie. Scott, she couldn't care less about.

"Sleep?" He let out a soft chuckle. "With you out there blasting away at errant wolves? Who could sleep through racket like that?"

She gave a watery laugh. "I'm sorry."

"Save that for when you've got something to be sorry about. Where are you now?"

"Looking at Be…" She caught herself before *Ben* slipped out. Odd, that. There really was no comparison. Burke was in pieces, cuts of meat and gnawed bone. Ben had been totally different. As she considered this, an image from memory flashed of Bubbe Sarah, kneeling by a buck she'd shot, hunting knife in hand. *This is how you do it so you don't spoil the meat.* And then, with a barely suppressed smirk: *Of course, it won't be strictly kosher because I'm not a shochet, but nu? What can you do? I'm sure God can take a joke.* For a woman who'd not spent a single year of her life in New York, Sarah could really lay on the schmaltz when she wanted.

"Looking at Burke," she said.

"Well, stop looking. You can't stand there all night. Earl and Hunter need you. You've done what you can. Now, go on. Walk. Get back to the fire. Get warm."

She started back to the fire on legs that felt like pegs. As she drew closer, she heard Hunter shouting and called back to let him know she was all right and would be in to check on him in a second. She told him not to worry, as if squeezing off a couple two, three rounds was par for the course, normal, no big deal. Once she was within sight of the fire, she brought the walkie-talkie back to her mouth. "Okay, I'm back. Please, Will, go to sleep."

"You're sure? We've got extra batteries. I can stay on. We can talk. I can read *The Times*."

That made her laugh. "That'll put me right to sleep.

Really, I'm positive. You get some rest. See you in the morning."

"All right." Another crackling silence. "Please stay safe, Emma."

"On my to-do," she managed around a sudden lump in her throat. "Will, I…I'm…" She wanted to say…what? For a split second, she saw the two of them in that one sleeping bag, with nothing between them but air, could almost feel the glide of his hand over her hip, the warmth of his palms cupping her breasts, and…

"Yes?" He waited a moment, and when his voice came back again, only a fool could miss that gentle note. "I know. Me, too." Another pause. "We're all scared."

And she was insane. He was married. His wife would be waiting when they stepped off that rescue chopper. She was nothing *but* baggage and unfinished business.

"Yeah," she said, her voice shaky. "Out."

AS SHE SLID another thick split of pine into the flames, Earl said, "You did…the right thing."

"Don't talk." At the sudden introduction of colder wood, the flames retreated before flaring back to lick at the wood with greedy golden tongues. After a few seconds, the resin heated enough to pop and sputter.

"Nothing else to do." Pause. "I'm afraid to go…to sleep. Might not…wake up."

She didn't know what to say to that. "I'm sorry, Earl."

His head moved in a weak nod. "Would've liked…to see Joshua."

"I'm sorry," she said again.

"Way it goes." At that moment, Hunter let out another plaintive call, and Earl said, "You gonna tell him? About his dad? That's what…what the wolves were…about, right?"

"Yeah." Why was this her responsibility? "Should I?"

"Best not to lie."

"Right." She gave Earl's shoulder a squeeze. "Be right back."

She'd expected tears, and there were a few, but Hunter didn't cry much. Maybe when your plane has crashed, your legs are trapped, there's blood in the cockpit, and your dad's disappeared, you expect miracles to be few and far between.

"Thanks for chasing them off." Hunter's eyes shimmered from a cocoon of space blankets and parka. "But what now? You can't leave him there. I mean, I know you can't do anything tonight, but..."

Well, she *could*, but from her story on Thule, she knew the Inuit left their dead to the elements all the time. Without a backhoe, digging a grave in frozen ground was a non-starter. "I don't know." Interesting question, though. So far, they'd not had to deal with dead people. "What do you want us to do?"

"Maybe rewind the last four days?" A weird, croaky laugh floated on a breath cloud that Hunter choked off. "I know you can't bury him. Ground's frozen. Maybe rocks?" Averting his face, Hunter burrowed deeper into his blankets and parka. "I need to think about it."

"Sure. I'm sorry, but with everything that's happened, I forgot to bring your broth and some hot water for your face. Would you like me to do that now?" They were running low on broth; pooling what was left from Burke's MREs and Will's two remaining ramen packs, they had about six watery servings left between the two camps. But it was the only humane thing to do.

"No." Pause. "I mean, maybe later. It's nice of you,

but I kind of need some time. Weird, huh? Been nothing *but* alone pretty much."

"It's okay. I'll come back in a little while."

"I'm not going anywhere." As she started to back out, he said, "I'm not going to make it out of here."

It had not been a question. "We don't know that."

"Don't bullshit a bullshitter. Blind man could see it with a cane. That Will, he's all right. He said he'd bring tools, and I know he'll try his damnedest. I can tell he's that kind of guy. I was a real prick to him, too."

"I think Will lets a lot of things roll off."

"I can't feel my feet anymore, can't wiggle my toes. I've never had frostbite, but even I know not feeling nothing's bad."

"People come back from frostbite." She'd seen pictures and knew the basics. "If we can get you out, get your feet and legs into warm water, get some circulation back…"

"You don't know me real well. I'm not a nice guy, okay? I've done a bunch of things, and I bullshit a lot. So, I'm telling you, don't bullshit a bullshitter."

"No bullshit." She really did know of a few cases where soldiers developed frostbitten toes, fingers, ears. A nose. "It doesn't all have to end bad, if we can get you out and warm you up." It would also be nice if a rescue plane found them already.

"Lot of ifs." Hunter sank back into in a black brood. "Lot of fucking ifs."

She waited a few beats then turned to leave. "I'll be back—"

"Watch out for that Scott," Hunter said with sudden vehemence. "I mean it."

She stared at him. "Why do you say that?"

"Because I heard him. He was threatening that old man. Said the old guy was lucky he hadn't suffocated him for his coat. That black eye Scott's got? That's not from the crash. The old guy tagged him."

"You saw this happen?"

"No, but I heard it. Heard him threaten that old man, and I thought I better keep my mouth shut or he'd come after me next. Turns out the old guy had a bag of jelly-beans he was saving for that girl, Mattie in a pocket. Scott accused him of hoarding 'em, but I think the old guy forgot he had them. Anyway, I heard him telling Scott to share and share alike, to eat only a couple and bring me some? Well, he didn't. Instead, Scott kept them for himself. Said the old guy wasn't going to last much longer anyway, no point in wasting food on him or me. He probably thought I couldn't hear, or maybe he didn't care. I'm telling you, I know guys like him. He's either coming down or just out of rehab. You gotta watch out. His wife and the little girl? If they get in his way, he'll do whatever he has to so long as he gets what he needs." His eyes held hers. "Don't think he won't do the same to you. For a guy like that? As easy as swatting a fly."

CHAPTER 9

"Thought you'd fallen in," Earl said as she emerged from the cockpit.

It was something Bubbe Sarah would've said. Her other go-to whenever someone headed for the bathroom: *Hope everything comes out all right.* Despite everything, she laughed. "We got to talking."

"About?"

She debated about lying then decided to hell with it. "Scott."

"Ah." The other man was quiet a moment. "Never liked him. But he's the father...of my grandkid."

"You don't owe me an explanation, Earl."

"She's my daughter." He subsided then said, "Kill for her...but I can't live her life. Can only help...when she makes a mistake."

Scott was a big mistake. On the other hand, it wasn't as if she hadn't made one helluva mistake herself. "You would've liked my grandmother. She'd have told you to knock out a couple of Scott's teeth for good measure."

Earl spluttered a laugh that degenerated into a phlegmy coughing fit. She couldn't get him into a sit. Will had warned about more damage to Earl's spine. She settled for slipping a hand under his shoulders and giving him a couple of thumps with a fist until Earl hawked up something and spat. When he was settled again, she dumped snow into the cookpot they'd unpacked from Burke's stash and set that on the fire to melt. "Let's get something warm into you."

"No." At her look, he gave a weak wave of a hand, "Save it. You'll…" He focused on breathing then said, "Save it."

"Okay." She put a hand on his chest. She didn't know why. For a while, they sat together, and her hand rode the swell and fall of the tides of his breath. Then she said, "I'm pregnant."

He was quiet a moment. "The father…"

"Isn't a good person. My husband's dead. Been dead eighteen months." She drew in a shuddery breath. "I've made a terrible mistake."

"Your parents…?"

"Both dead. Three months after my husband. Car crash, the police said. Drunk driver."

He waited a beat. "Doesn't sound like you believe that."

"Because I don't, any more than I believe what they said about Ben." Some proof to back any of that up would've been nice.

"Grandmother?"

"Gone. I've got a sister. She's got three kids, all little. She's married to a nice guy."

"If you've made a mistake…why are you…"

"Still pregnant?" She shook her hand. "I don't know. I came close. I made the appointment and then I…I couldn't do it. I still have the pills." Even if she took them now, she wasn't sure they would work. But she hung onto them for reasons she didn't understand. They were talismans of the person she always thought she was: independent, decisive. Fearless. Follow that damn story wherever it led and to hell with everything else.

That hadn't worked out so well.

His gloved hand cupped the back of her own. "God's kept you…safe. He got you this far."

She didn't want to be cruel, but she wouldn't let that pass either. "I'm sorry, Earl, but a god has nothing to do with it. If a god did, Jews wouldn't have been led into gas chambers still mumbling meaningless prayers. My husband would be alive. My parents wouldn't have been…" She almost said *murdered to make a point*. She really had no proof. "We wouldn't have crashed, and you'd be walking out of here. You wouldn't—" She grabbed the rest before it could fly from her mouth. "I'm sorry, but please don't talk to me about any kind of god."

"All right." He kept his hand on hers. "We'll…watch the fire then. Keepers of the flame. You heard…of them?" When she shook her head, he said, "Learned about them from…friend of mine. Alaska. Eskimo man makes this lamp…*qulliq,* it's called. Gives it to his wife. A gift. Without his wife to keep the fire burning…there would be no home. They'd all die." He patted her hand.

213

"They know. Without a woman...to protect that flame inside...there is no life."

It was a good story and, as Hunter would've said, a blind man could see that metaphor with a cane. She knew Earl meant well, too, even if all of it was so much sentimental treacle worthy of Hallmark. But she liked this old man and, for the rest of that night, she made it her business not to fall asleep and let the fire die. She kept that flame going.

But she couldn't do the same for Earl.

THE DRONE

CHAPTER 1

ON THE FIFTH MORNING...

"OKAY, ENOUGH." Will caught her by a forearm as she dropped another armload of wood onto the pile she'd been building up for the last two hours. "Stop. Go back and get some rest. You're beat. You also haven't eaten enough to feed a tick."

"I'm not that hungry." Her head was pulsing as if some mini-me monster were inside having a temper tantrum. In another minute, her brain was going to liquefy and dribble out of her ears. Before Will and Scott had appeared, she'd forced down a cup of tea, waited to see if it would stay down, and then followed with half a packet of ramen and broth. That did her in. Five minutes after she was done, a woozy kind of heaviness mantled her brain, and she heaved everything back up again in great, racking spasms that left her stomach sore and her throat burning with acid. Disgusted, she kicked snow over the mess and wondered when the hell the vomiting was going to stop. There was no good time to survive an airplane crash, but not being able to keep down food was going to make her no good to anyone, least of all herself.

Eventually, Will would say something, and then what? She kept remembering his expression, the way his eyes had narrowed almost imperceptibly when feeling her belly. Her waist had thickened, but could he have felt, well, something else? She wondered if there was some graceful way she could get out of eating in the mornings. Somehow, she didn't think saying she wasn't a morning person would cut it.

And why do you even care? He's married. He has a life.

"Hungry or not, you have to eat." Reaching into his pack, Will pulled out an energy bar. "Eat it," he said before she could protest. "The last thing we need is for you to get all light-headed and slip on a rock."

"Fine." She unwrapped the bar and caught a whiff of peanut butter and chocolate. Her stomach cramped. All of a sudden, she was ravenous—and that was as scary as her morning heaves. There was this *thing* in charge, growing inside, asserting its control. Maybe she needed to take those pills after all. But that might not be smart out here. First thing after they were rescued, though... "There's still a lot to do," she said, taking a tiny experimental nip and nearly fainting because the bar tasted so good.

"Which is true, but it's already noon, and you've gone more than thirty-six hours without sleep."

"We need more wood." She'd never truly appreciated

how hard people in third world countries had it. A person could spend her whole day gathering wood and hauling water.

"Scott can do that while I work on getting Hunter out." He gestured at a spread of tools and the inflatable raft which he and Scott had brought over from the fuselage that morning. "Really, we got this."

No, really, you don't. She eyed the two glass cockpit displays Will had already managed to jimmy free from Hunter's side of the cockpit. Those displays represented over three hours of work which had done diddly squat. The only thing decluttering the cockpit had accomplished was to give them a better sense of what the situation actually was. They weren't talking about a bent console or an easy fix for Hunter here. The impact had jammed the cockpit's frame in upon itself, crumpling and folding metal into large folds like a deflated accordion. No screwdriver or hammer or crowbar…they didn't have a crowbar, but just supposing…none of that was going to make a dent here. What they needed was a blow torch or jaws of life, something that could cut through metal. They could probably take out every display and every knob, and it wouldn't make a difference. The situation reminded her of that hiker, the one James Franco played in the movie, who'd slipped and gotten his arm wedged between boulders where he'd hung for a week before cutting off his arm.

"We got this," Will said again. "Please, go get some rest. I'll call you as soon as we get Hunter out. Then we probably will need an extra pair of hands to get the raft up that slope."

"Man, if someone was saying I should go lie down, I'd sure do it." Hands in pockets, Scott crouched in a dispirited hunch near the fire. "Maybe I should. I'm not feeling too good." Using a thumb, Scott blocked a nostril and blew a runner of snot from the other. "I think I've caught something. I think I'm getting sick. On account of the cold."

"Yeah?" said Hunter. Will had jimmied out Hunter's side window, the better to get at the various displays and now, holding up an arm to block the bolts of sun splashing into the cockpit, Hunter squinted at the other man. "Happy to trade places, man."

"I think you can probably muscle through this, Scott." She'd dug deep, trying to find a squeak of sympathy for the guy but had come up empty. She took another nibble of her energy bar then rewrapped and tucked it into a pocket. Best not to push it. "At least you get to walk away."

"Barely." Scott dragged a sleeve across his nose. "If you guys hadn't come, I'd be some wolf's dinner by now."

She sincerely doubted this. In fact, she wouldn't put it past Scott for him to back off and let the wolves or that mountain lion take Earl and Hunter first. "If he needs to go back, I can stay," she said to Will.

"Scott will pull through," Will said, dryly. "Sometimes the best medicine is to get your mind off your own worries and focus on how fortunate you are."

"Who said that?" demanded Scott.

"Me," said Will and then to Emma, "Go."

"Yeah, please. Seriously, you look worse than me."

Hunter's mouth moved in a wan grin. "And I look like shit."

What he looked like was a very sick man. Even with the bruising to mask it, she saw the high flush of fever in his cheeks. Despite the cold, his face shone with sweat, and his eyes were glassy. She remembered how bluff and big he was, but he seemed to have collapsed and shrunken into himself.

Will was also right. Her body was wobbly, her legs were water-weak, and she was starting to stumble over her own boots. If she could've curled up right then and there to sleep, she would've. Still, as relieved as she had been to see the sun rise and that awful night end, she didn't want to leave. There was so much left undone. She cast a glance at Earl's body. The old man seemed much smaller in only his blue jeans and shirt. Everything else Will had stripped from the body. Hunter got the parka, scarf, hat, and gloves. The boots were two sizes too big for Hunter, but Will said when they got Hunter out, they'd probably have to cut off his boots. So, they needed a spare pair.

It all seemed a little barbaric. She understood that Earl would have no more use for any of these things, that survivors had done this over the centuries. But it still felt vaguely obscene. She'd gone through his pockets and pulled out a wallet, a pocket watch, and a small folding knife with a staghorn handle, all of which she would give to Rachel. (Scott had offered to hang onto the items, but she'd refused.)

There was still the problem of what to do with the

body—and also with Burke, who still lay in pieces, and whom no one had touched yet.

"What we do about Earl will be Rachel's call," Will said when she had brought it up.

"Rachel's not awake," she pointed out. She didn't add that the other woman might never wake up.

"Makes me his next of kin, then," said Scott.

"Actually, no, that would be Mattie," Will said.

"C'mon, she's a kid."

"What did you have in mind?" asked Emma.

"Well…"Scott had sucked on his teeth. "We can't bury him."

"No." She'd looked around in mock dismay. "Really?"

"Emma," Will warned.

Scott ignored her. "Could pile rocks, but that's a lot of work."

"Yeah. Work," she said. "Perish the thought."

Scott rounded, a fist already bunched. "*Listen*, bi—" He stopped, shot a glance at Will, and jammed the fist into a pocket. "You got a better idea? Maybe leave 'im out for the animals? Oh yeah. I bet Rachel would *love* that."

"Eskimos did it." Hunter shrugged. "I mean, look, wolves already got my dad. It's not like they can kill him more."

"That's sick."

"No, it's an option," Will said. "But I don't think it's one we should take either. Once the bodies are gone, it's not as if there isn't more meat for the taking. I don't think I want to chance wolves and a couple mountain lions sniffing around."

There was one other option no one had mentioned. "What about cremation?" In answer to the men's collective stare, she said, "It's an option. There's wood."

"Wellll." Will rubbed the back of his neck with his good hand. "It takes a fair amount of heat to burn a body. That would mean a lot of wood burning at high heat for a long time, like two or three hours. It's so cold, I don't see how that would work."

"What about the extra fuel?"

"You mean, squirt 'em like charcoal briquets?" Scott laughed. "Barbecue!"

"It's not funny." God what an asswipe. She looked at Hunter. "I'm sorry he's such a jerk."

Scott flushed purple. "Who the fuck you calling a jerk?"

"You. Stop being one, and I'll stop saying it." She looked at Will. "What do you think?"

"It's a good thought, Emma," Will said, "but I still think you have the same problem of maintaining the right amount of heat for a long period of time. Constructing a cairn's probably better."

Scott frowned. "A what?"

"A rock mound, only it'd be a tomb. Yeah." Hunter rubbed his mouth with a gloved hand. "Better than leaving my dad out in the open to get chewed on."

"Sounds like a plan." Will nodded. "Scott can get a start while I work on you, Hunter."

"Oh, right. Like I got the energy for this?" Scott protested. "Why me?"

"Because I have a bum arm I can't use much, and as much as I like Emma, I'll take a pass on her relocating my shoulder again," Will said, calmly. "Scott, we're all hungry—"

"Yeah, fuck with this," Scott flared. "You want me to work, I got to eat! And where the fuck are those rescue planes, hunh? It's been five *days.*"

"The storm only let up day before yesterday. You have to give rescuers time."

"That's supposed to make me feel better? We're going to starve to death, man, unless we start eating each other—"

"Scott, are you always this much of an asshole," Emma asked, "or do you only practice in front of the mirror when you're alone?"

"Emma, stop. And you." Will put a restraining hand on Scott's shoulder. "Cool off."

"Yeah?" Scott was practically vibrating. "Tell your girlfriend to watch her mouth."

"Fine." Will turned to Emma. "Would you please watch your mouth?"

"You guys. Comedians." Hunter let go of a bitter laugh. "You do realize I'm dying here, right? Every minute I'm still in this fucking plane is another minute I get closer to fucking...*dying.* Do you not *get* that?"

"Yeah, sure," Scott blustered. "But that doesn't change the fact we're stuck, it's going on five days now, and we got to think about where we put our energy."

"Oh, yeah." Hunter showed his teeth in a nasty grin. "Heaven forbid you spend energy helping out a guy."

Scott ignored him. "Maybe we need to be thinking of rescuing ourselves. Maybe we have to leave."

"You can't leave me," Hunter said.

"No?" Cocking his head, Scott gazed up at blue, empty sky. "You hear any planes? Helicopters? Snow-mobiles down valley? Yeah, me neither. Did it ever occur to you that us getting out now might actually help you?"

"You know it wouldn't." Hunter's mouth trembled. Tears stood in his eyes. "You leave, you might as well put a bullet in my head."

"No one's going to leave," Will said.

She hated to do it, but it had to be said. "Could there be something wrong with the ELT? All we know for sure is the antenna's good."

"No, the ELT has to be working. I checked the remote switch by Burke's seat. It's on."

"But we haven't actually looked at the unit."

"Because it's locked. Unless we find a key, I don't see how we can check it out."

Yeah, what was with Burke and his obsession with keeping things locked up? "What if we did find a key?"

Will scratched the back of his head. "If we can get the panel open, and the unit's not working, I don't know how to fix it."

"What about you, Hunter?"

Hunter shook his head. "I don't know much about electronics. I wouldn't even know how to tell if it's working or not."

"There's got to be an off-on switch."

"I guess? It's got its own battery, I know that, but…" Hunter shrugged.

"Well, is there anything else? What about the flight plan? How come no one's searching along that?"

Hunter hesitated then said, his gaze slipping from hers, "I dunno. Bad luck?"

"Bad luck?" she echoed.

At the same moment, Will broke in. "Emma, we already went over this. We're probably off course. It'll take rescue time to backtrack, look at the weather patterns, figure out where we might have ended up. In a pinch, they could rely on our radar pings, but that presupposes the ELT's not working and no flight plan which wouldn't happen because if you fly IFR, you're required by law to file a flight plan."

But what if Burke hadn't originally thought he would be flying via instruments? Were the rules the same?

Scott scowled. "What are pings?"

"Every air traffic control at every airport tracks planes via primary radar," she said. "It happens automatically. The reflected waves give air traffic control a way of knowing, roughly, where a plane is, whether the pilot wants to be tracked or not." The only way around that would be to fly low, beneath the radar. She recalled Burke's boast about doing precisely that in Vietnam. So he *could* have done so if he wanted, but the conditions had forced him higher. Why would he even need to fly below the radar? She could think of only a handful of reasons, all of them both bad and nonsense. Burke had been carrying *passengers*, for God's sake. "Even if an ELT stopped working, it should be possible to extrapolate a bearing on the basis of the last ping. It all depends on how far back the last ping happened and how radically we changed course after that."

"Oh." Scott digested this. "How often does that work? The pings thing?"

"Let's put it this way," Will said. "You remember that Malaysian airliner that went down somewhere over the ocean? Everyone knew where the plane was because of primary and secondary radar until it got over the ocean where's there no radar. Air traffic control then has to rely on high-frequency radio and GPS, if it's available. Even knowing a projected course, even pulling up satellite data later on, even though the plane regularly sent out pings…they've never found that plane."

Scott pulled at his lower lip. "So, you're saying that if they're going by these pings…they might never find us."

Will nodded. "It's a possibility. We have to hope for the best."

"Hunh," Scott grunted. "Or plan for the worst."

CHAPTER 2

"AH, FUCK ME." Backing up a step, Scott put a hand to his mouth as his shoulders heaved. "That's fucking...I can't..." Rounding swiftly, he stumbled a few steps away and then bent from the waist and retched.

She looked away, not from any sense of wanting not to embarrass the jerk but to keep herself from doing the same. Lucky for her, she was upwind, so she didn't have to smell it.

Not that looking at what was left of Burke was any better. While seeing this had been bad enough last night, daylight and the cold only sharpened the horror, cutting the tableau from the icy air the way a diamond scored glass. Haloed by chunked red and pink snow, the man was simply in pieces: frozen hunks of half-gnawed flesh, jagged and splintered twigs of bones sticking from shredded clothing. A slop of dusky bowel spooled on top of a spaghetti coil of blued intestines mantled with a frozen curtain of yellow fat. These lay in a mound next to the blackish crater of Burke's abdomen,

from which the edible organs—liver, spleen, kidneys—
had been hollowed out. Once into Burke's belly, the
wolves had burrowed up into his chest, tearing out the
diaphragm to get at the heart and lungs, which were
also gone. The crotch of his jeans were in tatters, the
wolves having ripped through denim to get at the soft
genitals, and she could see the curds of fat where they'd
dug out his buttocks. The body was intact, though, from
the knees down, and Burke's boots were still laced to his
feet.

Her gaze tracked to the ruin of Burke's face. His
head had been almost completely severed from his
neck. She could imagine powerful jaws clamping tight,
crunching through bone and cartilage. A worm of
Burke's windpipe flopped from what was left his
ravaged neck. Most of his face had been eaten away, the
scalp torn from its moorings to lie in a frozen flap of
matted hair to reveal a dome of naked skull. Instead of a
nose, there were two black pits. The wolves had
stripped his lips, leaving Burke's teeth, yellowed and
crooked, bared in a skeletal snarl. Only a nubbin of
tongue remained. Enough was gone that she could see a
glimmer of gold molar on the left.

*They were probably at him for a long time before I woke
up.* Her gaze sharpened on one of Burke's eyeballs that
was frozen to his left ear and still attached to the brain
by a strand of optic nerve. The right eyeball was gone,
cored from its socket the way she might hollow out an
avocado. *They had to be for so much of him to be gone.*

She should be vomiting like Scott. That would be the
human thing to do. On the other hand, she'd seen a lot

of gore, and she hadn't really known this man. Maybe this is what happened to combat soldiers. See enough blasted human beings, nothing shocked you anymore.

"I'm not doing that." Sticking his hands in the pockets of Earl's parka, Scott hunched his shoulders around his ears. He'd appropriated both the parka and Earl's watch cap, arguing that he needed two layers and his own watch cap had vanished. "I moved Earl. I was okay with that. But I'm not touching any of that shit, any of those pieces of that other guy."

"You can use the shovel." Seeing Scott in Earl's clothes pissed her off to an unreasonable degree. It shouldn't. It wasn't as if Earl would mind, and Scott was a thin guy, without a lot of body fat for insulation. That didn't mean she had to like it. Her mind kept darting back to what Hunter had claimed about Scott's threats. Although it had been the taking of Earl's candy, the jellybeans he'd been saving for Mattie, that made her want to blacken Scott's other eye. "It's all frozen, Scott. If you do it fast…"

"You deaf?" A smear of puke glistened on his jaw. Backhanding the slime, he cursed then wiped his glove in snow. "I'm not doing it at all." Digging into a breast pocket, he pulled out a cigarette, screwed that into the corner of his mouth, lit up, and sucked. "End of story," he said, smoke jetting from his nose. As if to put the period on that, he jammed the point of the camp shovel into snowpack and headed back toward the low mound of rocks they'd heaped. "You want to move him over here, you do that," he called over a shoulder. "If it was me, I'd leave him and let the wolves have the rest."

The snark—*Yeah, of course, you would*—teetered on the tip of her tongue before she swallowed it back. Sniping at Scott might be satisfying. She really was spoiling for a fight with the guy, which was crazy. It wasn't like she was a secret agent or some ninja-assassin. Still, she would love to pound that needle-nose into his skull. Actually, what was crazy was her being out here. Will was right; she needed rest. Except this would never get done if she didn't do it. Will would pick up the slack, but Hunter was a priority. They had to get him out before night came again. So, tag. There wasn't anyone else.

Thirty minutes with the camp shovel was all she needed to scrape all of Burke's pieces into a mound. It was only when she was socking rocks into place around the body that her gaze fell on a chunky gold band with a faceted, square blue stone around Burke's right ring finger. Probably a class ring. A wedding band encircled the ring finger on his left.

Shit. She should've thought of this. Unlike Earl, she hadn't gone through the dead man's pockets or twisted off a ring or a watch. Hunter might want those rings, or his mom would. Certainly, the authorities would need any identification Earl might have in a wallet.

As luck would have it, she could work off only the bigger, chunkier ring which turned out to be from a high school, *Robert E. Peary*, she'd never heard of. Try as she might, she couldn't work the wedding band over Burke's knuckle and finally left it. There was no way she was cutting off the guy's finger. His shirt was mostly in ribbons, and though she remembered he'd tucked a pack of cigarettes and a Bic lighter into a breast pocket, they were gone. He apparently had not bothered with a watch, which seemed a little odd for a guy who was a pilot, but whatever. Other than a small brass parrot clasp secured to a belt loop—which was both odd and familiar, as if she ought to know what that was about— his front pockets were empty. This sucked. Ben had never carried a wallet and always kept his cards and money on a clip. Burke had not and probably had a wallet.

Which meant she had to roll him.

It wasn't as bad as it might have been, principally because, without his guts and missing most of his muscle mass, Burke wasn't that heavy anymore. Shoving him up on his left hip took very little effort, though it freaked her out a little when she dipped a hand into a hip pocket and felt a huge divot where a butt cheek ought to have been but wasn't because the wolves had eaten that out from the front.

She found his wallet in his right hip pocket. Sliding it out, she lowered the body back onto the snow. The wallet was a trifold, cracked with age, and curved from years of resting on Burke's butt. Unfolding the creased leather revealed a fan of pictures in plastic on one side, slots with a few cards. A much-younger Burke stared from a North Dakota driver's license. He carried only a little cash, two twenties, a ten, and three ragged dollar bills.

As she stood and tucked the ring and wallet into a pocket, she noticed a glint of yellow on the snow by Burke's left hip. *That clasp.* Her gaze darted to the brass parrot's beak clamped around a belt loop. Burke had carried something on a chain. Not his wallet; she had that. What was this? Kneeling, she spotted a length of linked brass chain that must've fallen out of a front pocket then been buried by the wolves as they rummaged. Digging the chain from crusted snow, she pinched links between her fingers and tugged. There was something heavy at the other end.

Something clicked. She also understood why Burke had no wristwatch.

The pocket watch was thick and looked old. She knew at a glance it was half-hunter, which meant that only the back was covered by a brass case. The glass over the face was intact, though the second sweep had stilled and the black hands showed the watch had stopped at twenty past eleven.

Interesting. There was a big round ball of brass at the top with a ring to which the chain link was attached. Old watches had stems you could wind. This wasn't that. Then how would you set the time? Turning the watch over, she studied the smooth back then held the watch the way she might inspect the white icing layered between two halves of an Oreo. At one end was a tiny hinge, and now she could clearly see there were layers to the watch's back, like two half-shells from an oyster piled one on top of the other.

Wait a minute. I know this. Bubbe Sarah's husband, Chaim, had died young of pneumonia, leaving behind a widow with three children, a few pictures, a fifty-dollar life insurance policy…and an antique wind-up pocket watch from the old country. The watch still worked but had to be wound with a special key Sarah had long since misplaced. But her grandmother had shown her how this kind of watch worked.

The watch's face and guts were nestled in two brass cases. Opening the first revealed a hole into which a watch key could be inserted and then turned to wind the watch. Beneath the second sat the watch's mainspring and barrel. Clicking the two back cases closed again, she turned the watch face up then slid her nails under the brass rim of the glass cover. The cover lifted on a hinge and there, where the hour and minute hands were attached at the center, was a tiny raised square brass peg.

So, where was the key? Burke's watch had been torn from its pocket, probably by the wolves. *And they pulled pretty hard.* She feathered snow from where she'd unearthed the watch. *Hard enough to break the chain.* A tiny watch might have been flung pretty far, too.

But it had not—because it had been attached to something heavy enough for it simply to drop into the snow.

Wow. She cradled the items in her left palm. The watch key didn't look like a proper key at all but more like the stump of a thick brass toothpick with a square opening at one end and a ring at the other to which it was attached by another smaller ring to a heavy brass airplane-shaped fob. With the fob was another, much larger, more traditional silver key, the kind you might use for a—

What? She suddenly straightened. Had she heard something? The sound had been odd and out-of-place, one that reminded her of her grandmother's garden in high summer when there were a lot of—

Bees. She jerked her head toward the sky. A buzz, she'd heard a buzzing and…she sucked in a sudden gasp of chilled air. "Guys, guys!" She was on her feet now, arms waving above her head in a crazy semaphore. "Here!" she screamed. "Over here, down here!"

She heard Will, who was over by the cockpit, call her name, his voice rising in a question but then Scott was shouting and pointing. "Look, look, it's a drone. It's a fucking *drone*!"

Oh my God.. She'd seen plenty of drones in her time, though most had either missiles or cameras. This drone was smaller than she expected, but that might also be an illusion because of altitude; the thing had to be a hundred feet in the air if not more. The drone looked almost military: a jet-black streamlined bullet with a thin proboscis of an antennae, long, narrow wings with upturned tips, and a tail-mounted propeller. Well, why not? Joe Kuntz was ex-military. He or Patterson might have pulled strings. *Honey, I will take what I can get.* Spotting the camera nestled in a small dome on the drone's belly, she waved at it. "We're here. We're here!"

By now, they were all yelling. Even Hunter was screaming, his right arm sticking out of his empty window and waving in a frantic semaphore. The drone hovered a moment, seeming to take in the scene, before slowing drifting away, heading for the woods and, probably, the fuselage beyond. God, she hoped Mattie had kept that fire going.

"Give me your radio," she said to Will, who'd come

up alongside. Depressing the send, she shouted into the mike, "Mattie, Mattie! Are you outside? You got the fire going, right?"

"Emma?" Mattie sounded alarmed. "What's wrong? No, I'm inside, with Mom. Are you all—"

"There's a drone, there's a *drone*! Get outside, right now! Make sure they see you!"

"Oh!" There was nothing for a few moments, probably because the girl was squirming through their tunnel. Then: "I'm out and...oh, here, *here*! I'm down here! Emma, should I light my flare, too? So they know?"

"No need if you've got the fire going, Mattie." Will was close enough that when she turned, they could've brushed lips. "But if it's hovering, write the number six in the snow, okay? They need to know how many of us there are."

"Okay." Ten seconds. "Okay," Mattie came back. "I did it. I don't know if it's looking, but it hasn't left. It's spending a lot of time looking at the plane...oh, it's turning, starting to head back your way."

Now that she knew what to listen for, she heard the buzz well before the black arrow of the drone came into view. It was still going slowly, sketching a wide circle in the sky. "We see it. Good work, honey."

"Does this... Emma, it means they found us, right?"

"Yes, it does." She was grinning like a maniac. "We are saved."

"WELL?" Outside the fuselage, Mattie jumped up from a seat they'd dragged over to the fire. "Where are they? When are we getting rescued?" She looked around Emma in the direction of the forest. "Where's Will?"

She answered the last question first. "He'll be here later to check on your mom. He wanted to get in as much time as possible on the cockpit before it got too dark for him to get back in time to see your mom and then hustle back to stay with Hunter." She was so tired, her eyeballs were going to merge above her nose. It had been all she could do to pull herself up the rock scramble. She supposed it was the tail-off of adrenaline conspiring with lack of sleep and little food that made her want only to curl up in a sleeping bag and sleep until the rescuers arrived with a one-way ticket out of here.

"Is Scott coming back tonight?" Mattie swallowed. "To stay?"

The poor kid sounded as if she hoped her stepdad

might trip into a black hole and get sucked away to the Delta quadrant. "I don't think so. It's the guys' turn tonight."

"Oh. Good." Mattie's shoulders relaxed. "I mean, I don't like that Will has to stay out but... Oooh, careful!" Mattie pointed. "Don't mess up the six. Why aren't we getting rescued tonight?"

"Well, drones have a pretty long range." Skirting the wobbly numeral Mattie had sketched in the snow, she dropped into the seat the girl had vacated. "So, I guess a rescue team could be a day or so away."

"Really?" Mattie's forehead wrinkled. "But if it's got a camera, and they know we're here, why not send a helicopter or something?"

She'd thought of that. After she'd finished with Burke, she'd asked Will the same question. There was only one thing either of them came up with that made sense. "It's possible there isn't a good place for a helicopter to land." That, she'd pointed out to Will, only sort of made sense unless there was something about the mountain they didn't know about. *We're not up that high,* she'd said. *The only other thing that might be a problem is the slope.* On a steep incline, a helicopter would have trouble maintaining a stable hover. Most people tended to overlook the fact that a helicopter was never truly stationary but constantly matching its speed to the rotation of the earth beneath it. A steep slope made sticking to a single point extremely difficult.

"Really?" Planting her fists in her hips, Mattie turned a circle, scanning the small ellipse of their plateau. "This isn't big enough for a helicopter?"

"A small one, maybe, but beats me. It might be that there's more than one team, or they want to bring in something big enough to get us all off at the same time. They could already have a team or two on the ground in the general area, too."

"And they'll climb up?"

"Or take snowmobiles, but yeah. That could be." She watched Mattie turn that over. "What?"

"Welll," Mattie drawled, "if they couldn't land or anything, couldn't a helicopter at least have dropped some food or something?"

"I…" she began then stopped. Not even Will had thought of that. But it was an excellent question, wasn't it? "I don't know what they're thinking, Mattie. But it's enough that they saw us. That's what counts. By this time tomorrow, we'll probably be off this rock. So… what are you going to eat first when we do?"

"Pizza," Mattie declared. "With extra cheese and pepperoni and sausage. Mom always makes me have vegetarian because she says it's healthier and good for the environment, and I know she's right, but…" Mattie let out a dreamy sigh. "I like really want *grease*, you know? Ooo, and French fries with mayonnaise. And a *cheeseburger* with mushrooms and bacon. What about you?"

They spent the next few minutes talking food until their stomachs growled, and Emma finally pushed to a stand. "Come on, let's feed the fire and go eat something."

"That's all I think about." Mattie tugged at her sagging pants. "I can barely keep these up."

Hers were also loose, which was worrisome in more ways than one. And to think she'd been worried about how tight her clothes were getting around the middle. "How many MREs are left?"

"Two."

"Two?" She was in the middle of stooping to worm through their tunnel but now turned back. They'd rationed themselves to one a day for the three of them and, along with a packet of ramen, Will had left a whole one for her to dole out between her, Earl, and Hunter. She'd given the lion's share to Hunter. "We had five a day ago."

"Scott ate a whole one and then another half all by himself." Emotions warred on Mattie's face. "I didn't want him to, but Will said he needed the calories."

Well, he probably had. Hadn't she done the same with Hunter? Although, with Scott now in the mix, and in light of what Hunter had said, she wasn't sure how safe their food supply was if they left Scott here unsupervised. On the other hand, Scott wasn't *stupid.* If he scarfed down their food, he'd be out that much faster, and it wasn't as if Scott could go running off on his own. There was nowhere to run, for starters, and no reason either, now that rescue was on the way. Besides, there *were* wolves out there and at least one mountain lion. Although she wouldn't put it past Scott to try and sneak food while Will slept. He would, too, and then claim Will must've miscounted or whatever. Still, the good news was if he did that, grabbed something to eat and then snuck off somewhere into the night to stuff his face, the wolves might catch a whiff and decide Scott-tartar wasn't a half-bad idea. (Yes. Mean.) The bad news was the wolves might decide Scott-tartar was only the first course. Hunter was the definition of a sitting duck. She made a mental note to remind Will to be on the lookout.

Once she was inside, she brushed snow from her pants and, with a groan, lowered herself next to Mattie "You want to eat now or wait?"

"We should wait," Mattie replied. "At least an hour or so past dark. Do you want to play cards, or maybe I could read to you?"

"Sure, let's hear more quantum cat," she said, catching a yawn in a cupped hand. The combination of snow mounded on the fuselage and the day's sun meant the fuselage was almost cozy, though the air was close with the combined smells of too many people crammed into too small a space.

Mattie opened her mouth, closed it again then said, "Well, I have another book. It was in my luggage. I packed it under a sweater so Mom didn't see."

"Yeah?" The kid was acting like it was contraband. "What book?"

Mattie nibbled at the chapped skin of her lower lip. *"Charlotte's Web."*

"Really?" She'd never have guessed. "Aren't you a little old for that?" At the sudden pinched look on Mattie's face, she said, "I'm sorry. I shouldn't have said that. I love that book. It's that I'm surprised because you seem so…"

"Brainy?" Mattie said it as if the word tasted bad. "Advanced?"

241

"Well, you have to admit that *Charlotte's Web* isn't exactly a quantum cat."

"I know." Mattie studied her fingers. "Mom says it's too baby, but I bet if I had a favorite teddy bear or old doll, she wouldn't be so...so negative. Some people have security blankets and stuffed animals. I have a book. What's so wrong with that?"

"Nothing?" She'd never heard of anyone ever having a *security* book but so what? It was the story *behind* the teddy bear or blanket or whatever that mattered.

"Exactly. My mom thinks I ought to be reading all these classics and stuff, and I do, but some of them aren't so great. Did you know she was going to name me after Amelia in *Vanity Fair*? I'm so glad my real dad talked her out of it. I mean, Amelia's such a *dork*."

Not her favorite character either. She'd always been partial to Becky Sharp. Now, there was a woman who did things. As she remembered it, her high school English teacher said Thackery fell in love with the character a little too much himself. *It's why there's that abrupt turnaround from admiring her pluck to deciding she's a snake in the Garden of Eden.* "I didn't read that book until high school."

"My mom's always doing that, getting me to read *classics*, like books are a kind of medicine, something someone's decided is good for you, and so you *have* to read them even if they're stupid and don't have anything to do with life *now* and God, *Amelia!*" Mattie rolled her eyes. "She doesn't do anything except fall in love with the wrong guy who doesn't love her, only then George gets killed, but she's pregnant and then she's this noble widow-type, hanging onto the image of this perfect guy, except George was a complete jerk! Yeah, it turns out okay in the end because Dobbins has loved her all along and waited for her to get over George."

"So, why is *Charlotte's Web* contraband?"

"I told you. She's thinks it's for babies, but that's ridiculous. That's like saying *Watership Down* isn't a great novel because it's about rabbits. I think *Charlotte* is, you know, it's really deep in a way my mom can't let herself see."

"Why not?"

"Because it's all about death, really. From the very first, right? Fern saves Wilbur from getting killed because he's different and a burden? The whole book is like that because what it's really about is what happens when you figure out your family's not forever. Like, you know, your mom's going to die." She paused. "Or your dad. I always cry when I get to the part where Charlotte dies all alone. It's so sad."

"Me, too." Her sister's kids were so worried when she couldn't stop bawling, they'd called for their mom. On the other hand, Ben was only three months in his grave at the time, so maybe she was entitled to a little nervous breakdown now and then. "Your mom doesn't want you to cry?"

"She can't stand it when I do. I think that's what gets to my mom the most. She thinks the book is…she called it my way of always picking open the scab."

"About your dad?" When Mattie nodded, she asked, "What happened to your dad?"

"He was a cop, and he got shot."

"Oh?" Her chest tightened with a sudden clutch of dread. "How did that happen?"

"It happened because Scott's a jerk. He was my dad's partner." Mattie's face hardened. "Drugs."

"They were undercover." Like her Ben. "Why was Scott a jerk?" She already thought she knew, though.

"He got to like it too much. When you're a cop, you're not supposed to use or anything, but I guess they do. They get trapped into it, you know? They have to prove themselves. Dad said that once. He and Mom were in the kitchen. They thought I was asleep. Mom was asking him what was wrong, and Dad was, like, I think I can't go so deep anymore, it's messing me up."

"Did you understand what he meant?"

Mattie gave her a *duh* look. "He was having to be an actor in a play, but he could never walk off the stage for very long. He was never out of costume. You know he got tattoos? On his back." Mattie pointed to a spot at the small of her own. "A spider and then barbed wire up here." She touched a biceps. "And other stuff, a skull and a knife. Not a ton of tattoos, but he never had them before. I didn't like them, but he said they were like makeup. Only tattoos are forever, pretty much. Makeup, at least, you take off. I think that's what happened with Scott. He got so it wasn't makeup with him anymore. It was everything. I don't know the whole story because they think I'm only a stupid little kid. Like I don't have ears and can't think and haven't been reading books on my own since I was four. All Mom said was Scott got into trouble and then Dad tried to get him out only when all the shooting started, it was my dad who got killed and not Scott." Her eyes watered. "Like Charlotte, except he died all alone on a basement floor instead of an empty barn."

"I'm sorry."

"Everyone's always sorry." Mattie's features knotted as if she'd tasted something sour. "Mom says Scott still feels guilty. Well, he should. He got my dad killed, and he got kicked out of the cops, and he's lucky he's not in jail because he should be. I don't see why feeling sorry for somebody means you have to marry him either. You know what it's like to get up every morning, and there's the jerk who got your dad shot walking around in his bare feet and having cereal? He's got hair on his *toes*. It's disgusting. I think Mom is sorry they got married."

"Why did they?"

"On account of her getting pregnant with Joshua. I don't understand why she did that."

Oh, she could. "Maybe being with Scott was a way for her to still be with your dad."

"That's what Grampa says. He says I should be understanding. But why should *I* have to? Why can't the grown-ups act like grown-ups? And now I'm going to have a little brother who should've been my brother from my *real* dad. They're even using the name my real dad wanted for when they had their next kid. Only now Joshua will be half *Scott*, and *Scott's* who caused all the trouble in the first place. It's not fair. It's not as if Mom couldn't get...you know...not have it while there was still time not to." Her face contorted with sudden ferocity. "It's not like she would have killed a real *baby*. Back then, when there was time, it was only a bunch of *cells*."

"Uh…" She swallowed. "How much do you—"

"I'm twelve, not two. I know all about it," Mattie interrupted irritably. "Mom and Dad told me where babies come from when I was five on account of Mom used to go on marches for women's rights and everything. But she gets pregnant and it's like all that went away, and do you know that disgusting that is? That my mom and *Scott* made a baby? It's *gross*. But now it's too late to do anything, and I'm going to have a brother, and I have to move and leave all my friends because of Scott and my mom. Nobody asked me. It's not right. Fine, mess up your own lives, but why do you get to mess up mine?"

"Because sometimes adults are stupid. They think they know how they'll act if something happens only, when it does, all of a sudden, it's different. It's not a thought experiment like Schrödinger's cat. You know what I'm saying?" At the girl's look, she gave a wry smile. "Yeah, yeah, you're twelve, not two. But reality can be different than imagination and something that's not happened yet. Your mom opened the box and, all of a sudden, it wasn't a choice for her anymore. Maybe your mom would've gotten an abortion if your dad hadn't died the way he did. In a funny way, she might even believe that Joshua *is* your dad's because he wanted that."

Mattie picked at a thumbnail. "You sound like our therapist."

Yup, been there, done that, bought the T-shirt. "Doesn't mean it's not true."

"That's what Grampa says. The only good thing

about moving is I get to live on a farm, and Grampa said there are lots of chores to do, and I'll get to ride a horse and learn to shoot."

Oh no. It suddenly hit her. *Mattie doesn't know about Earl.* Emma had waited until she knew Will was on the trail down to the cockpit before telling him about Earl precisely because she hadn't wanted Mattie to over-hear. Why Will had decided not to tell Mattie how badly injured Earl was remained a mystery, but… *Damn.*

Mattie's jaw set. "You know what? Maybe *I'll* become a cop or a Mountie or something. Then I'll get those guys who killed my dad. I'll put *everybody* in jail where they can't hurt people—"

She interrupted. "Mattie, what did Will say about your grandfather?"

"What?" Mattie's eyebrows crinkled in confusion at the sudden shift. "That he was hurt and couldn't walk and that you were going to stay with him and Hunter. I asked Scott when Will went outside for something if maybe we should go see Grampa, but he told me to be quiet. Actually, he told me to shut my mouth or he'd give me something to be upset about. Why? I was so excited about the drone I forgot to ask. Is Grampa coming back tomorrow? Was he better this morning?"

"No, Mattie." She swallowed. "He wasn't."

"Oh." The girl's face stilled into the watchful expres-sion of someone who knows there's more bad news "How hurt was he?" As if hearing herself, she said, "*Is* he?"

There was no right way to say this, and Mattie was a

247

smart kid who deserved the truth. "Bad. Will was pretty sure his back was broken."

"Wait. You said *was*. Why?"

"Because he…he went to sleep in the middle of the night, only he didn't wake up."

Mattie went utterly still. "You mean…" She stopped as if afraid saying the words made them true. "Did he… is my…he *died*?"

She remembered the moment she found Ben. She had read about military families who refused to answer the door when they saw men in uniform walking up their drive because so long as no one spoke the words, their son or daughter or father or wife was still alive. She'd felt that as soon as she walked into her bathroom, while she still believed they had years ahead, and she was thinking of lamb chops with rosemary the way Ben liked them and asparagus with lemon and a baked potato for their supper when she opened the lid of the metaphorical box that was their bathroom and Ben, who'd been alive in her thoughts only seconds before, wasn't.

"Yes," she said. "Your Grampa Earl died really early this morning."

"Oh." A slab of granite held more expression than Mattie's face. "Why didn't anyone tell me? Why didn't Will? Is it because he thinks I'm stupid? That I'll cry? That I don't already *know* what this is like?" All at once, her composure shattered. Every muscle shivered, her body quaked, and then Mattie was screaming, "That I haven't *ever* had anyone I love *die* and get *shot* and all because someone else messed *up*?"

"Will didn't know for sure until he was already on the trail. Don't blame him." Emma's eyes filled. Mattie's grief was horrible to watch and even worse to bear, but there was no one else who could do this with her. "If you want to be angry with someone, be angry with me. I could've called last night, but I didn't."

Mattie's face purpled. "Then why didn't *you* tell me right away?" She slammed a fist on her thigh. "Why did you let me talk about pizza and cheeseburgers and sound so *dumb*?" Mattie hit herself again and then again and again, caught up in a tornado of fury and grief. "You grown-ups are *always* doing this to me, you're always *doing* this, you're *always...*"

"Stop." Her hands shot forward and snagged Mattie's wrists. "Stop beating yourself up because you're mad at me—"

With something like a roar, Mattie wrenched free. "Stop *telling* me what to do!" she howled. "Stop telling me how to *feel*—"

Mattie's fist rocketed for her face in a blur. The impact was like a bomb going off under her left eye. Pain detonated in a blinding white starburst, and she reeled, nearly falling onto her back.

"Oh." Mattie froze. She clapped her hands to her mouth. "Oh, Emma, Emma, I'm sorry, I'm so sorry, I'm—"

"It's okay." Her cheek stung where her teeth had torn the soft flesh. She swallowed back a ball of blood. "You didn't mean it."

"I always mess up." Mattie's voice hitched against a sob, and her eyes welled. "If I were older, if I knew how to make my mom happy, if I hadn't *told* Dad to go away…it's all my fault!"

"What are you talking about?"

"He called the night before he…" Tears streamed down the girl's cheeks. "We were supposed to go to a movie. He'd been away for ten days, and he *promised.* Only he said he had to work, and I said, *fine.* Fine, go *work* because you're never home anyway, and he…and he…" Mattie wailed and dove into Emma's chest. "He went because of *me*! He went to work and died because I told him to!"

He died because he was doing his job. She pressed the weeping girl close. *He died trying to save a friend.* Or Mattie's father, like Earl, had died for no reason at all because he was in the wrong place at exactly the wrong time and the universe was random, nothing made sense, and a person could pray until the words blurred and became meaningless because there was no purpose and no design, and a good man followed a lead his wife fed him, and horrible things happened to really good people.

Oh, Ben. She pressed her face into the top of Mattie's head. *I'm so sorry I got you killed.*

CHAPTER 4

WHEN SHE WOKE, she was spooned against Mattie's back, and the light was gone.

She held herself still a moment, getting her bearings. Her cheek still ached, and her mouth tasted of dead blood. Her brain was fuzzy, and her lashes were crusted with salt and sleep. The only truly pointed sensation was the sharp beaky feeling in the pit of her gut as if she'd swallowed a giant parrot that was trying to gnaw its way out through her belly button.

Starving. On the other hand, what was new? Since they'd crashed she'd been either puking her guts out or trying to pretend three mouthfuls felt like thirty. She was going to have to talk to Will tomorrow about scouting more, maybe figuring out if there was any game up here or a lake or something. She doubted they'd find anything. Except for the wolves and that mountain lion's prints, she'd seen no other animal trails, which wasn't surprising. In winter, animals kept to the lower elevations where they had a better chance of finding food. The only reason predators were skulking around up here was because *they* were potential prey. God, Hunter was, for sure; she'd caught a whiff of what smelled like rotting meat when she'd helped him wash his face this morning. Plus, there were bodies to scavenge with the promise of more to come.

What time was it, anyway? She raised an arm to squint at her watch. Almost nine. They'd slept for nearly six hours.

Moving in slow motion, she disentangled herself, freezing when Mattie let out a soft moan. When the girl's breathing evened out again, she slid away, forked hair from her face then patted around her parka until she found the pocket where she'd shoved in her flashlight. As she pulled it out, something tumbled onto the sleeping bag with a muted but brassy tickle.

Mattie's voice, still half-asleep: "What was that?"

The kid had radar. "Something I found in the..." She almost said *pilot's pocket* but caught herself, certain that if no one had told Mattie about her grandfather, they'd not elaborated about Burke either. "In the snow. Near the wreck. It's an old-fashioned pocket watch. See?"

"A watch?" Mattie's tone held only a smidgeon of interest, but she sat up, sweeping hair from her face. Her cheeks were creased from the sleeping bag. She scrubbed her eyes with the ball of a fist. "How do you know it's old-fashioned?"

"Because it takes a special key to wind it. See?" Opening the back, she inserted the slim watch key into the hole in the case and gave it a twist and then another. The movement made the plane-shaped fob and the other silver key clash together. "Why don't you try it? A couple twists is all you need."

Mattie gave the key a few dispirited turns, withdrew it, and then held it to an ear. "Okay, so it's ticking." Turning it over, she frowned how at the dial. "It's the wrong time."

"That's because you need the key to move the hands." She showed the girl how to slot the key over the center peg. "And see, now, when you turn it, the hands move. Why don't you set it for nine-ten while I see what we've got for food."

"Not much." Mattie worked the key with all the enthusiasm of the condemned. "I counted. We have to do something, Emma. Like, hurray, there was a drone, but it's been hours, and there's nothing. We can't wait around for someone to rescue us. I don't get that anyway. The drone doesn't make sense."

"Your guess is as good as mine," she said, reaching for the pack of their provisions. "The only thing I can figure is we're someplace that takes a long time to get to."

"No." Mattie gave an emphatic shake of her head. "It doesn't make sense. Because now that we've seen the drone, we can't leave, can we? Or we shouldn't? It's almost like it was a tease. Like, ha-ha, sit tight, we'll be back soonest."

"Oh, no, I don't think," she began—and then stopped. *Wait, she's right.* She and Will hadn't thought of that either.

"It's weird. If you see something that says, oh, rescue's on the way, you're not going to wander off even to look for food. You're going to wait for rescue to get here, but if you have no idea when rescue *might* show up…"

"You could be waiting a long time." They stared at one another, and then Emma ventured, "Checking us out?"

"Or waiting for us to get weaker or seeing how many of us are left? Or all three?" Mattie nodded. "Doesn't it feel like that to you?"

It did. Any of what Mattie had suggested was possible. But why?

"Do you think Hunter knows?"

I always knew this business would come back to bite us if we stayed in too long. She'd found it curious when Hunter said it then; she really wondered now. "I don't know. He might. I would have to ask him."

"If he'd even tell you."

"The guy's trapped, and he needs us. I think he'd tell us."

"Unless he's worried it will only make you mad and then you'll leave him." Then Mattie said, without a hint of irony, "It's something Scott would do."

This girl was way too grown-up for her own good.

After a moment's silence, Mattie prodded, "We have to do something to get ready."

"Whatever we do depends on what we find out."

"Then we need to think of all the possibilities and plan for them."

"Such as?"

"Such as, I don't know…*leave*? We would have to think about that no matter what, right?" Leaning against a pack, Mattie let the watch dangle like a mesmerist trying to hypnotize a volunteer. The fob and keys tinkled. "Come on, Emma, I'm only twelve, and I know we're in big trouble, drone or no drone or maybe *because* of the drone."

Now she felt like the slow student. "If they're not here to rescue us."

"Especially if they're not. It's been five days and now, with Scott and Hunter, we don't have enough food to last even another two. That means tomorrow has to be about making a plan, finding food, and maybe getting out of here, except how is that supposed to work? What about my mom? Yeah, we can dribble water into her mouth and she swallows and pees and she pooped, but that's all she does. What about if Will and Scott can't get Hunter out by tomorrow? Or what if they do? Will said the guy's feet are toast and probably most of his legs from the knees down. That means if we leave, we have to carry him *and* my mom. How do we do that?"

"We have the raft."

"Which means we'll be really slow unless we split up, like…you know…an advance scout to go hunting and the rest of us catching up. They did it in wagon trains."

Everything Mattie said made sense…but there was the *drone*. How did they *dare* to leave now that they'd seen it and vice versa? "It's like the Kobayashi Maru." She waved away the girl's frown. "Never mind. I still have to talk to Will tonight. We'll think of something."

"But what if we can't?"

"I don't know. Panic?"

"Ha-ha. Bet next you're going to tell me to look on the bright side of life."

"Never." Although a line from Monty Python did flit through her mind. "So," she said, inserting a note of cheer she did not feel, "what'll it be? Chili mac or beef ravioli?"

"Which tastes better?"

"From my experience? Chili mac." Although she was hungry enough to eat the packaging.

"Uhm...chili mac, I guess. Say, Emma?" Mattie was studying the silver key. "What does this key open?"

Peering through the gloom, she shrugged. "Beats me." Then it hit her how dark it was. "Mattie, when was the last time you fed the signal fire?"

"Oh, crap. Right before you came." Clambering to her feet, Mattie cupped her hands and peered through Will's window. "*Crap.* It's burned down to almost nothing. I see a couple of coals, but...*crap.*" The girl whirled from the window. "I can't believe I'm so stupid."

"Relax, even it's out, we can start it again in the morning, Mattie. No big deal."

"Yes, it *is.*" Sweeping up a boot, Mattie jammed in a foot and began to furiously lace up. "It was my only job, the *only* thing Will asked me to do and I *blew* it. I was supposed to keep the flame *going.*"

She heard the ghost of Earl's words in the girl's own. "And you will. We will. I can come help if you want. It's late. We always bank the fire now anyway."

"Oh. yeah." Mattie paused, her left boot only half-laced. "I guess that's right. You know what would be really good? If we could figure out a way to carry the fire with us so we don't have to keep starting from scratch or for when we run out of matches or lighters or whatever. Native Americans know how. So do Eskimos. I read it in a book."

"Did the book have instructions?" She reached for her own boots. It occurred to her that Will might know how to do this, too, but it might be important to let Mattie try first.

"Sort of?" Mattie finished lacing up but much more slowly as she thought about it. "You would need air. That is, for the embers you'd carry? Can't smother them, but it would be the same as banking a fire. You know, using ash and punk wood to protect the ember and not kill it. I have to think about it."

"You do that, then. Now, come on." She held out a hand. "Let's go keep that flame alive."

THE FIRE *WAS* MOSTLY OUT, and if it had been up to her, she'd have started over fresh in the morning. But she kept it zipped and only held the flashlight, moving it whenever Mattie said so the girl could see what she was doing. As Mattie fussed, she threw a quick look at their wood supply sheltered under its lean-to of Visqueen. If they did leave here, they would have to start all over, every day: a shelter, a fire, a woodpile, food, water. Worse, much of what they'd already managed...the lean-to, the wood pile, this signal fire, even their stupid latrine...all that would be left in their rear view. They could pack out a lot but not everything, especially if they were also taking out Rachel and Hunter on the raft or whatever half-assed stretcher they could rig. Maybe both would fit on the raft and maybe not, but no matter what, that was a two-person operation and heaven help them when it got to a rock scramble or steep downhill.

So, maybe only one of us should go. Dropping to her belly, she followed Mattie and wriggled back into their shelter. But go for what? To hunt? She thought again of the drone. Or not wait and get the hell out of Dodge?

As she shucked her boots, she looked over at Mattie who'd gone to check on her mother. "Still in the mood for chili mac?"

"Yeah." Mattie was studying her mother by flashlight. "What time is it anyway?"

"Late. Past ten. How's your mom?"

"The same, although…"

She stilled, her fingers poised to rip open the MRE's pouch. "Although what?"

"I think." Mattie pulled her head over a shoulder to look back at Emma. "I think she's dreaming."

"Really?" Abandoning the pouch, she scuttled down and wedged herself next to the girl. "Show me."

"Watch her eyeballs…there." Mattie pointed. "See? They're rolling."

The girl was right. Emma's gaze sharpened on the woman's face. Rachel's nostrils flared at irregular intervals, and the tiny muscles along her mouth twitched. Her breathing had become more irregular, too, and Emma thought back to her grandmother's mouser, Timmy. Whenever Timmy's whiskers would quiver and his paws twitch, Sarah quipped, *Got himself another critter.*

"Dreaming," Mattie said slowly, "is good. Right?"

Dreaming was normal. Did people in comas dream? Will would know. "I know people dream at different times of night."

"And lots of the time right before they wake up." Mattie's tone was tentative. "I read that in a book. I think we need to ask Will. Aren't you supposed to talk to him anyway?"

"Yes, but this isn't an emergency. Come on. We need to eat." She set about preparing their meal, ripping open the MRE's plastic pouch then pulling out packets and the flameless heater. (MREs were never *amazing*, but choking them down cold only added insult to injury.)

As she poured water into the flameless heater, Mattie asked, "Can we light candles now?"

"Sure. This will take about ten minutes. Why don't you set them up?" After slipping in the pouch of chili mac, she propped the heater on a boot near the entrance where there was a draft, started the timer on her watch then scooted back to where Mattie was screwing candles into the travel menorah. "You want to do the honors?"

"Yeah." After touching the tip of the burning *shamash* to each candle in turn, Mattie screwed the *shamash* back into place. *"Yehi 'or."*

"Yehi 'or." She caught Mattie giving her a look. "What?"

"Why don't you ever say the blessings? The Hebrew ones on the back of the box?" Mattie hesitated then added, "Will did. He didn't even have to look. He knew them by heart. I asked Will if he knew why you won't, and he said he didn't, but that I should ask you. So, you know, I'm asking."

Well, that answered the question about whether Will was Jewish. "Your grandfather and I had this same talk, more or less. I don't believe in any of that, Mattie.

PROTECTING THE FLAME

They'd be only words, and I don't see the point in saying thanks to something I don't believe in."

"You don't believe in God at all?" When she shook her head, the girl asked, "Do you believe in miracles?"

"I believe there are things we think are miracles because we can't explain them." She cocked her head. "You know science, Mattie, and math. What do you believe?"

"Sort of the same thing, especially after my dad. But then there are times when I see something really cool, like a pretty sunset or when I finally got to see Saturn through a telescope and then I get this *feeling*." Mattie pressed a bunched fist over her heart. "Right here, like something is so beautiful, so *amazing* my whole body fills up, and I feel like I'm going to burst. Sometimes, in the woods, if I'm walking and there's a bird singing, I feel the same way. Really…*big* inside like there's another part of me connected to something larger, and I like it. Why make us this way if there isn't a reason for it? That's what I don't understand."

"Me neither." Emma shrugged. "But feeling spiritual isn't the same as believing in a god or belonging to a religion."

"Then why do you wear that?" Mattie pointed. "Your star."

Her fingers caressed the pendant. "Because it belonged to my grandmother, and I like feeling close to her. It has nothing to do with a god or religion. Religions are nothing but systems people made up to explain the world. I mean, Mattie, look around." She gestured at the fuselage. "This is totally random. There's no purpose here or some god's plan. That would be like saying your dad got shot or your grandfather died for a good reason where there is none."

"Well…but Grampa dying means there's a little more food." At her expression, the girl said in a rush, "I know that sounds bad, but I bet he would've pretended not to be hungry so Mom and I would have more. If we hadn't crashed, I wouldn't have met you or Will." Mattie thought another moment. "If my dad hadn't died, like… would there be a Joshua now? Even if half of him is Scott?"

Or there might well have been a Joshua that was half her dad, but she didn't say that. And, seriously, there was a purpose to her grandfather's death? "I guess not believing is my choice, and—" Her watch beeped, and she said, "And I think it's time for dinner." Slipping out the pouch of chili mac, she ripped off the top. An aroma of hot tomato sauce, spicy beef, and macaroni ballooned out on a pillow of steam.

"Oh, wow," Mattie sighed. "That smells *so*…"

"Mmm."

They both froze. After a beat, Mattie said, "You didn't…"

"No," Emma said, and they both turned.

"Hey." Rachel's mouth moved in a weak smile. "That smells good."

"Oh my God," Emma said.

"Yeah." Mattie's mouth stretched in a joyous smile. "*Yehi 'or.*"

"THEY LOOK PRETTY NORMAL," Emma said into her handset. "One pupil's not bigger than the other."

"Will," Rachel called, "I feel fine. Well, except for the headache."

Will came back through a crackle of static. "We'll give you something for the headache, but I need Emma to finish checking you out. More importantly, how's the baby? Is it moving?"

"Oh, yeah." Now sitting, Rachel put a hand to her belly. "Kicking to beat the band."

"He's probably hungry," Mattie said.

"I know I am," said Rachel.

"Then, let's get some food into you, but I want you to go slow. What you need right now are hot fluids and plenty of them. You have a couple packets of broth tonight and maybe some crackers…Emma, do we have any crackers?"

"They were in the MRE we opened," she said.

"Then broth and crackers first and, if you keep that

down, Rachel, I don't see why you shouldn't eat as much as you want. Well, can," he amended. "Our rations are pretty tight. But we saw that drone, so…" He opted for an upbeat note. "It won't be much longer."

She felt Mattie's eyes and gave the girl a little shake of warning. *Not now.*

"Is…" Rachel raised a timid hand like a kid worried about giving the wrong answer. "Is Scott there? Can I speak to him?"

Emma thought that pause went on a beat too long. "Sure, he went to have a smoke, but let me get him. Hang on."

Figures. Leaving the handset with Rachel, Emma moved to the front of the shelter, lifted a small corner of their plastic sheeting to allow for ventilation, and lit Will's small canister stove. *The guy's wife wakes up, and he wanders off to have a smoke.* But she was being unfair. That might be the way Scott handled stress. Dumping a packet of chicken broth into their pot, she followed with what was left in her water bottle and stirred, listening with half an ear to one end of what sounded like a pretty stilted conversation: lots of *uh-huhs* and *okays.*

"Are you *sure* you're all right, Scott?" Rachel asked. "You don't sound good."

"Well, you know…hungry. Tired." Scott coughed. "I'd be out of smokes if I hadn't got that pack off of Burke."

The guy was really such a dick. "Soup's on, Rachel," she said. "Get it while it's hot."

Rachel held up a finger: *one second.* "I've got to go, Scott. See you tomorrow. Let me talk to Will one more time, okay?" When Will came on, Rachel said, "Can I *please* take this thing off my neck?" Inserting a finger over the top of the SAM still wrapped around her throat, Rachel gave the splint a little tug. "My neck is fine, and it's really kind of itchy."

"Sure. You don't know how relieved I am you're awake. See you tomorrow," Will said and cut the connection.

"Makes at least three of us," Emma said, and then thought she was being mean. Scott might not be one of those expansive type of guys, the kind who showered a woman with little things like, oh, *I love you* and *I was so worried.* She held out a mug of broth. "Trade you for the handset. Mattie, you want to get some crackers and peanut butter for your mom?" Bending, she scooped up the pocket watch and chain with its fob and keys where Mattie had left them, dropped them into a pocket then held up her empty water bottle. "I'm going to go out and fill this up with some snow."

Once she was outside, she moved away from the entrance, took out the handset, and touched off their prearranged signal: *break-break-break.* A few moments later, Will was back. "What's on your mind?" he asked.

A lot of things, actually, and some were contradictory. She could feel the war inside herself between wanting to believe that the drone meant something *good* versus a darker suspicion that it was not. "If we stay, I have a couple ideas about getting food. One is that I leave and go find game and bring it back."

"I hate that idea, and we shouldn't split up. Next." He

listened and then said exactly what she'd thought he would. "You can't be serious. Are you nuts?"

"No, I'm being practical. Will, we have to do *something.* Mattie's right. That drone is just too damned weird and, I swear to God, I think Hunter knows something he's not saying or is too scared to say. I don't know which it is, and it doesn't matter. Plus, we will have no food at all by the day after tomorrow unless you want to try your luck shooting a wolf." She'd actually not thought about *that* until this second.

"Well, Liam Neeson did it."

"In a movie." As she recalled, the characters complained that wolf tasted terrible. "But calories are calories."

"Uh-huh. And for bait, you would use…?"

"I'm thinking…" She pulled in a long breath. "It's something you're not going to like."

"Hit me." She did, and he said, "You're right. I don't like it."

"But it *would* work, Will." Boy, what did it say about *her* that she'd thought of it in the first place? This was like something out of the Ukrainian famine way back in the thirties when parents roasted their children or one of those apocalyptic survivalist novels, the ones where the power grids crash, and people start thinking about which juicy little kid they'll barbecue next. This wouldn't be *quite* so bad. Would it? "Besides, I'm not suggesting we use *him.* We use his clothes. They're in tatters to begin with, they're soaked in blood, and it's not as if we have any use for them."

"You do realize Hunter's trapped, right?"

"What does that have to do with this?"

"Everything. You'd be drawing in wolves using human scent and blood as bait. Fine, they're only Burke's bloody clothes, but the wolves won't differentiate. If we do this, someone has to be with Hunter all the time, which means that person gets the gun. But the fuselage isn't that far away. All those wolves have to do is follow their noses."

"You've been reading too much Jack London. Wolves don't operate like that."

"Mountain lions do."

She hadn't considered that. "Well, look, do you have a better idea? If we don't bring the game to us, that means we have to go get it and if someone has to do that, that means that person will need a weapon, and we only have one. Since you don't want to split up, that means we starve. If we stay, a wolf's all we've got."

"Unless a rescue team comes."

"We're still talking about that? Listen to me. Hunter would be a sitting duck, no matter what. How close are you guys to getting him out?" She got only the crackle of dead air and thought, *Shit.* "Are you serious, Will? You can't?"

"I'm not done trying yet."

That didn't sound hopeful. "Did you ever see that James Franco movie?"

"The one about Ralston?" Another pause. "Yeah, and I heard him speak at a conference. That was a much different situation."

"How? Hunter's legs are already starting to rot. I could smell it. So it's not different."

"No, it is, actually, because of two things. First off, the bones Ralston had to break were in his forearm not his leg. The ulna and radius aren't as thick; they're easier to break. But you have to stand on your legs and walk around. By definition, those bones must be thicker and stronger. Second, the mechanics were on Ralston's side. Because he was literally trapped between a rock and a hard place, it was as if his arm was in a vise. He was able to use torque to break it, but to do that, he had to be able to move the rest of his body. Hunter can't do that at all. See what I'm saying? I would have to figure a way to break both his legs and then amputate, but I... Jesus, Emma, I'm not a surgeon. I used to push drugs to kill cancers, not cut them out."

"You think Ralston was a surgeon?" It was brutal, but it wasn't like they had a ton of options here. "He broke the bones, he put on a tourniquet, he cut off his arm, and he got out. We're not talking neurosurgery, Will. We're talking giving Hunter a fighting chance and getting the hell out of here. He wouldn't be able to walk even if you could get him out, right? So we're going to be carrying him out, no matter what. How much longer can Hunter last if we don't get him out?"

"Another couple of days, maybe three. It's the hypothermia that's going to kill him before the sepsis can. I can warm him up a little but not enough. Even if we get him out now, I'm not sure he'll make it. He needs antibiotics, debridement." Will gave a bleak laugh. "The guy needs an entire trauma team. Where the hell are the planes, the rescue? I don't get it, I don't get it!"

"I'm telling you, that drone was weird. It might not

be related to a rescue or even the crash at all. What if it was…I don't know…some *guy* somewhere?"

"Who wouldn't notify anyone?"

"If his drone is illegal, maybe he wouldn't." That hadn't occurred to her either until this second.

"But how did it find us?"

"The ELT?" Then she thought, *Uh-oh.* "Will, if *that's* true…"

"Yeah, I know. If that drone homed in on the transponder, why hasn't anyone else?"

"So it could be a true, true unrelated. Yeah, we crashed. Yeah, there's a drone."

"And neither has anything to do with the other." A pause. "If we could only *get* to the thing and see if it's working."

"But we need a—" She stopped talking.

"Emma?"

Oh, my God. "Hang on a second, Will." She didn't want to jinx anything by saying what she was thinking out loud. Following her flashlight, she made her way around to rear of the plane and fanned her light over the tail.

The antenna was as she'd found it days ago: a slim white stalk with a bulbous end protruding from the plane about a foot away from the tail and rudder assembly. Below the antenna and along the left hand side of this section was a panel one find might covering a wall safe but instead of a combination, the panel was secured via lock and key. *It can't be that simple.* Dipping a hand into a pocket, she came out with the watch chain to which was attached that fob, the watch key… *And you.*

"Emma?"

"Hang on," she said again. The steel key winked a dull silver. Why hadn't she thought of this earlier? Maybe being half-starving and dealing with a guy in pieces had something to do with it. *But I'm here now.* She eyed the panel lock. There was no way to tell by looking. Sliding the key home, listening to the slight chatter of metal teeth against metal, she thought, *You watch, it won't work.*

But the key turned.

"Emma, what is it?"

"I found a key." Her voice sounded very far away or maybe it was that her pulse was beating a timpani in her temples. That odd smell she'd noticed that very first day fumed around her face and up her nostrils, and her mind conjured not only of smoke and late-night bars but of earthy peat and fire-blackened logs and expensive decanters and nice cut-crystal tumblers. "It fits. I got it open."

"Oh, my God. Is there a unit? Is it on?"

"Yeah, there's a unit. There are two, actually." Only one looked familiar. But there was other stuff crammed in here that also looked familiar—and made both no sense and all the sense in the world.

"What? Two? Well," Will amended, "unless he decided to mount a second unit that could transmit GPS. Those are pretty new, though."

"I don't think that's it." ELTs were of a type: thick, bulky orange rectangles bolted into place from which there were normally two wires. One was for the antenna, the other fed through the body of the plane to an audio alert and remote switch on the pilot's side of the cockpit. "Will, do you remember checking the remote switch?"

"For the ELT? On Burke's side? Yes, I told you it's on. Why?"

"Because the unit's off."

"What?" The word was flat. "The unit is…"

"Off, Will. As in it's not on. The main rocker switch is set to off, and there's no readout on the display."

"But that…he would've had to…"

She waited for him to finish and, when he didn't, she did it for him. "He turned it off, Will. Burke turned off the ELT before takeoff. But this other unit?" She studied the digital readout. "It's active."

"What's the frequency?" After she read out the numbers, he said, "That's not right. Standard for search and rescue is four-oh-six megahertz."

"Well, that's not this." She had an idea why, too. "Will, remember when we were talking to Scott about how they'd find us, and you mentioned a flight plan? Well, I don't think Burke filed one."

She waited while he absorbed that. "Because he thought he would be VFR, not flying by instruments," he said.

"No. I don't think he wanted a record of his exact route." That also explained why he'd turned off the main ELT but left this secondary unit, set to an entirely different frequency no one would think to monitor, active.

"But that makes no sense."

"Yeah, it does." Reaching in, she pulled out a very

large, very heavy block wrapped in opaque plastic and secured with industrial-strength duct tape. When she did, she heard a tiny slosh of liquid and a slight *chik* of glass. Liquid dripped from the block. Of course, this wouldn't have completely frozen. The really good Scotches, the ones designed for a celebration, were about seventy percent alcohol. Turning her light into the cavity, she remembered what Burke said about installing that new belly tank so he'd had plenty of fuel, which she'd found odd. Why bother with bladders of extra gas if they had all this extra fuel?

Because. Who said a tank could carry only fuel?

"Emma? Why does it make sense?"

"Because." In the light, the blocks were brighter than snow…and those bricks of bills looked awfully, awfully green. "It depends on who you're flying to meet."

YEHI 'OR

CHAPTER 1

ON THE MORNING of the sixth day...

"YOU'RE SHITTING ME," Will said. He and Emma were crouched around Hunter, still trapped in his copilot's seat. Emma had hustled down at first light and sent Scott back, ostensibly to be with Rachel and Mattie, but mostly to get him out of the way. Not that Emma thought letting an ex-addict anywhere near a whole lot of heroin and who knew how many bricks of banded twenties and tens was all that safe, but she'd not told Mattie what she'd found, only locked the panel back up again and kept the key.

"Are you serious, Hunter?" Will's gloved hands balled, and Emma was pretty sure that if Hunter wasn't a literal sitting duck, Will would've beat him silly. He might anyway, on general principle. "A smuggler?"

"No, a *mule*." Cocooned by his parka's hood, Hunter's

head was skull-like. His pallor gave him a spectral look, something the hectic glitter of fever in his sunken eyes did not dispel. Over the course of the past twenty-four hours, his skin had drawn down so tightly over his cheekbones, it was a wonder his face hadn't split in two. "He gets paid for the delivery, that's it. He doesn't get a cut of the sales."

"Yeah, I suppose that makes it all better. The hell you guys thinking? Drugs and money and booze, and you guys took on passengers?"

"That's why they hired him. It was part of the deal. Passengers make the flights look less suspicious. No one checks, and if you don't file a flight plan—" When Will interrupted with a curse, Hunter held up his gloved hands in surrender. "It's not mandatory if you're VFR, which we were."

"Until we got socked in, which your dad had to know about because he knew where we'd be flying. Did he happen to tell you where he was really going?"

"Yeah." Hunter slicked pearls of sweat from an upper lip. "South. After he dropped you all off."

"South *where*?"

"Not far. Wyoming. Yellowstone."

"Oh, for God's..." Will aimed that comment at the sky, which was overcast today. "So, you're saying that if anyone is looking for the plane, where it was supposed to end up at the very end of the day, they're looking for us hundreds of miles from here."

"But there are the radar pings." With the cloud cover, the air was not as cold and held a scent of a chilled beer can. More snow, Emma thought, and soon. "Will, there won't be any south of us. They'll still be looking in this general area."

"Yes, but with no help from an ELT. No one's going to think about trying another frequency." Will looked back down at Hunter. "That's what the drone was about, wasn't it? If anything happened to the plane, your employers would know where to look, right?"

"Look, they're not *my* employers, okay? That's what we were arguing about when you guys got there. Dad said he was getting out of the business. I honestly thought he was serious about that, too. It made sense when he outfitted the plane with a new belly tank and all because he *was* talking about doing more winter runs into Canada. I swear to God, I didn't have a clue until I saw those avgas bladders, and then I knew. He was going to fill that third one up, but I talked him out of it."

That explained the empty bladder. *Hot water for a bath, my eye.* "That's why you were worried about weight," she said.

"Shit, yeah. I'd seen the weather. I knew we weren't going to get a lot of miles fighting that headwind."

"But, Hunter, why did the engines stop? It wasn't because of the weight."

He shook his head. "I think...my dad...when he got the new belly tank, he replaced the wing tanks, too. If you put the selector in backward, the thing that controls which tank you're drawing fuel from..."

"I know what a selector is," Will interrupted. "You're saying your dad switched to an empty tank when he thought he was switching to a full one." At Hunter's nod, Will closed his eyes. "Well, that does explain it."

"Who are these guys?" Emma asked Hunter.

Hunter let his head fall back. "I told you, I don't know their *names* or even where they come from. But if they're the ones operating that drone, they know where we are, and they've got two alternatives. You need me to draw a map?"

"Yeah, actually, if that would get us the hell out of here," she sniped.

"Cut it out," Will rapped. "The choice is obvious. Whether we die or leave, they're not going to care. All they'll want is the cargo."

And they'd helpfully told them how many people to expect. Well, they had the advantage there because whoever was coming didn't know *they* knew why. "I haven't heard any more drones," she said.

"Which would suggest they're on their way." Will gnawed skin on a lower lip split and chapped by cold and wind. "You have to wonder, too. That drone wasn't, you know, something you buy at Walmart. It had to have some range, but it's also easier to overlook because people *are* looking for us. These guys can't chance an airplane or helicopter because that might get them the wrong kind of attention. So that means they've got to be coming on foot or, more likely, snowmobile, and then they have to climb, unless there's a way up opposite where we are that we don't know about because we haven't gone far in that direction. We've been focused on the cockpit."

"You think they're close."

"Now? Absolutely, but not at first. They've had all of yesterday afternoon and evening and this morning." He checked his watch. "It's half past nine. If they were close, I bet they could have walked here on their knuckles by now. That suggests…a little distance? A fair amount in terms of resources? Where do people get good long-range drones?"

"Military."

"Or border patrol. On either side. Yeah. Wouldn't be the first dirty agents in history."

She could tell him a thing or two about that. "So, what do we do, Will?"

"I don't know, Emma. I am coming up empty here." His bruises had gone a sickly yellow-green as the blood decayed and was reabsorbed, but Will had worked harder and longer than even she, and the elements, fatigue, and hunger were starting to show. Small fissures scored his cheeks, and there was a quarter-sized spot near his left ear that was fish-belly white with the beginning stages of frostbite. For the first time since this whole nightmare began, he'd not bothered to shave. "We have one weapon. Hunter is still trapped. I have to check her out, but I'm assuming Rachel can walk—"

"Walk?" Hunter straightened as far as he was able. "Wait a minute."

Emma ignored him. "She can walk. Mattie and I are fine." She didn't mention Scott. Let him drag his own sorry ass. She wished she could feel sorry or even sympathy for the guy. "But, at the risk of sounding like a racist stereotype, I truly know nothing about birthing babies."

Will managed a thin smile. "You'd manage. All I'm saying is that slogging through snow for umpteen miles won't help her or the baby, if it comes."

"You said yourself, the baby seems fine, and she feels all right. The thing is, we know *they're* coming, They have to be. It could be today, tomorrow, the day after that—"

"Or they wait for a spring thaw."

She shook her head. "All that money and the drugs? I wouldn't take that chance. People are probably still looking for us and they know it. I'm saying we strip the plane and leave. Let them have their shit."

"No, wait, you can't leave me." Hunter's face shivered with emotion. His eyes pooled. "I'm a sitting fucking duck. If they don't get me, the wolves will or that mountain lion or, shit, I'll rot and die that way. You might as well put a bullet in my brain right now."

"Not everyone's leaving," she said, keeping her eyes on Will. She saw the moment the words registered.

"Wait a minute," he said, his eyes widening. "You can't be serious. You?"

"You see anyone else who can?" She ticked the items off on her fingers. "One, you're the only doctor. Two, that means Rachel needs you. Hell, it means everyone does. Mattie could fall and break a leg or whatever. Third, Scott is…let's just say he's unreliable. He also happens to be Rachel's husband and that's his kid she's carrying. He should be with them." Turning her hands palms up, she finished with a shrug. "That leaves only one person to stay with Hunter."

"No, it doesn't, and you know it." He took her by the

elbows, his grip steady and strong, and drew her close enough she saw the flecks of gold in his eyes and her reflection captured there.

"Damn you," he said, a tremor in his voice. "It means leaving two."

CHAPTER 2

AFTER BUILDING UP THE FIRE, they left Hunter, reasoning he'd be safe for the short time it would take for her to gather a few supplies she'd need for the long night and return. Clambering back up the cliff path took all their breath and not a little of her strength. By the time she made it to the top, she felt as rubbery as Gumby. She could understand why, in all those stories of forced marches, people sometimes fell and couldn't make their feet again. She didn't know what she could do about that either.

God. If I'm running low on gas, what about you? She almost put a hand on her belly but caught herself in the nick of time. She was not going down that road. This thing growing in her wasn't a *you*. It was cells. A powerful cluster of cells, yes, enough to play hell with her hormones and make her sick in the mornings and change her body. But she sure as hell wasn't going to go all maternal here.

"You okay?" Will asked.

"Fine." She kept her eyes on the well-worn path they'd carved over days of moving back and forth between the cockpit and fuselage. "How long have you known?"

"Since the first day. When I examined you, I could feel your womb and your..." He cleared his throat. "Women's breasts change when they're pregnant. But I would be lying if I said I was a hundred percent sure."

She kept her gaze fixed on the trees straight ahead. In a few more minutes, she should be able to see the orange spark of their signal fire. "What changed?"

"Well, there's you being sick every morning. You can only blame the altitude and shock for so much. But then the night you stayed with Hunter, when Mattie and I lit the menorah—"

"Oh." The realization broke over her mind the way a shaft of sun pierces thick clouds. She'd kept the menorah and candles in her pack. "You found the pills."

"Actually, Mattie did. Don't worry. I said they were some kind of medicine for headaches or something. But, yeah." They crunched over snow for a few seconds before he asked, "By my exam, you're further along than for the time frame the meds are designed for. They're best by eight weeks at the latest. And you're—?"

"About eleven weeks." By Christmas...God...if this was the sixth day of Hanukkah, that meant Christmas was two days away, and she would be three months along, through the first trimester. She would still have plenty of time for an abortion. The procedure would only be more involved, that was all.

"Well, I don't know if the pills would work, but I'm

not an obstetrician. They might, if you wanted to try. Do you?"

"I don't know. I know I didn't want to do it now, *here*. I was thinking when we're back in civilization would be nice. I do know that if there's something wrong with the fetus, I will. I won't even hesitate. I know other people make different choices about what to do if they've got a fetus with Down's or some other congenital problem. But I know me."

"I'm a doctor. You don't have to justify anything to me. I respect whatever choice you make. But I'm not the one who's pregnant. It's why I didn't say anything until today. This is none of my business. I figured you would tell me yourself if and when you were ready."

"Yeah." She didn't know how she felt that he knew. She ought to be ashamed. She'd gotten herself into this mess and still wasn't sure how to fix it. "That's why you kept after me to eat. It's why you gave me your energy bars."

"At least you kept them down. Look, I'm sorry I sprang it on you this way. I wasn't going to say anything, but you didn't give me much choice." He stopped walking and turned to face her. "I can't let you risk this. You can't stay by yourself."

"I'm pregnant, Will, not sick." It hit her that she hadn't been queasy at all this morning. "Women have been pregnant for centuries in harsher conditions than this. If I were back on base, I'd still be doing PT or whatever. I think the only thing I'd get out of is standing at parade rest for longer than fifteen minutes and riding in a vehicle on unpaved roads. Apparently, they worry about the vibrations."

He let out a silent dog's laugh. "I would suspect there's nothing in regs about airplane crashes."

She smiled back up at him. "Apparently not, although they might have had something to say about all that turbulence."

"What about the father?"

"What about him?"

"Does he—"

She cut him off. "Yes. He wants nothing to do with it or me. In fact, he told me to get rid of it. He's married, got kids. It was a mistake. I was stupid. He—"

"You don't owe me an explanation."

"But I want to tell you. He was Ben's CO." Saying that made her face flame. "At first, it was him making condolence calls, you know? An invite to come to his office, go for a walk, and then it was a drink and then meeting for more drinks and then…" She slicked her lips. "I…we ended up in bed. More than once. It was…I was…it went on a while. Three, four months."

"Hey." He still wore a sling to rest his shoulder, and now he circled the fingers of his good hand around her left wrist. "It's okay. I understand. I told you." His thumb found her naked, scarred skin. "I know grief when I touch it."

"Yeah. It was a way for me to remember Ben, I guess. He would talk about what a good investigator Ben was, but how the pressure must've gotten to him, that kind of thing. Then, one night, he asked me how much Ben had told me about what he was working on because it was highly classified and blah, blah." She blew out a shaky breath. "That's when I knew."

"Knew what?"

"That Ben hadn't killed himself. *I* gave Ben the idea, not the other way around. *I* was the one who'd heard about a smuggling ring from a sergeant I knew and passed it to Ben. He was working this strictly off the books. He didn't tell anyone in his command, not even his partner."

She watched as Will sorted through this information. "You're saying the CO was involved? In the smuggling ring?"

"It wouldn't be the first time. A Special Forces guy was arrested down at Elgin in Florida for the same thing. This was back in October. They got him with ninety pounds of cocaine. You're talking a street value of several million, and they think this is only the tip of the iceberg because the Special Forces guy was part of a unit involved in counter-drug operations in Mexico and South America."

"Where did your source think this smuggling ring operated out of?"

"Idaho, mostly. Big ring in Boise, but Wyoming, too, like Burke's people. Both are perfect because you've got all this land and no people to speak of."

"And you think Ben's CO had your husband murdered because he got too close?"

She nodded. "He told me the higher-ups had investigated and found there was nothing there. Ben killed himself, and I needed to accept that."

"But you obviously don't."

"I…I think it's hard to know. Undercover work is…"

He interrupted. "Is that why you tried to kill your-self?" When she nodded, he said, "Not because of the baby?"

"God, no." Despair washed through her veins. "I thought that maybe Ben's CO might be right. That kind of work can swallow you up." In the month leading to his death, Ben *had* become moodier and more with-drawn. "So, there are days when I think, yeah, he took his service weapon and blew his brains out all over our bathroom. Then, there are others when I think whoever was pulling the strings on this operation, whether it was his CO or someone else, caught up with him because there are my parents, too, dying in that car crash. You can say coincidence, sure. But that happened when I started making noise. Except I can't prove anything. My tip is only a tip, that sergeant is sure as hell not going to talk to me anymore, and everything Ben did was classi-fied. Anything I know is in my head. There's my sister and her children, too. I can't risk it. I have to let it go." Not to mention the fact that she was now responsible for yet another life, a child Ben and she had talked of having, eventually. She thought of Mattie and her rage at her mother for carrying a baby Mattie's father had wanted. Emma wasn't all that different from Rachel.

"So, what are you going to do? Leave the military?"

"Don't think I haven't thought of that, but to do what? I'm a journalist. Newspapers are dying. Eking out a living as a stringer isn't appealing. Besides, do you know how hard it is for a single mother, in general? The world's a pretty messed up place, Will, and right now, with climate change and right-wing governments, and all the rest, it feels as if it's only getting worse. Who in their right mind brings a baby into a world like this?"

"I suspect people have been asking that question for generations."

"Doesn't mean it's not true." She debated then said, "My grandmother had a sister, Klara. She went back to Poland in the early thirties."

"That sounds like incredibly bad timing."

"How about the worst? She met a man named Robert. They got married and settled down."

"Where?"

"Warsaw."

She heard his intake of breath. "Oh, Jesus," he said. "They were in the ghetto?"

She nodded. "He ran a newspaper. She liked books and wanted to be a writer. They joined up with this secret underground research organization, the *Oyneg Shabes*."

"Joy of the Sabbath. Interesting name."

"The group used to meet after Shabbos services to talk about that week's work, but Sarah once said it was because, on Shabbos, you've lit candles, you've welcomed the Sabbath Queen, and, if you're really orthodox, you believe the lights to the gates of the Torah are open and you're that much closer to God. She thought they ought to have called themselves 'Protectors of the Flame.'" That made her think of Earl and what he'd said about Inuit women.

"Did they call themselves that?"

"No. They said they were 'The Librarians.' They

made it their mission to document everything about life in the ghetto, so we're talking gathering and publishing books, memoirs, letters, poetry. They even kept train tickets and candy wrappers. They wanted to make sure people knew who they'd been, but they were also worried of being discovered so a lot of it was done piecemeal, like in cells? That way, if anyone was caught, they couldn't give up the whole show. My grandmother's sister ran a soup kitchen, a *folkskikh*. It was the real deal, but it was also a good cover for passing documents back and forth. When things got really bad, right before the ghetto uprising in 1943, they buried it all. No one found any of the materials until 1946, but the archive still exists. It's in New York now."

"What happened to them? To Klara and Robert?"

This was something she'd only told Ben. "The Uprising and then Treblinka happened. Well, that is, Treblinka happened to Robert. After the Uprising, Klara got sent to a labor camp. She knew she was pregnant when the Nazis emptied the ghetto. She'd been *this* close to having an abortion, but either she dithered too long or there was no time...I don't really know. All I do know is if she'd been showing, they'd probably have killed her right there and then. There were doctors in some camps—most of them were doing abortions, of course—but there were also a couple of midwives. For whatever reason, some women were allowed to come to term, which was pretty cruel because they would kill the babies right away. But my bubbe said, my grandmother Sarah?"

"I know what a bubbe is." He showed a faint smile.

"My grandfather always said, *Oyb di bobe volt gehat a bord, volt zi geven a zeyde.*"

"Oooh." She knew what that meant. *If Grandma had a beard, she'd be Grandpa.* "Nice guy."

He gave his silent dog's laugh. "He had his moments. Great accent, though."

"Where did your family come from?"

"England, believe or not. My great-grandfather had a tea shop, the first in Whitechapel and then a second, much bigger and swankier place in Hampstead. The family apocrypha's that he met Freud."

"You're kidding."

"Scout's honor. This happened a couple months after Freud escaped from Germany. So the story goes that Freud invited Virginia and Leonard Woolf for tea, but they needed cakes because their baker fell through at the last second or something and everyone knows that tea is about the cakes and sandwiches. Is it true?" He shrugged. "Virginia Woolf noted the tea in her diary. So, it's not impossible. But we're not talking about me. What happened with Klara?"

"Sarah thought Klara was allowed to come to term because she didn't fit the stereotype of a Jew. She was this gorgeous blue-eyed, blond-haired, very Aryan-looking woman. Right around that time, some camps would take Jewish babies from mothers who could easily pass and gave them to Nazis to raise as their own. The program was called *Lebensborn.* That's what happened with Klara's little girl. They took the baby and, even though Klara survived, she never saw that child again. She looked, too. For years."

She fell silent. For a few heartbeats, they simply stood together, hand in hand, and there was nothing but the hollow moan of wind through trees, a *whump* as heavy snow slid from a bough. Then, Will said, quietly, "Why did you tell me that?"

"Because." She breathed out, watching as the wind carried the word away. "I think of Klara, despite everything, having that baby in the worst possible conditions, and yet she still came out the other side, and I can't figure out what the bigger miracle: that she lived or her baby did. And then here I am, and I've made a mess of things."

"No, you haven't," Will said. "You've helped make a life."

CHAPTER 3

WILL and the others left before noon. The last she heard from them, she'd been down at the cockpit and they were two miles distant from the crash site and at the very edge of their walkie-talkies' range.

"You could follow," Will said. "Mattie's leaving blazes the whole way, and you should be able to follow our tracks."

The temptation to do that pricked at her neck. "You know I can't. We decided. Someone has to stay with Hunter and that's me. So," she changed the topic, "how's it look?"

A long, static-filled silence followed, and she was about to repeat the question when he said, "I don't know. We're headed downhill, so that's good, but all I see are mountains and more mountains. Best we can hope for is we come on a game trail or maybe an old fire road. If we're really lucky, we find an old hunting cabin or something. Like that movie with Anthony Hopkins."

"Oh, uh…" She knew which one he meant. "Plane crash, happens in Alaska, they get stalked by a grizzly."

"That's it. I remember I thought Alec Baldwin's teeth were too white for a guy who'd been out in the wilderness for a week or something. But they found a cabin and a boat."

"It was a movie."

"And this is reality, Greg."

"*E.T.*"

"I was always partial to *Close Encounters* myself."

"Why?" Then she laughed. "Right. Because you wanted to be an astronaut." She'd have pulled a Roy Neary, too, and gone off with the aliens. Man, if she got out of this, she was making a massive amount of popcorn and hunkering down with Netflix and Amazon Prime for a solid month. "Everyone else okay?"

"Well, considering that we only left you two hours ago, we're fine. Mattie's pissed, but she'll get over it. She wanted me to tell you not to light the menorah again until we're all together. Oh, and she said that if you eat the Almond Joy without her, you're a dead man."

"Deal." Though she wasn't sure she could honor that promise. "Is she there?"

"No, I moved off into the woods a good ways, you know, in case Hunter had…"

"Sure." She listened to the air fizz and thought of all the things they'd left unsaid. "We better stop talking then. Save your batteries."

"Right. Listen, turn on your unit about every six hours starting now, okay? Leave it on this band and when you come on, do three quick breaks. That'll take less energy, but that will tell someone you're there. I'm betting that if we find help or someone stumbles on us, they'll probably have better handsets. Once they figure out you're on, they can talk to you, let you know they're on their way, probably even triangulate on your signal, okay?"

"Good idea." She didn't want to sign off. "I'd better go. Good luck, Will. Thanks for..." *Being my friend. Being a good man.* For being someone she wanted to hold close, skin to skin, with no barriers or regrets. His wife was one lucky lady. "Everything."

"Thank me later," he said. "You and I? We're not done yet."

CHAPTER 4

"THAT'S EN-ENOUGH, TH-TH-THAT'S ENOUGH." Averting his face, Hunter gave her hand a weak shove. He sucked a dribble of broth from his lower lip. "Don't waste any more food on me."

"Come on," she coaxed, trying to maneuver the steaming mug back to his mouth. "You have to stay hydrated at the very least, and Will said the salt was good."

"Huh. G-g-good for *yuh-you*." Hunter let out a weak laugh that nevertheless fizzed with both despair and a sort of hysteria. Shuddering, he hunched down in his seat as if trying to capture as much heat as he could. "C-c-can't stop sh-shaking. That's b-b-b-bad, isn't it?"

Well, it certainly couldn't be good. It was early afternoon of the seventh day. The day before, she'd disassembled enough of the cockpit to move both the fire and reflective barrier closer to Hunter. The cockpit was open to the night sky and would never be toasty, but heat pulsed at her back, and she'd dragged off her watch cap. She might be weak from lack of food, but at least she was warm.

"Look," she said, sponging fever sweat from Hunter's forehead, "you need to keep drinking like Will said. So you've got to cooperate, Hunter. Otherwise, what are we doing here?"

"G-g-good," Hunter stammered then forced out the rest, "*question*. W-watching me d-d-die?"

She bit back the urge to snap. "You know why I'm here. I'm trying to keep you alive so you *don't* die before they find us. You have to have faith, Hunter." My God, what was she saying? But she *did* have faith and how weird was that? She had faith in Will. She might even have found a little faith in herself. After all, she was still here and Will was right: there was a life, a small flame inside, she had to protect. If she didn't, no one would.

"F-f-faith?" Hunter gave that hysterical hyena's cry again. "You th-think W-W-Will...if the g-g-guys my d-dad get h-here..."

"I know, I know." She didn't need chapter and verse again. Earlier, she'd thought she'd caught a faint grumble of something like a motor drifting up from the valley. She'd gone absolutely still, trying to parse that out, but the sound had been as ephemeral as a soap bubble and did not come again. Hunter hadn't commented either. Probably her imagination, then.

She glanced at her watch. Almost two. Already, though, the distant hazy peaks were beginning to purple, and shadows gathered in the lower, northern slopes and along the valley's floor.

"There's only about three hours of daylight left, and it's been two days since the drone," she said. "Not much time left today for any bad guys to put in an appearance unless they're into roughing it for a night." Which they might be. Anybody who did hike or ride in would have to be ready for that possibility, but she kept coming back to the reality that people were looking for them. Surely, they couldn't be so far off-course the plane wouldn't be spotted, or the fires she kept going both here at the cockpit and back at the fuselage.

She and Will had discussed that, whether it made sense for her to keep shifting between the two locations, but she'd pointed out she would have little else to do, and staying on the move would be better than remaining in place. Besides, the more fires there were, the better the chance someone—like Hank Patterson's people, that Kujo guy—might spot the thermal signature via the *right* kind of drone or helicopter. Although they'd switched on the ELT and switched *off* the other transmitter, the simple fact of no search planes or helicopters having appeared wasn't a hopeful sign. On the other hand, military drones didn't necessarily operate where they would be spotted or heard because this defeated the purpose of, say, sneaking up on the bad guys.

"Listen." Squaring the mug on a bit of intact console near Hunter's left hand, she stood, but too fast. A swoon of vertigo swirled through her head, and she staggered, nearly falling back into the fire.

"H-h-hey!" Hunter's hand shot out and grabbed her coat to steady her. "Are y-you…"

"I'm fine." She swallowed back against another swoop of dizziness. Her mouth was sour and rank, though she wasn't worried about tossing her cookies. She had absolutely nothing in her stomach to vomit.

And therein was the problem. Other than a cup of broth drunk under Will's careful eye the day before, she'd had only water. Her blood sugar had to be in the basement. It wasn't that she had no appetite. She was trying to make the half an MRE and two energy bars, all the food she had standing between her and outright starvation, last. Well, there was the Almond Joy, but she would only touch that when she'd exhausted every other option. Tearing into it before then would be a complete jinx. Yes, call her superstitious.

Though she could still bait the wolves. It wasn't a bad idea, except she didn't have any weapon now other than the hand axe, KA-BAR, and her flare. That had been quite the discussion, too. Will wanted to leave the rifle, but that would mean *them* traveling with only a knife or axe and no ability to hunt. She would have the fires. So long as she tended them, she was reasonably certain she would be safe. She would also be *starving*, but six of one, half dozen of the other.

It was the afterward part, if Hunter died before help or the bad guys came, she was a little fuzzy about. The plan was for her to follow the trail the others would leave. It was, in fact, a decent idea. If worse came to absolute worst and Hunter died, she could either hunker down in place or leave. Without a rifle, she wouldn't be able to take out the wolves or a cougar (or its friends; geez, she hoped it didn't have friends). She could snare food, but she would have to be farther down-valley for that.

Oh, stop. She was tired of thinking and rethinking the same thoughts. "I'm going back to bank the fire at the fuselage. It won't be dark for a couple hours yet, but I want to give myself plenty of time." As Hunter opened his mouth to protest, she put a hand on his shoulder. "I'm not leaving you. I won't be long, but I do have to do this. The more hot spots I keep going, the better the chance someone will see."

"Oh-oh-k-kay." Swallowing hard, Hunter jerked a nod. "Ok-kay. J-just b-be b-b-back before the wuh-wuh-*wolves*…"

"I won't let the wolves get you." Dragging on her watch cap seemed to take a lot longer than it ought to, but she still managed a smile. "You know what we really need? You ever seen *Dracula*? Not the one with Bela Lugosi but the remake with Gary Oldman. Coppola film?"

"Uh…" Hunter's brow crinkled. "N-n-no. Who's C-C-Coppola?"

"Director? *Apocalypse Now*? Never mind," she said, waving away Hunter's perplexed expression. "Anyway, there's this great scene where Anthony Hopkins, who's Van Helsing…do you know the *Dracula* story at all?" When Hunter shook his head, she sighed. "Well, you do know he's a vampire, right? So, the good guys are out to stop Dracula only they get surrounded by these vampire brides in the woods, and so Professor Van Helsing lights this circle of fire to keep them out. It's really cool. Anyway, that's what we need, a ring of fire to keep the baddies at bay. Something that would burn a long time. Torches, maybe, or something."

Hunter opened his mouth, closed it then said, "We m-might could d-do that."

CHAPTER 5

Tools. Hunter had specified which tools she needed to bring back. *A Phillips No. 2, a monkey wrench.* She kept going over the list in her head as she made her way back, which seemed to be taking her longer and longer. *Hungry. Getting weak and...* She pushed all that away with an impatient mental shove. She had to focus here. *Monkey wrench. Wire cutters to be on the safe side.*

But you'll probably get by with the Phillips, if it comes down to it, Hunter had said. *All you have to do is unscrew all the cowl fasteners that are still intact.*

"Right," she panted as she tried to make her feet move faster. "Piece of cake."

What else? Oooh, something to catch liquids. A bucket. She needed to bring the bucket they'd been using for a chamber pot. Maybe also spare clothes? Clothes could be dunked, fashioned into torches, and oil theoretically ought to burn for a long time.

It was amazing they hadn't thought of this before. Why not use the ton of avgas, too? Hunter said it burned well in a container at a rate of about three minutes an ounce but wasn't something you'd put in a bucket or next to a fire. *I don't know if sparks would make it go ka-BOOM*, Hunter had said, *but I'm not real anxious to find out either.*

Actually, she knew the answer to this one because she'd asked the same question about the scene in *Thelma and Louise* where the two women shoot the fuel tanker of a creepy guy who's been leering at them for most of the movie. Of course, the tanker went up in a huge fireball. Except the *MythBusters* guys said that couldn't happen. A gunshot wouldn't cause an explosion, but a spark could.

If there was one thing all these firs and pines had it was plenty of resin, which meant plenty of sparks.

So, the gas was out for her big Van Helsing fire-ring, unless she could figure a way of burning only small amounts. Maybe line small depressions in the snow with Visqueen? That could keep water from mixing with the gas. She could almost visualize it, too, like the oil cups of a menorah. An image of Bubbe Sarah, head covered with a lacy veil, lighting her old-fashioned nine-branched oil candelabra floated to the front of her brain.

I bet I can do that. She could use clothes for wicks and then they'd have something that would be exactly like a menorah, too, but on an industrial scale because while the Chieftain's engine cowling was damaged, the engine was intact—and so was the oil pan.

"How much oil are we talking?" she'd asked when Hunter suggested it. "And what kind?" Synthetic oil wouldn't burn for long. It was designed not to in order to cut down on engine fires.

"M-mineral oil," Hunter had said. "About eight qu-quarts. Engine's n-new, s-so you d-don't use synthetic. G-g-gunks up the works."

She wondered how long mineral oil would burn. Maybe a pretty long time if they were talking pure. Her bubbe had used a special grade of olive oil for her menorah because the rules were that the oil or a candle must burn for a minimum of thirty minutes every night. The flames in Sarah's menorah didn't go out until near midnight most evenings, same as the candles her own mother had used. She remembered being little and wandering down to the kitchen well after her parents had gone to bed to find the menorah, which her mother had put in the sink to guard against fire, still burning.

Wheezing from the exertion, she paused at the verge and studied the Chieftain's remains. Only that morning, she'd thought how the thing really *felt* like a wreck, a husk of something long abandoned. Even the trickle of smoke from the fire she was tasked to keep burning seemed more like something from the aftermath of some calamity. In some ways, she'd actually dreaded coming here to stoke this fire because she was never sure if Hunter would be alive when she got back. This morning, she'd actually considered letting the damn thing go out. Then, she'd stay with Hunter until...well, until whatever happened did.

But now we have a plan. We have a way of lighting up the night.

First things first: stoke this fire. That wouldn't take

long. Then grab the tools, the bucket. *And cloth and the gas with some plastic liner.* Ooh, wait. The Visqueen might not be the best idea. Carrying the gas in that spare bladder would work, but *burning* it in plastic could be pretty toxic…She chuckled at that. Toxic gases were the least of her worries. Still, it would be nice not to kill herself any sooner than absolutely necessary. She might still decide the gas was too much trouble, but she was totally down with whatever burned and kept burning.

The woods were still, even more so than normal. Her steps were loud in the quiet, the snow made crunchy from several days of softening by the sun only to freeze back up as soon as the light was gone. The tracks and chunked snow left by the others were clearly visible. She could pick out Mattie's smaller prints alongside her mother's. When she'd seen them off, Will had been in the lead, a smooth slight trough showing where he'd been towing the inflatable raft, while Scott brought up the rear. Mattie had waved frantically until the very last, when they'd come to a bend and were swallowed up by trees. Even Scott had tossed a look back…though there was something in the set of his shoulders that made her a little uneasy. She wasn't sure why, but she bet he sensed she and Will were leaving him out of something and that this didn't sit well.

Well, yeah. Using the hand axe, she hacked off small twigs for kindling. *A cop with a drug problem?* Leaving Scott out of this particular loop seemed wise.

Sliding branches atop orange embers, she smiled as the fir caught with sputters and pops, the resin providing a ready, easily flammable medium. Once the fire was crackling, she ducked into their now-abandoned fuselage. The place seemed enormous now that there was no one inside. Her sleeping bag was still spread on the deck as was her backpack. Shrugging off a lighter, smaller pack she used to carry items back and forth, she went to the cargo locker and opened the lid. The locker was empty of everything except the toolbox, several lighters, a package of batteries, a roll of extreme weather duct tape, and a packet of firesticks. Opening the toolbox, she selected the Phillips, the wire cutter, and a socket wrench. Transferring her flare from a parka pocket to her hip, she slipped the tools into her jacket.

As she stood, her gaze fell on that empty avgas bladder still in the cargo hold. Maybe she *should* try the avgas trick. If oil burned, certainly oil and avgas were better, right?

Grabbing the bladder, she worked her way out, made another quick check of the fire then went around to the other side where she'd dragged the still-full bladders. Unpacking the extra, she unfurled a short hose attached to one of the containers already filled with gas, released the clamp, and listened as fluid gurgled and sloshed. *Don't fill it too much.* She kept hefting the rapidly filling bladder. *Liquids always weigh a ton—*

"What are you doing?"

"Oh!" Startled, she jumped back, dislodging the hose, which flew from the bladder's mouth, releasing a spray of avgas.

"Jesus!" Scott shouted as gas sprayed the front of his parka and jeans. He hopped back, his boots making splashing sounds in the gas still gushing out of the hose. "What the *fuck*?"

"*Scott.*" Bending, she fumbled with the clamp and stopped the flood of fuel. "What are you doing—"

She stopped when she saw the two men standing behind Scott. One was young with the crooked nose of a brawler. The other, older man had a jowly, hangdog look that reminded her of Tommy Lee Jones. Both wore big, kitted-out black balaclavas they'd rolled up to their foreheads, snowsuits, heavyweight Pac boots, expedition ski mitts, and black turtlenecks. From the snaps on the collars of their snowsuits, she also saw she'd been right about what she'd heard earlier in the day. The snaps were for riders to snap to snowmobile helmets.

"Who are you?" she asked.

"Agent Talbot." The Tommy Lee Jones lookalike extended a gloved hand. "DEA."

"Oh, my God." She automatically took the offered hand, but what she really wanted was to fall down. She was suddenly even weaker, but now with relief. "How did you get here? Did Will...are they, is everybody..."

"They're good. Met up with these guys and a whole rescue party on the trail. Will sent me back to help out with the DEA. You know." Scott shrugged. "Seeing as how it's my job and all."

He got my dad killed, and he got kicked out of the cops. That's what Mattie had said. *And he's lucky he's not in jail because he should be.*

"Yes," Talbot seconded, still gripping her hand. "Detective Paisley here says you have something we very much want to see."

"Oh," she said. "Well, wow, you don't know how good it is to see you guys. I don't know if we could've made it through another day."

Another day? Hah.

Chances were she had no more than five minutes left.

CHAPTER 6

"You've got the key?" Talbot was inspecting the locked panel where she'd found the drugs and cash.

"Yes." No point in lying about it. They knew she had it because Scott knew. Scott must've pried the information from Mattie somehow, or maybe he'd overhead the girl talking to her mother.

Think. Pulling the key from a pocket, she fiddled with detaching it from the watch chain. She could've handed the chain to Talbot, but she needed every second she could manage to figure out what to do. "How did you find us, Agent Talbot? We've been stuck up here for days. Was that your drone we saw? We heard it a couple days ago, but boy, it really took you guys—"

"You need help with that?' It was the younger guy. "Why don't you—"

"No, no, I got it." Slipping the key from the chain, she offered it to Talbot. "Sorry, a little shaky. I haven't had anything to—" She dropped the key as Talbot extended his hand. "Oh God, I' so sorry. I…"

"It's fine." Pulling off a glove, Talbot scooped the key from the snow. He wiped it and his hand dry on his snow pants.

"So how did you find us?" she asked, pocketing the chain and fob again. Instead of shoving on her gloves, she stuffed them into a pocket then slipped her hands into her hip pockets. The right was a tight fit, what with the flare. She took a step back, mindful where she put her feet, then wondered if that would even matter.

"They found us first," Scott said before Talbot could respond. "Will was checking, you know, dialing through the frequencies, and then these guys came on."

"Oh." What had happened to Will and the others?

Talbot was playing with the lock. "We'd picked up an extraneous signal we'd seen before. It was a band of a known smuggling ring. We were finally able to pinpoint your location, but it took a while to mobilize people. We had to coordinate with the Canadians. You're actually straddling the border here."

"Yeah, we wondered about that." This story was plausible enough to be true. Maybe something had happened to Will or Scott had overheard Will talking to the agents and then volunteered to lead them here. Will would want to stay with Rachel. *But wait, if they really have been rescued, those people would have doctors, right? Or medics?* Will would have no reason to stay with Rachel. He would be itching to get back to her and Hunter.

"I'm surprised Will didn't tell you about checking

309

the frequency and letting me know. We had a signal worked out."

"Yeah?" Scott frowned. "You did?"

"Yes." *Oh, Will.* She had to do something.

"Damn this thing." Straightening, Talbot let out an exasperated sigh. "It's frozen."

"Yeah, it does that. I had to use a lighter the first time around. Sorry, it must've gotten blocked up with ice." She made a show of patting pockets then pulled out a lighter. "Here. Try this."

"Thanks." Flicking the striker wheel, Talbot got a flame going then held it to the lock. "That's got it…ah." Socking in the key, Talbot gave it a twist. "There we go."

"Holy shit." Scott crowded in on Talbot's right as the younger guy, snow boots splishing, came up on Talbot's left. Reaching in, Scott came out with a wad of banded cash. "How much are we talking here? A million?"

"Try more like three," Talbot said, handing a brick to the younger guy. "Check that."

"No sweat, but why the fuck is it wet? Is that—" The younger guy gave the packet a sniff. "Is that Scotch?"

"Yeah, there were broken bottles in there." Her right hand found what she was looking for, and now she carefully twisted. "Careful. Don't want to cut yourself."

"I'll watch myself," the younger guy said, " though it's not like there isn't plenty here to kill the pain." Digging out a small knife, he cut a small slit, dipped in the tip of his knife, gave the white powder a sniff then flicked out the tip of his tongue and made a face. "It's good."

"So is that heroin? Or cocaine? What's that taste like anyway?" Snagging the cap, she jammed that back in her hip pocket before it could fall to the snow. The loop was exactly where Will said it would be. "You know, in movies, they're always tasting and rubbing stuff on their gums."

"That's for cocaine." Talbot was looking at the younger guy. "Well?"

"Bitter as shit." Turning to Scott, who was jamming wads of cash into his jacket, the young guy hooked a thumb. "Hey, not like that. Evidence, man. Bags are back with the Snowgos. Go grab a couple."

"You don't have to tell me twice." Scott slipped in a brick, though. "And one to grow on," he said and jogged in the direction of the woods where Will and the others had gone.

"What an asshole," the young guy said.

"Well." Talbot was hauling out bricks and setting them on the snow. "You won't have to suffer with him much longer." As if catching the innuendo, Talbot flashed her a grin. "In a manner of speaking. You neither."

"Great," she said.

She watched as the men pulled out brick and brick, wad after wad. She didn't have much time. Scott would be back any second and, knowing Scott, he'd make sure he got his cut no matter what.

So I have to do this. The avgas bladders were to her left, and she edged that way now. But hadn't Will also said she'd helped to make a life? She was responsible for two lives now. *Somebody, tell me what to do.* She eyed the men, but they had their backs to her, so it really was now or never. Sliding another slow inch to her left and then another, she felt her left hand brush the siphon hose. Carefully, she nudged the hose until the open bore rested over the half-empty bladder and then released the clamp. She felt cold liquid on her fingers but heard nothing as the avgas sheeted over fabric. *Good.*

"Say," she said, already backing up, "do you guys mind if I go get my pack? I left it on the other side next to the signal fire."

"Sure." This time, Talbot's smile didn't make it to his eyes, which were, she saw now, the lifeless gray of a shark's skin. "But don't run off."

"Are you kidding?" She was the edge of the fuselage. Maybe twenty feet, thirty max. *It will have to do.* Still facing them, she reached for her right hip pocket. "You guys are my heroes—"

"Hey!"

They all wheeled. Scott stood at the verge, black duffels in his hand. "Hey, she's got something in her pocket, she's got something, she's got—"

Damn him. In one swift moment, she pulled the flare from her pocket and jerked the string. There was an audible *crack* and then a shower of sparks as the flare caught and bloomed a red-hot flame that sounded like a blowtorch.

Talbot and the younger guy rounded, setting up ripples in the puddles at their feet. "The *hell?*" Talbot cried. "What are you—"

"*Yehi 'or*, you fuck!" Tossing the flare, she whirled around and thought, *Run, Emma, run, run, run as fast as you—*

She discovered that the *MythBusters* guys had been right. Sparks were the necessary ingredient.

In the next second, the last of that day erupted in a sheet of heat and flame, and with a roar.

And she knew nothing more.

AND THERE WAS...

CHAPTER 1

THE HOSPITAL ROOM was decorated with tiny lights. Soft Christmas music trickled from a ceiling speaker outside her door. At the moment, a jazzy rendition of "Jingle Bell Rock" competed with the soft and intermittent *tick-tick-tick* of a blood pressure cuff that self-inflated every twenty minutes and always got tight enough it was a wonder her left hand hadn't gotten gangrene and fallen off. She'd complained to a nurse that her blood pressure never went above one-twenty, and the cuff was inflating to over two-twenty, which she was certain was stroke territory. The nurse, a cranky woman who probably was pretty pissed she got tagged to work on Christmas Day, had only shrugged, and Emma decided to deal. There were, she had discovered, many worse things in the world. Although if she had suffered through another rendition of Elvis crooning about his blue, blue Christmas, she might be moved to do violence. At times, she found herself almost wishing for Burl Ives.

"It was a rancher," Will was saying. He perched on

317

the edge of her hospital bed. "Nice guy named Judd. He said he'd like to visit soon as you're feeling up for it."

"I'm up for it," she croaked. Her throat was still sore from that rush of superheated air as the concussive blast, which had knocked her flying, sheeted her body. *Good thinking,* her doctor had said, *you putting that part of the plane between you and the fire.* If she'd been any closer or in a contained space, she'd have probably flash-fried her lungs. *It's what happens to people in burning buildings,* the doctor said. *One big inhale, and their lungs are toast.*

"Actually," she said to Will, "I'm up for *leaving.*"

"Tomorrow. Don't rush it. Where do you have to go anyway?"

Anyplace that isn't a hospital? She still had her interviews with Kujo's people to do, too. Although all that seemed almost trivial now. She should write all *this* up, get it down while it was fresh. She bet *Outside* magazine would take it. Ooh, and then if she included the rescue, Kuntz's people and all…this had possibilities, but not if she was stuck here. She wondered how many other stringers were here already, camped around the hospital. Probably dozens.

She was surprised, actually, that there wasn't a throng of reporters at her door now. She wondered if maybe Will had something to do with that. Or the hospital might care about its *other* patients. She'd known an older friend of a friend who'd been an intern when Reagan was shot. Talk about ancient history. The friend said the police escorted her into the hospital every day. She had *nothing* to do with the president's care and wasn't even on the surgical team, but reporters still stuck mikes in her face, hoping for a scoop. Journalists were like vultures over roadkill when it came to a story. That, at least, the movies got right.

"Tell me about Judd," she said.

"He was out with his cows. He said he heard the plane go down but didn't realize it *was* a plane until almost a week later when he heard it on the news. He was the one who got word to the search parties. We were right, too. They were looking in the wrong place. Even so, everyone kind of brushed him off except for that friend of yours, Kuntz?"

"He's not my friend." Her throat moved in a painful swallow, and she said, thinly, "He's only a guy I was going to interview."

"Here." Taking a cup of ice water from a tray, he held the straw steady so she could sip. "You want more?" he asked when she came up for air.

She shook her head. What she wanted was food. She eyed the cubes of red Jell-O on her hospital tray and a half-congealed lump of something the nurse said was cream of wheat but that looked like something a cat brought up. The doctor said if she did well with soft foods today, she could have something approaching real food tomorrow. *After all,* the doctor said, *we don't want to tax your digestive system here.*

Was he freaking kidding? It had taken all her willpower not to chuck applesauce at the guy. Her stomach *wanted* to get back to work.

At her stomach's sudden, loud grumble, Will cocked an eyebrow. "Someone's awake."

"Oh, ha-ha." Maybe *Will* would smuggle something

in. Like, like...*doughnuts.* The soft type with chocolate crème. Or maybe Mexican? No, no, pizza, dripping with grease... *My God, would you stop?* She forced herself to focus. "So, what happened with Kuntz?"

"He got in touch with somebody back in Washington...Patterson? Anyway, the guy's got friends. They rerouted a border patrol drone. It saw the signal fires you kept burning. So their people were heading up on foot when their drones saw the snowmobiles. They got there in time to get us, but Scott and the other two were already long gone and headed back your way by then. I think if they'd left more than one person to watch us, it might have been worse. As it was, all of a sudden, these red fireflies are lighting up the guy watching us, and they're shouting for him to freeze and gets his hands up." Will's dimple showed. "It was like the movies. Oh, and the feds got into Burke's safe, the one on the plane? A lot of maps and contact numbers. The DEA will be busy for a while."

"Cool." She rested a hand on her belly. Other than the jab of her hipbones...the doctor said she'd shed ten pounds...nothing felt different. "Can I ask you a question? The very first day, you made that comment about the black market and habits being hard to break. Did you know?"

"I wondered. The extra avgas when you've got a big belly tank made me sit up and then Hunter and Burke were going on about weight. So..." He shrugged. "It crossed my mind. I was thinking of putting a bug in someone's ear once we got where we were going."

"Speaking of which, how is Hunter?"

"They took both legs in below-the-knee amputations. Me, I think he'll lose even more, but they wanted to give him a chance with as much viable tissue as possible." He put a hand atop hers. "You are a nut and a maniac and one extremely, amazingly lucky woman. A little charred, but look at the bright side. If you hadn't already been turned around, you might have lost your eyebrows."

Instead of only the three inches of hair spilling from her watch cap, which had instantly crisped. "How's Rachel doing?"

"About Scott? Not great. But the baby's fine. He seems happy to wait to put in an appearance, but she's pretty close, so you never know. You realize that if this had been a Harlequin novel, she'd have given birth, and you'd have delivered it."

"Yeah, instead, we got sucky real life." Then she blew out, impatient with herself. "I'm sorry. I should be grateful, I know. It'd be a lot worse if we were all dead." Or if they'd been as unlucky as Hunter, Earl, Burke. Even Scott. "I guess what I meant is…"

"How does Rachel feel about you?" Will sighed. He, too, had lost weight. His cheekbones were sharp as axe heads, but that made him look stronger. A little feral, actually. It was a nice look. "I don't get the sense she and Scott were destined for a long and happy life, especially after Scott pretty much gave us up when Talbot showed. But he was the father, and she's also lost her dad. Give her time."

They fell silent for a few moments. In the hall, Dolly

Parton and Kenny Rogers were warbling on about once upon a Christmas.

"Tell me about your wife," she said. "Tell me what really happened with Becca. You didn't divorce." She didn't know how she knew this, but she thought that was right.

If caught off-guard, that didn't show on his face. "There's not much to say. We wanted children, and then when we thought she was pregnant..." He paused. "Cancer's a thief, you know. It steals everything. By the time she died, she had so many mets...metastases to the brain, she didn't know who I was anymore."

"And that's when you stopped."

"Being an oncologist, yeah. It was like that really bad joke about the universe laughing behind your back. I couldn't save my wife. All I could do in the end was help her die."

"How many years ago?"

"Seven. I still think of her every day. It would be odd not to, don't you think? But everything people say about time and memory is right. It doesn't really hurt anymore. But sometimes I'll see something, a beautiful sunset, for example, and I'll think how Becca would've loved that and how sad it is that she hasn't gotten that chance. But I can still see it and enjoy it, and until now, doing that on my own...that's been all right. But... oooh." He turned to stare at her cardiac monitor, which was pitching a fit, and a heart rate that was practically galloping across the screen. "We're not excited, are we?"

"Oh, ha-ha." She felt a flush that had nothing to do with the really bad sunburn she'd given herself. It had been seven years for Will, but less than two for her. Maybe that was long enough. She wanted to be part of something living, for a change. In fact, if her heart rate was any indication, that wasn't a maybe. "But what?"

"But it's not all right now. If you'll let me…" He put a hand on the swell of her belly. "If you'll let me, I'd like to see how all this turns out. I'm not making promises, but I'm a pretty steady guy. I'm kind of demanding, though."

"Yeah?" She was suddenly having a tough time catching her breath. She liked the weight of his hand. "In what way?

"In all ways. I want to be the person with whom you wake every morning," he said, "and who tells you to please brush your teeth because, you know, sex with morning breath only really works in movies. And the rest is commentary." He waited until she was done laughing then said, "What do *you* want?"

She had asked herself that same question earlier in the day when the doctor had wheeled in a portable ultrasound, applied warm goop to her belly, and then pressed the transducer to her abdomen. She'd avoided having an ultrasound until now, avoided any kind of exam, in fact, except on the day she visited the abortion clinic then chickened out for reasons she couldn't understand. Now, though, she'd heard the baby's heart, a hollow but rapid beat that reminded her of a runaway horse. *Oooh,* the doctor said and turned the monitor around so she could see. *That's one happy baby.*

She held Will's gaze. "I want to name her Klara, if it's a girl, and Robert, if it's a boy."

He was bending down—to kiss her, she was sure of

323

it—when her stomach picked that moment to complain so loudly they both broke into laughter instead.

"Another party heard from," he said, slipping a finger beneath her grandmother's necklace to caress her collarbone. "And your stomach is correct. *Di liebe is zees, nor zi iz gut mit broyt.*"

The old Yiddish saying was right. Love *was* good and probably better with bread.

But get real.

Love was even better with pizza.

CHAPTER 2

"EMMA?"

She jerked awake with a gasp. Her door was ajar, but the overhead in her room was out. The small Christmas lights still twinkled, enough for her to piece together a face, but she'd have known the voice anywhere. "Mattie. Honey, what are you doing here?"

"They wouldn't let me visit until now," she said.

"But visiting hours are over."

"Okay, fine, so I lied. I'm not supposed to be here, but I waited until I saw the nurse leave."

"Where's your mom?" She checked the time; it was only a little past six. Will was due back at eight and he'd promised a gooey, loaded veggie pizza if he had to bring it in under a trench coat.

"Downstairs. My dad's mom, my *real* grandmother, is here. Joshua's coming."

She sat up. "You're kidding. Will said it was going to be another week or something."

"I guess Joshua has different ideas. Kind of like a

movie, you know? Him being born on Christmas? I actually kind of feel sorry for him. He'll get totally gypped out of presents every year."

She bit back a laugh. "I hadn't considered that." She reached out to touch the girl's shoulder. "I'm really glad to see you."

"I…" Mattie gave an audible swallow. "I was really scared I was never going to see you again. I'm so sorry about Scott. I think he heard me talking to Mom and…"

"Sweetie, don't worry about it. It's past now. It doesn't matter. You didn't do anything wrong. Scott had…he had his problems."

"Yeah." Drawing in a shaky breath, Mattie dragged a forearm over her eyes. "I didn't like him, but I didn't want him to die either."

"You don't know if he's dead." In fact, the odds were against it. By the time rescuers got to her, Scott had vanished, and one of the snowmobiles was missing. Knowing Scott, he was probably in Canada now, spending his money and figuring out what to do with that brick of heroin.

"True. But now, Mom's all alone again."

She thought Rachel had been alone for some time, ever since her husband didn't come out of that drug house. She said nothing.

"Do you think things will get better?" Mattie asked.

"I think they'll be different. Better in some ways, maybe worse in others." Although that was hard to imagine. "Where will you guys go?"

"Probably to Grampa's ranch. It's ours, now. I don't know anything about ranching."

"Maybe you'll like it."

"Maybe. There's a lot to work out. Anyway." Mattie thrust out the paper bag. "I brought you something."

She was about to refuse, to say that it wasn't her holiday then got disgusted with herself. *Oh, give it a rest, will you?* Switching on a small bedside lamp, she opened the bag and peered inside. "Oh, Mattie."

"I did the best I could. I know it's not the same," the girl said. "Your pack got all messed up in the fire."

Her pack. She hadn't even thought of it until now. That meant her camera and lenses were gone. Ben's copy of *The Waste Land* was now only so much ash. Well, maybe that was all right. Although she really had liked her camera and those lenses cost a fortune.

She pulled out Mattie's gift. The menorah was small and golden. It was Sarah's candelabra in miniature. "It's beautiful."

"And it's like your necklace, see?" Mattie pointed to a very tiny red crystal in the center of a Star of David. "That way, when you light it, you can think of your grandmother. You're going to have a lot of extra candles, though," Mattie said as Emma squared the box of candles next to the menorah. "It's Christmas and *last* night was the last night of Hanukkah, so…"

"We're going to light them anyway." Really, God or a god or whatever could take a joke. "And I'll have a head start on next year. But, oh." Grinning, Emma drew out the candy bar. "I thought I smelled chocolate and coconut."

"And almonds," Mattie said. "Because sometimes you feel like a nut."

They smiled at one another for a moment and then Emma said, "Shall we light the candles now?"

"Are we allowed?"

"I kind of doubt it." Although she wasn't on oxygen or anything. "Tell you what. Why don't we wait for Will to come back? He's bringing pizza. It's not sausage or anything, only veggie." Bubbe Sarah would've been pleased. "Is that okay?"

"Are you kidding? I've done nothing *but* eat, and I still want to gnaw on your arm." Mattie paused. "Can we say the blessings for real this time?"

"Absolutely."

"That would be nice." Sliding her arms around Emma, Mattie buried her face in Emma's neck. "*Yehi 'or*, Emma."

"Yes." Emma held the girl close. "Light."

CHAPTER 3

C'MON, c'mon, light, you motherfucker, light!

Scott was shaking so hard he could barely hang onto the lighter to flick his Bic. Gritting his teeth, he forced his icy thumbs to bend and stroked the Bic's wheel again and again. Tiny sparks sputtered briefly to life but quickly died.

Light, light!

Calm, he had to calm down. Shuddering with cold, he forced himself to stop and jammed his hands under his armpits. He'd lost his gloves somewhere along the way, he didn't know where, probably back at the fuselage when he'd cut and run right before Emma, that bitch, that *bitch*, torched the place. Squatting in the snow before his sorry pile of twigs and crumpled bills laid atop rocks because even *he* knew you couldn't start a fire in the *snow*...and, yes, he was going to burn his own fucking money because he didn't have a knife either and no way to find tinder or kindling or whatever the hell you called that shit because he'd grabbed the one snowmobile that doesn't have *any* gear, no matches, no clothes, no food, not even a gun... But at least by the time those helicopters appeared, the machine had gotten him far enough away before running out of gas. He'd bet everyone was so busy looking at that fireball and zeroing in on the wreck, no one even thought about, say, hadn't there been *three* guys?

He'd been lucky. But he was a lucky guy. That bullet Dave took? Totally meant for him. He ducked faster, was all, and then he got the hell out of there.

So, yeah, okay, he wasn't a fucking Boy Scout. He also didn't know what he was doing here. He'd watched Mattie fuss at that signal fire, but she at least had wood and lighters, and she wasn't *freezing* and *starving*.

Calm down. He had to calm down. He dragged in a sobbing breath. He couldn't feel his face anymore. His cheeks were numb, and so was his nose. He was going to die if he couldn't calm down and get a fire going. The problem was the damn lighter. There was only *this* much fuel left, and most of that probably vapors. God, he should never have gone through all those smokes! Rachel had always been after him to quit. *Think of the baby and the secondhand smoke.*

Yeah, yeah, yeah. Get through this night, this one night. It was Christmas. Hell, nothing bad happened to people on Christmas, right? He was on a mountain, he knew that, but lower than before. Right before dark, he'd spotted the twinkle of lights in a far-off valley. Ten miles, he thought. Maybe twenty. He couldn't tell distance, but it didn't matter because there were lights.

A ranch, he bet. In the stillness, if he held his breath, he could *swear* he heard the moo of cows. So, that was good. People in the country were solid, good, decent folks. They'd help him. All he had to do was get there. Well, he could do that. It would be all downhill come morning, ha-ha, and…

"What was that?" he said. He popped out of his slouch. He'd heard something off to his right. Not a snap or crack but a very soft, almost inaudible shushing that was the sound of plush slippers over a shag rug. He tried to listen above the fierce chattering of his own teeth but couldn't still himself enough to be sure. He twisted right and then left. Nothing.

The fire. Light the fire.

"Please." He held that lighter the way a penitent clutched a rosary… Christ. When was the last time he'd taken Communion? Been in a confessional? *Well, I promise, God.* He was quaking so hard the lighter jittered in his hands. He was worse than a drunk with DTS. The feel of the wheel was distant, more of an impression, his thumbs wooden. He stroked the wheel but so weakly there wasn't even a spark. *I promise. Get me out of this.* He closed his eyes. *One more time, last time, I promise. I'll get clean, I'll change. Please, just one light, just one.*

He rolled the wheel as fast and hard as he could, thinking this was it, this was all she wrote, he couldn't possibly…

The Bic caught with a tiny, thin, yellow flame.

For a second, he was so stupefied, he only stared. Then he laughed. "There, there!" Cupping the flame, he touched it to a twenty and then laughed again, an almost maniacal cackle, as the bill caught. *"Yes!"* The Bic died, but it didn't matter. He didn't care. He held his hands over his burning stash. So he torched some money. So what? He had a duffel half full of the stuff. Thank God, he'd stuffed his pockets before he left. There was still the heroin, too. That was going to get him big money. Grinning, he fed more bills to the hungry flames. The fire was tiny, but hell, it was hot and going and that was all that mattered. He was going to be all right. It was like that really, really old movie with the gangster guy: *Look at me, Ma! I'm on top of the—*

That was when he happened to look up and to his right.

For a second, he only...he just...his brain simply hung there. If he'd been a cartoon, there would have been one of those thought bubbles filled with question marks over his head.

But then, time started up again.

CHAPTER 4

"DID YOU HEAR THAT?" Looking up from her knitting, Jess reached for the radio, turned down the volume at the same time old Burl was winding himself up about not knowing if there'd be snow, and twisted on her stool toward the barn door. "I heard something."

"Yeah?" Randall Cobb was trembling now; her tail was kinked the way Judd's dad said it always did, and the hay around the cow's hooves was wet. That calf was coming anytime now. "What did you hear?"

"Sounded like a scream. Way far off."

He shot a glance at Carson...if there'd really been something, his dog was nearly as good as radar...but the shepherd was snoozing and deep into dreaming from the looks of those twitchy paws and that nose. "North or south?"

Jess thought about it. "North."

Black Wolf Mountains then. "Boy scream or a girl scream?"

"There's a difference?"

"Of course." You'd think the woman had lived her whole life in a condo in the middle of New York where the only chickens anyone ever saw came wrapped in cellophane. Pulling his new Packers watch cap down over his ears, he said, "A girl scream, then it's probably a mountain lion or a bobcat, but to carry this far, I'm thinking mountain lion. A boy scream, well…then it was probably a person." All his time in 'Nam, seeing men holding onto their guts to keep them from slopping onto the ground or looking for that leg they didn't have anymore, he'd heard a lot of screaming.

"Oh." Jess looked troubled. "I couldn't tell. It was only the one. Could've been a girl-girl screaming."

"Maybe. If there was only the one, I guess we'll never know." Cobb was really huffing and puffing now. Another pinkish stream of liquid squirted to course down the cow's back legs. A second later, there came another, more intense gush.

"That calf sounds like it's in a hurry," Jess remarked.

"I'm thinking so."

"Good. I'm thinking some eggnog afterward might be nice."

"Long as you hold the nog," he quipped.

"Oh, you," she mock-scolded as if he hadn't said that same line every single Christmas of their marriage and for the season before when he'd courted her. "That's all we need, you with a snootful dancing around the kitchen."

They laughed, and he thought how it was a damn fine life, yet another fine Christmas. He was where he ought to be: in his barn, with his girls mumbling at their feed, the seven calves he'd helped birth suckling at their mother's teats, Jess's knitting needles going *click-click-click*, and the promise of eggnog without the nog and a warm kitchen and an even warmer bed with this woman who had earned every wrinkle and all her beauty.

Yes, he thought, pulling on gloves and squaring himself to help turn the calf if it was breech (or back the heck away fast so he wouldn't get himself kicked if it wasn't), it was like that movie with Jimmy Stewart and Donna Reeve and Old Clarence. Even though he'd seen it every Christmas for well over half a century, he never tired of it. Always got kind of choked up and misty because, my, they just didn't make them that way anymore.

"Turn up the radio, would you, Jess?" He got himself ready to welcome this new little life to his ranch and this world. "I love that song."

DRAW THE DARK

Star Trek Novels and Stories

- STAR TREK: THE LOST ERA: WELL OF
  SOULS
- STAR TREK STARFLEET CORPS OF
  ENGINEERS
- WOUNDS, Part One and Two
- GHOST
- LOST TIME
- "A Ribbon for Rosie," in STAR TREK:
  STRANGE NEW WORLDS II
- "Shadows, in the Dark," in STAR TREK:
  STRANGE NEW WORLDS IV
- "Alice, on the Edge of Night," in STAR TREK:
  NEW FRONTIER: NO LIMITS
- "Bottomless," in STAR TREK: VOYAGER:
  DISTANT SHORES

Mechwarrior Dark Age Novels

- BLOOD AVATAR
- DRAGON RISING
- DAUGHTER OF THE DRAGON

ABOUT ILSA J. BICK

Ilsa J. Bick is a child psychiatrist, as well as a film and television scholar, surgeon wannabe, former Air Force major—and an award-winning, best-selling author of dozens of short stories and novels. Her work spans established universes such as *Star Trek*, *Battletech*, *Battlecorps*, *Mechwarrior Dark Age*, and *Shadowrun*. Her original novels include such critically acclaimed and award-winning books as The *ASHES* Trilogy, *Drowning Instinct*, *The Sin-Eater's Confession*, and *White Space* (longlisted for the Stoker).

Ilsa's also written in *New York Times* best-selling author Elle James's BROTHERHOOD PROTECTORS. Her four-part *SOLDIER'S HEART* series features Kate McEvoy, a cybernetically-enhanced Afghan vet and Sarah Grant, a veterinarian struggling to help her dead lover's traumatized war dog, Soldier.

Currently a cheesehead-in-exile, Ilsa lives in Alabama with the husband and several furry creatures. On occasion, she even feeds them.

Drop by for a visit at www.ilsajbick.com or and check out her Friday's Cocktails and Sunday's Cakes and other assorted effluvia on
Facebook

(https://www.facebook.com/ilsa.j.bick
and
https://www.facebook.com/ilsajbickauthor/),

Twitter (@ilsajbick),
and
Instagram (@ilsajbick).

facebook.com/ilsa.j.bick

twitter.com/ilsabick

instagram.com/ilsabick

BROTHERHOOD PROTECTORS

ORIGINAL SERIES BY ELLE JAMES

ABOUT ELLE JAMES

ELLE JAMES also writing as MYLA JACKSON is a *New York Times* and *USA Today* Bestselling author of books including cowboys, intrigues and paranormal adventures that keep her readers on the edges of their seats. With over eighty works in a variety of sub-genres and lengths she has published with Harlequin, Samhain, Ellora's Cave, Kensington, Cleis Press, and Avon. When she's not at her computer, she's traveling, snow skiing, boating, or riding her ATV, dreaming up new stories. Learn more about Elle James at www.ellejames.com

Website | Facebook | Twitter | GoodReads | Newsletter | BookBub | Amazon

Follow Elle!
www.ellejames.com
ellejames@ellejames.com

facebook.com/ellejamesauthor
twitter.com/ElleJamesAuthor